THE
BUCCANEERS
OF AMERICA

In the Original English
Translation of 1684

THE
BUCCANEERS
OF AMERICA
In the Original English
Translation of 1684

JOHN ESQUEMELING

NEW YORK

The Buccaneers of America
Cover © 2007 Cosimo, Inc.

For information, address:

Cosimo, P.O. Box 416
Old Chelsea Station
New York, NY 10113-0416

or visit our website at:
www.cosimobooks.com

The Buccaneers of America was originally published in 1678.

Cover design by www.kerndesign.net

ISBN: 978-1-60206-100-2

One of the Pirates was wounded with an arrow in his back,
which pierced his body to the other side. This instantly he pulled out...
and putting it into his musket, he shot it back into the castle.

—from Chapter IV

CONTENTS

ENGRAVED PLATES

THE BUCCANEERS OF AMERICA.

PART I.

CHAPTER I.

The Author sets forth towards the Western Islands, in the Service of the West India Company of France. They meet with an English frigate, and arrive at the Island of Tortuga.

WE set sail from Havre de Grace, in France, in a ship called *St. John*, the second day of May, in the year 1666 Our vessel was equipped with eight and twenty guns, twenty mariners, and two hundred and twenty passengers, including in this number those whom the Company sent as free passengers, as being in their service. Soon after we came to an anchor under the Cape of Barfleur, there to join seven other ships of the same West India Company, which were to come from Dieppe under the convoy of a man-of-war, mounted with seven and thirty guns and two hundred and fifty men. Of these ships two were bound for Senegal, five for the Caribbee Islands, and ours for the Island of Tortuga. In the same place there gathered unto us about twenty sail of other ships that were bound for Newfoundland, with some Dutch vessels that were going for Nantes, Rochelle, and St. Martins ; so that in all we made a fleet of thirty sail. Here we prepared to fight, putting ourselves into a convenient posture of defence, as having notice that four English frigates, of threescore guns each, lay in wait

for us about the Isle of Ornay.   Our Admiral, the
Chevalier Sourdis, having distributed what orders he
thought convenient, we set sail from thence with a favourable gale of wind.   Presently after, some mists arising,
these totally impeded the English frigates from discover-
ing our fleet at sea.   We steered our course as near as
we could under the coast of France, for fear of the enemy.
As we sailed along, we met a vessel of Ostend, who
complained to our Admiral that a French privateer had
robbed him that very morning.   This complaint being
heard, we endeavoured to pursue the said pirate ; but our
labour was in vain, as not being able to overtake him.

Our fleet, as we went along, caused no small fears and
alarms to the inhabitants of the coasts of France, these
judging us to be English, and that we sought some convenient place for landing.   To allay their frights, we used
to hang out our colours ; but, notwithstanding, they would
not trust us.   After this we came to an anchor in the
Bay of Conquet, in Brittany, near the Isle of Ushant,
there to take in water.   Having stored ourselves with
fresh provisions at this place, we prosecuted our voyage,
designing to pass by the Ras of Fonteneau and not
expose ourselves to the Sorlingues, fearing the English
vessels that were cruising thereabouts to meet us.   This
river Ras is of a current very strong and rapid, which,
rolling over many rocks, disgorges itself into the sea on
the coast of France, in the latitude of eight and forty
degrees and ten minutes.   For which reason this passage
is very dangerous, all the rocks as yet being not thoroughly known.

Here I shall not omit to mention the ceremony which
at this passage, and some other places, is used by the
mariners, and by them called Baptism, although it may
seem either little to our purpose or of no use.   The
Master's Mate clothed himself with a ridiculous sort of
garment that reached to his feet, and on his head he put
a suitable cap, which was made very burlesque.   In his

right hand he placed a naked wooden sword, and in his left a pot full of ink. His face was horribly blacked with soot, and his neck adorned with a collar of many little pieces of wood. Being thus apparelled, he commanded to be called before him every one of them who never had passed that dangerous place before. And then causing them to kneel down in his presence, he made the sign of the Cross upon their foreheads with ink, and gave each one a stroke on the shoulders with his wooden sword. Meanwhile the standers-by cast a bucket of water upon every man's head; and this was the conclusion of the ceremony. But, that being ended, every one of the baptized is obliged to give a bottle of brandy for his offering, placing it near the main-mast, and without speaking a word; even those who have no such liquor being not excused from this performance. In case the vessel never passed that way before, the Captain is obliged to distribute some wine among the mariners and other people in the ship. But as for other gifts which the newly baptized frequently offer, they are divided among the old seamen, and of them they make a banquet among themselves.

The Hollanders likewise baptize such as never passed that way before. And not only at the passage above-mentioned, but also at the rocks called Berlingues, near the coast of Portugal, in the latitude of thirty-nine degrees and forty minutes, being a passage very dangerous, especially by night, when through the obscurity thereof the rocks are not distinguishable. But their manner of baptizing is quite distinct from that which we have described above as performed by the French. He, therefore, that is to be baptized is fastened, and hoisted up three times at the main-yard's end, as if he were a criminal. If he be hoisted the fourth time, in the name of the Prince of Orange or of the Captain of the vessel, his honour is more than ordinary. Thus they are dipped, every one, several times into the main ocean. But he that is the

first dipped has the honour of being saluted with a gun.
Such as are not willing to fall are bound to pay twelve
pence for their ransom ; if he be an officer in the ship,
two shillings ; and if a passenger, according to his
pleasure.   In case the ship never passed that way
before, the Captain is bound to give a small runlet of
wine, which, if he does not perform, the mariners may cut
off the stem of the vessel.   All the profit which accrues by
this ceremony is kept by the Master's Mate, who after
reaching their port usually lays it out in wine, which is
drunk amongst the ancient seamen.   Some say this ceremony was instituted by the Emperor Charles the Fifth ;
howsoever, it is not found amongst his Laws.   But here I
leave these customs of the sea, and shall return to our
voyage.

Having passed the river Ras, we met with very good
weather until we came to Cape Finisterre.   Here a huge
tempest of wind surprised us, and separated our ship
from the rest that were in our company.   This storm
continued for the space of eight days, in which time it
would move compassion to see how miserably the passengers were tumbled to and fro on all sides of the ship ;
insomuch as the mariners in the performance of their duty
were compelled to tread upon them everywhere.   This
uncouthsome weather being spent, we had again the
use of very favourable gales until we came to the Tropic
of Cancer.   This Tropic is nothing but an imaginary
circle which astrologers have invented in the heavens,
and serves as a period to the progress of the sun
towards the North Pole.   It is placed in the latitude
of three and twenty degrees and thirty minutes, under
the line.   Here we were baptized the second time, after
the same manner as before.   The French always perform
this ceremony at this Tropic, as also under the Tropic
of Capricorn, towards the South.   In this part of the
world we had very favourable weather, at which we were
infinitely gladdened by reason of our great necessity

of water.   For at this time that element was already sc
scarce with us that we were stinted to two half-pints pe
man every day.

Being about the latitude of Barbados, we met an
English frigate, or privateer, who first began to give us
chase ; but finding himself not to exceed us in strength,
presently steered away from us.   This flight gave us
occasion to pursue the said frigate, as we did, shooting at
him several guns of eight pound carriage.   But at length
he escaped, and we returned to our course.   Not long
after, we came within sight of the Isle of Martinique.
Our endeavours were bent towards the coast of the Isle
of St. Peter.   But these were frustrated by reason of a
storm, which took us hereabouts.   Hence we resolved to
steer to the Island of Guadaloupe.   Yet neither this
island could we reach by reason of the said storm, and
thus we directed our course to the Isle of Tortuga, which
was the very same land to which we were bound.   We
passed along the coast of the Isle of Porto Rico, which is
extremely delicious and agreeable to the view, as being
adorned with beautiful trees and woods, even to the tops
of the mountains.   After this, we discovered the Island
Hispaniola (of which I shall give a description in this
book), and we coasted about it until we came to the
Isle of Tortuga, our desired port.   Here we anchored the
seventh day of July in the same year, not having lost one
man in the whole voyage.   We unladed the goods that
belonged to the Company of the West Indies, and soon
after the ship was sent to Cul de Sac with some passengers.

CHAPTER II.

Description of the Island of Tortuga : of the fruits and plants there growing : how the French settled there, at two several times, and cast out the Spaniards, first masters thereof. The Author of this book was twice sold in the said Island.

THE Island of Tortuga is situated on the North side of the famous and great island called Hispaniola, near the Continent thereof and in the latitude of twenty degrees and thirty minutes. Its exact extent is threescore leagues about. The Spaniards, who gave name to this island, called it so from the shape of the land, which in some manner resembles a great sea tortoise, called by them *tortuga de mar*. The country is very mountainous and full of rocks, yet notwithstanding hugely thick of lofty trees that cease not to grow upon the hardest of those rocks without partaking of a softer soil. Hence it comes that their roots, for the greatest part, are seen all over entangled among the rocks, not unlike the branching of ivy against our walls. That part of this island which stretches towards the North is totally uninhabited. The reason is, first, because it has proved to be very incommodious and unhealthy, and, secondly, for the ruggedness of the coast, that gives no access to the shore, unless among rocks almost inaccessible. For this cause it is populated only on the Southern part, which has only one port that may be esteemed indifferently good. Yet this harbour has two several entries, or channels, which afford passage to ships of seventy guns, the port itself being without danger and capable of receiving a great number

6

of vessels. That part which is inhabited is divided into four other parts, of which the first is called the Low-land, or Low-country. This is the chief of them all, because it contains the aforesaid port. The town is called Cayona, and here live the chief and richest planters of the island. The second part is called the Middle Plantation. Its territory, or soil, is hitherto almost new, as being only known to be good for the culture of tobacco. The third is named Ringot. These places are situated towards the Western part of the island. The fourth, and last, is called The Mountain, in which place were made the first plantations that were cultivated upon this island.

As to the wood that grows on the island, we have already said that the trees are exceedingly tall and pleasing to the sight ; whence no man will doubt but they may be applied to several uses with great benefit. Such is the Yellow Saunder, which tree by the inhabitants of this country is called *Bois de Chandelle*, or in English Candlewood, because it burns like a candle, and serves them with light while they use their fishery in the night. Here also grows *Lignum Sanctum*, by others called *Guaiacum*, the virtues of which are very well known. The trees likewise that afford *Gummi Elemi* grow here in great abundance, and in like manner *Radix China*, or China Root ; yet this is not so good as that which comes from other parts of the Western world. It is very white and soft, and serves for pleasant food to the wild boars when they can find nothing else. This island also is not deficient in Aloes, nor an infinite number of other medicinal herbs, which may please the curiosity of such as are given to their contemplation. Moreover for the building of ships, or any other sort of architecture, here are found, in this spot of Neptune, several sorts of timber very convenient. The fruits, likewise, which here abundantly grow, are nothing inferior, as to their quantity or quality, to what the adjacent islands produce. I shall name only some of the most

ordinary and common.   Such are magniot,[1] potatoes,
Acajou apples, yannas,[2] bacones, paquayes, carosoles,
mamayns,[3] ananas and diverse other sorts, which, not to
be tedious, I omit to specify.   Here grow likewise in
huge number those trees called Palmetto, whence is
drawn a certain juice which serves the inhabitants instead
of wine, and whose leaves cover their houses instead of
tiles.

In this island abounds also, with daily increase, the
Wild Boar.   The Governor has prohibited the hunting
of them with dogs, fearing lest, the island being but
small, the whole race of those animals in short time
should be destroyed.   The reason why he thought convenient to preserve those wild beasts was that in case of
any invasion of an external enemy the inhabitants might
sustain themselves with their food, especially if they were
constrained to retire to the woods and mountains.   By
this means he judged they were enabled to maintain any
sudden assault or long persecution.   Yet this sort of game
is almost impeded by itself, by reason of the many rocks
and precipices, which for the greatest part are covered
with little shrubs, very green and thick, whence the
huntsmen have ofttimes precipitated themselves, and left
us the sad experience and grief of many memorable disasters.

At a certain time of the year huge flocks of Wild
Pigeons resort to this Island of Tortuga, at which
season the inhabitants feed on them very plentifully, having more than they can consume, and leaving totally to
their repose all other sorts of fowl, both wild and tame,
to the intent that in absence of the pigeons these may
supply their place.   But as nothing in the universe,
though never so pleasant, can be found but what has

[1] Probably the mango.   There is, however, a local term, "manihot,"
applied to cassava.
[2] Probably the yam.
[3] The mammee apple.

something of bitterness joined to it, the very symbol of this truth we see in the aforesaid pigeons. For these, the season being past wherein God has appointed them to afford delicious food to those people, can scarcely be touched with the tongue, they become so extremely lean and bitter even to admiration. The reason of this bitterness is attributed to a certain seed which they eat about that time, as bitter as gall. About the sea shores great multitudes of Crabs[1] are everywhere found, belonging both to the land and sea, and both sorts very big. These are good to feed servants and slaves, who find them very pleasing to the palate, yet withal very hurtful to the sight. Besides which symptom, being eaten too often, they also cause great giddiness in the head, with much weakness of the brain, insomuch that very frequently they are deprived of sight for the space of one quarter of an hour.

The French, having in 1625 established themselves in the Isle of St. Christopher, planted there a sort of trees, of which at present there possibly may be greater quantities. With the timber of those trees they made Longboats and Hoys, which they sent thence westward, well manned and victualled, to discover other islands. These, setting sail from St. Christopher, came within sight of the Island of Hispaniola, where at length they arrived with abundance of joy. Having landed, they marched into the country, where they found huge quantities of cattle, such as cows, bulls, horses and wild boars. But finding no great profit in those animals unless they could enclose them, and knowing likewise the island to be pretty well peopled by the Spaniards, they thought it convenient to enterprize upon and seize the Island of Tortuga. This they performed without any difficulty, there being upon the island no more than ten or twelve

---

[1] Land-crabs are abundant in the West Indies. The violet land-crab (*Gecarcinus ruricola*), living in communities, burrowing and travelling great distances, is the principal variety—it is a great delicacy.

Spaniards to guard it. These few men let the French come in peaceably and possess the island for the space of six months, without any trouble. In the meanwhile they passed and repassed with their canoes to Hispaniola, whence they transported many people, and at last began to plant the whole Isle of Tortuga. The few Spaniards remaining there, perceiving the French to increase their number daily, began at last to repine at their prosperity and grudge them the possession they had freely given. Hence they gave notice to others of their own nation, their neighbours, who sent several great boats, well armed and manned, to dispossess the French of that island. This expedition succeeded according to their desires. For the new possessors, seeing the great number of Spaniards that came against them, fled with all they had to the woods ; and hence by night they wafted over with canoes to the Isle of Hispaniola. This they more easily performed having no women or children with them, nor any great substance to carry away. Here they also retired into the woods, both to seek themselves food, and thence with secrecy to give intelligence to others of their own faction ; judging for certain that within a little while they should be in a capacity to hinder the Spaniards from fortifying in Tortuga.

Meanwhile the Spaniards of the greater island ceased not to seek after their new guests, the French, with intent to root them out of the woods, if possible, or cause them to perish with hunger. But this their design soon failed, having found that the French were masters both of good guns, powder and bullets. Here, therefore, the fugitives waited for a certain opportunity, wherein they knew the Spaniards were to come from Tortuga, with arms and great number of men, to join with those of the greater Island for their destruction. When this occasion proffered, they, in the meanwhile deserting the woods where they were, returned to Tortuga, and dispossessed the small number of Spaniards that remained at home. Having so done, they fortified themselves as best they could, thereby to prevent the return of the Spaniards, in case they should attempt it. Moreover, they sent immediately to the Governor of St. Christopher, in 1630, craving his aid and relief, and demanding of him to send them a Governor, the better to be united among themselves and strengthened on all occasions. The Governor of St. Christopher received their petition with expressions of much satisfaction, and without any delay sent to them Monsieur le Passeur in quality of a Governor, together with a ship full of men and all other things necessary both for their establishment and defence. No sooner had they received this recruit than the Governor commanded a fortress to be built upon the top of a high rock, whence he could hinder the access of any ships or other vessels that should design to enter the port. To this fort no other access could be had than by almost climbing through a very narrow passage, that was capable only of receiving two persons at once, and those not without difficulty. In the middle of this rock was a great cavity, which now serves for a storehouse ; and, besides, here was great convenience for raising a battery. The fort being finished, the Governor commanded two guns to be mounted, which could not be performed without huge toil and labour, as also a house to be built in the fort ; and, afterwards, the narrow way that led to the said fort to be broken and demolished, leaving no other ascent thereto than by a ladder. Within the fort a plentiful fountain of fresh water gushes out, which perpetually runs with a pure and crystalline stream sufficient to refresh a garrison of a thousand men. Being possessed of these conveniences, and the security these things might promise, the French began to people the island, and each of them to seek his living, some by the exercise of hunting, others by planting tobacco, and others by cruising and robbing upon the coasts of the Spanish Islands—which trade is continued by them to this day.

The Spaniards, notwithstanding, could not behold but
with jealous eyes the daily increase of the French in
Tortuga, fearing lest in time they might by them be dis
possessed also of Hispaniola.   Thus taking an opportunity, when many of the French were abroad at sea, and
others employed in hunting, with eight hundred men in
several canoes, they landed again in Tortuga, almost
without being perceived by the French.   But finding that
the Governor had cut down many trees, for the better
discovery of an enemy in case of any assault, also that
nothing of consequence could be done without great
guns, they consulted about the fittest place for raising a
battery.   This place was soon concluded to be the top of
a mountain which was in sight, seeing that thence alone
they could level their guns at the fort, which now lay open
to them, since the cutting down of the trees by the new
possessors.   Hence they resolved to open a way for
carriage of some pieces of ordnance to the top.   This
mountain is somewhat high, and the upper part plain,
whence the whole island may be viewed.   The sides
thereof are very rugged by reason of a huge number of
inaccessible rocks surrounding it everywhere ; so that the
ascent was very difficult, and would always have been the
same, had not the Spaniards undergone the immense
labour and toil of making the way aforementioned, as I
shall now relate.

The Spaniards had in their company many slaves, and
Indians, labouring men, whom they call *Matates*, or, in
English, half-yellow men.   To these they gave orders to
dig a way through the rocks with iron tools.   This they
performed with the greatest speed imaginable.   And
through this way, by the help of many ropes and pulleys,
they at last made shift to get up two sole cannon pieces,
wherewith they made a battery, and intended next day to
batter the fort.   Meanwhile the French were not ignorant of these designs, but rather prepared themselves for
a defence (while the Spaniards were busied about the

battery), sending notice everywhere to their companions requiring their help. Thus the hunters of the island all joined together, and with them all the pirates who were not already too far from home. These landed by night at Tortuga, lest they should be seen by the Spaniards. And under the same obscurity of the night, they all together by a back way climbed up the mountain where the Spaniards were posted ; which they more easily could perform as being acquainted with those rocks. They came thither at the very instant that the Spaniards, who were above, were preparing to shoot at the fort, not knowing in the least of their coming. Here they set upon them, at their backs, with such fury as forced the greatest part to precipitate themselves from the top to the bottom, and dash their bodies in pieces. Few or none escaped this attack, for if any remained alive they were all put to the sword, without giving quarter to the meanest. Some Spaniards still kept the bottom of the mountain, but hearing the shrieks and cries of them that were killed, and believing some tragical revolution to be above, fled immediately towards the sea, despairing, through this accident, to ever regain the Isle of Tortuga.

The Governors of this island always behaved themselves as proprietors and absolute lords thereof until the year 1664 ; at which time the West India Company of France took possession of it, and sent thither for their Governor, Monsieur Ogeron. These planted the colony for themselves, by the means of their factors and servants, thinking to drive some considerable trade thence with the Spaniards, even as the Hollanders do from Curaçoa. But this design did not answer their expectation. For with other nations they could drive no trade, by reason they could not establish any secure commerce from the beginning with their own. Forasmuch as at the first institution of this Company in France, they made an agreement with the pirates, hunters and planters, first

possessors of Tortuga, that these should buy all their
necessaries from the said Company, taking them upon
trust.   And although this agreement was put in execution, yet the factors of the Company soon after found that
they could not recover either monies or returns from
those people.   Insomuch as they were constrained to
bring some armed men into the island, in behalf of the
Company, to get in some of their payments.   But neither
this endeavour nor any other could prevail towards
settling a secure trade with those of the island.   And
hereupon the Company recalled their factors, giving
them orders to sell all that was their own in the said
plantation, both the servants belonging to the Company
(which were sold, some for twenty, others for thirty,
pieces of eight), as also all other merchandizes and pro-
perties which they had there.   With this resolution all
their designs fell to the ground.

In this occasion I was also sold, as being a servant
under the said Company, in whose service I came out of
France.   But my fortune was very bad, for I fell into the
hands of the most cruel tyrant and perfidious man that
ever was born of woman, who was then Governor, or
rather Lieutenant General, of that island.   This man
treated me with all the hard usages imaginable, even with
that of hunger, with which I thought I should have
perished inevitably.   Withal he was willing to let me buy
my freedom and liberty, but not under the rate of three
hundred pieces of eight, I not being master of one, at
that time, in the whole world.   At last through the
manifold miseries I endured, as also affliction of mind, I
was thrown into a dangerous fit of sickness.   This misfortune, being added to the rest of my calamities, was the
cause of my happiness.   For my wicked master, seeing
my condition, began to fear lest he should lose his monies
with my life.   Hereupon he sold me the second time to
a surgeon for the price of seventy pieces of eight.   Being
in the hands of this second master, I began soon after to

recover my health through the good usage I received
from him, as being much more humane and civil than
that of my first patron. He gave me both clothes and
very good food, and after I had served him but one year
he offered me my liberty, with only this condition, that I
should pay him one hundred pieces of eight when I was
in a capacity of wealth to do so. Which kind proposal of
his I could not choose but accept with infinite joy and
gratitude of mind.

Being now at liberty, though like unto Adam when he
was first created by the hands of his Maker—that is,
naked and destitute of all human necessaries, nor knowing
how to get my living—I determined to enter into the
wicked order of the Pirates, or Robbers at Sea. Into
this Society I was received with common consent both of
the superior and vulgar sort, and among them I continued
until the year 1672. Having assisted them in all their
designs and attempts, and served them in many notable
exploits, of which hereafter I shall give the reader a true
account, I returned to my own native country. But before I begin to relate the things above-mentioned, I shall
say something, for the satisfaction of such as are curious,
of the Island Hispaniola, which lies towards the Western
parts of America, as also give my reader a brief description thereof, according to my slender ability and experience.

CHAPTER III.

Description of the great and famous Island of Hispaniola.

THE very large and rich island called Hispaniola is
situate in the latitude of seventeen degrees and a half.
The greatest part thereof extends, from East to West,
twenty degrees Southern latitude.   The circumference
is three hundred leagues, the length one hundred and
twenty, its breadth almost fifty, being more or less
broad or narrow at certain places.   I shall not need here
to insert how this island was at first discovered, it
being known to the world that it was performed by
the means of Christopher Columbus, in the year 1492,
being sent for this purpose by Ferdinand, the Catholic,
then King of Spain.   From which time, to this
present, the Spaniards have been continually possessors
thereof.   There are on this island many very good

and strong cities, towns and hamlets; it also abounds in a great number of pleasant and delicious country-houses and plantations; all which are owing to the care and industry of the Spaniards, its inhabitants.

The chief city and metropolis of this island is called San Domingo, being dedicated to St. Dominic, from whom it derives this name. It is situated towards the South, in a place which affords a most excellent prospect, the country round about being embellished with innumerable rich plantations, also verdant meadows and fruitful gardens—all which produce plenty and variety of excellent and pleasant fruits, according to the nature of those countries. The Governor of the island makes his residence in this city, which is, as it were, the storehouse of all the other cities, towns and villages, which hence export and provide themselves with all necessaries whatsoever for human life. And yet has it this particularity, above many other cities in other places, that it entertains no external commerce with any other nation than its own, the Spaniards. The greatest part of the inhabitants are rich and substantial merchants, or such as are shopkeepers and sell by retail.

Another city of this island is named Santiago, or, in English, St. James, as being consecrated to the Apostle of that name. This is an open place, without either walls or castle, situate in the latitude of nineteen degrees South. The greatest part of the inhabitants are hunters and planters, the adjacent territory and soil being very proper for the said exercises of its constitution. The city is surrounded with large and delicious fields, as much pleasing to the view as those of San Domingo; and these abound with all sorts of beasts, both wild and tame, whence are taken a huge number of skins and hides, that afford to the owners a very considerable traffic.

Towards the Southern parts of this island is seen another city called Nuestra Señora del Alta Gracia.

The territory hereof produces great quantities of cacao, which occasions the inhabitants to make great store of the richest sort of chocolate. Here grows also much ginger and tobacco ; and much tallow is prepared of the beasts which hereabouts are hunted.

The inhabitants of this beautiful island of Hispaniola often go and come in their canoes to the Isle of Savona, not far distant thence, where is their chief fishery, especially of tortoises. Hither those fish constantly resort in huge multitudes at certain seasons of the year, there to lay their eggs, burying them in the sands of the shore. Thus by the heat of the sun, which in those parts is very ardent, they are hatched, and continue the propagation of their species. This island of Savona has little or nothing that is worthy consideration or may merit any particular description, as being so extremely barren, by reason of its sandy soil. True it is, that here grows some small quantity of *lignum sanctum* or *guaiacum*.

Westwards of the city of San Domingo is also situated another great village, called by the name of El Pueblo del Aso, or the Town of Aso. The inhabitants of this town drive a great commerce and traffic with those of another village, which is placed in the very middle of the island, and is called San Juan de Goave, or St. John of Goave. This place is environed with a magnificent prospect of gardens, woods and meadows. Its territory extends above twenty leagues in length, and grazes a huge number of wild bulls and cows. In this village scarce dwell any others than hunters and butchers, who flay the beasts that are killed. These are for the most part a mongrel sort of people of several bloods[1] ; some of which are born of white Euro-

---

[1] The offspring of a negro and Indian, or a person with three-fourths of black blood, is denominated a zambo or sambo ; a mixture of half white and half black is strictly the mulatto ; three parts white to one part black forms the quadroon ; one-eighth part of black blood marks the mustee or octoroon ; after the octoroon the mixed race are usually considered to be " white-washed," and rank as white. In the British

pean people and negroes, and these are called *Mulattos.* Others are born of Indians and white people, and such are termed *Mestizos.* But others are begotten of negroes and Indians, and these also have their peculiar name, being called *Alcatraces.* Besides which sorts of people, there are several other species and races, both here and in other places of the West Indies, of whom this account may be given, that the Spaniards love better the negro women, in those Western parts, or the tawny Indian females, than their own white European race, whereas peradventure the negroes and Indians have greater inclinations to the white women, or those that come near them, the tawny, than their own. From the said village are exported yearly vast quantities of tallow and hides, they exercising no other traffic nor toil. For as to the lands in this place, they are not cultivated, by reason of the excessive dryness of the soil. These are the chiefest places that the Spaniards possess in this island, from the Cape of Lobos towards St. John de Goave, to the Cape of Samana, near the sea, on the North side, and from the Eastern part, towards the sea, called Punta d'Espada. All the rest of the island is possessed by the French, who are also planters and hunters.

This island has very good ports for ships, from the Cape of Lobos to the Cape of Tiburon, which lies on the Western side thereof. In this space of land there are no less than four ports, which exceed in goodness, largeness and security even the very best of England. Besides these, from the Cape of Tiburon to the Cape of Donna Maria, there are two very excellent ports, and from this Cape to the Cape of St. Nicholas there are no less than twelve others. Every one of these ports has also the confluence of two or three good rivers, in which

West Indies very few of the negroes are of pure black blood, owing to the number of convicts and political prisoners who were sent to the plantations during the earlier settlements of the islands. In Montserrat (known as little Ireland), which was largely colonized by Irish prisoners, the negroes universally bear Irish surnames, and retain the Irish accent.

are found several sorts of fish, very pleasing to the palate, and also in great plenty. The country hereabouts is sufficiently watered with large and profound rivers and brooks, so that this part of the land may easily be cultivated without any great fear of droughts, it being certain that better streams are not to be found in any part of the world. The sea coasts and shores are also very pleasant, to which the tortoises resort in huge numbers, there to lay their eggs.

This island was formerly very well peopled on the North side with many towns and villages ; but these, being ruined by the Hollanders, were at last for the greatest part deserted by the Spaniards.

CHAPTER IV.

Of the Fruits, Trees and Animals that are found at Hispaniola.

THE spacious fields of this island commonly extend themselves to the length of five or six leagues, the beauty whereof is so pleasing to the eye that, together with the great variety of their natural productions, they infinitely applaud and captivate the senses of the contemplator. For here at once they not only, with diversity of objects, recreate the sight, but, with many of the same, also please the smell, and, with most, contribute abundancy of delights to the taste. With sundry diversities also they flatter and excite the appetite; but more especially with the multitude of oranges and lemons, here growing both sweet and sour, and those that participate of both tastes, and are only pleasantly tart. Besides which here abundantly grow several other sorts of the same fruit, such as are called citrons, toronjas and limes, in English not improperly called crab-lemons. True it is that, as to the lemons, they do not exceed here the bigness of a hen's egg; which smallness distinguishes them from those of Spain most frequently used in these our Northern countries. The date-trees, which here are seen to cover the whole extent of very spacious plains, are exceedingly tall in their proportion, which notwithstanding does not offend but rather delight the view. Their height is observed to be from 150 to 200 feet, being wholly destitute of branches to the very tops. Here it is there grows a certain pleasant white substance not unlike that of white cabbage, whence the branches and leaves sprout, and in which also the seed or dates are contained.

Every month one of those branches falls to the ground, and at the same time another sprouts out. But the seed ripens only once in the year. The dates are food extremely coveted by the hedgehogs. The white substance growing at the top of the tree is used by the Spaniards after the same manner for common sustenance as cabbage in Europe, they cutting it into slices, and boiling it in their *ollas*, or stews, with all sorts of meat. The leaves of this sort of date-tree are seven or eight foot in length and three or four in breadth, being very fit to cover houses with. For they defend from rain equally with the best tiles, though never so rudely huddled together. They make use of them also to wrap up smoked flesh with, and to make a certain sort of buckets wherewith to carry water, though no longer durable than the space of six, seven, or eight days. The cabbages of these trees, for so we may call them, are of a greenish colour on the outside, though inwardly very white, whence may be separated a sort of rind, which is very like parchment, being fit to write upon, as we do upon paper. The bodies of these trees are of an huge bulk or thickness, which two men can hardly compass with their arms. And yet they cannot properly be termed woody, but only three or four inches deep in thickness, all the rest of the internal part being very soft, insomuch that, paring off those three or four inches of woody substance, the remaining part of the body may be sliced like new cheese. They wound them three or four foot above the root, and, making an incision or broach in the body, thence gently distils a sort of liquor, which in short time by fermentation becomes as strong as the richest wine, and which easily inebriates if not used with moderation. The French call this sort of palm-trees *Frank-palms*, and they only grow, both here and elsewhere, in saltish grounds.

Besides these palm-trees of which we have made mention, there are also in Hispaniola four other species of palms, which are distinguished by the names of Latanier, Palma Espinosa or Prickle-palm, Palma à Chapelet or Rosary-palm, Palma Vinosa or Wine-palm. The Latanier-palm is not so tall as the Wine-palm, although it has almost the same shape, only that the leaves are very like the fans our women use. They grow mostly in gravelly and sandy ground, their circumference being of seven foot more or less. The body has many prickles or thorns of the length of half a foot, very sharp and pungent. It produces its seed after the same manner as that above-mentioned, which likewise serves for food to the wild beasts.

Another sort of these palm-trees is called Prickle-palm, as we said before, by reason it is infinitely full of prickles, from the root to the very leaves thereof, much more than the precedent. With these prickles some of the barbarous Indians torment their prisoners of war, whom they take in battle. They tie them to a tree, and then taking these thorns, they put them into little pellets of cotton, which they dip in oil, and thus stick them in the sides of the miserable prisoners, as thick as the bristles of a hedgehog; which of necessity cause an incredible torment to the patient. Afterwards they set them on fire, and if the tormented prisoner sings in the midst of his torments and flames, he is esteemed as a valiant and courageous soldier, who neither fears his enemies nor their torments. But if on the contrary he cries out, they esteem him but as a poltroon or coward, and unworthy of any memory. This custom was told me by an Indian, who said he had used his enemies thus oftentimes. The like cruelties to these, many Christians have seen while they lived among those barbarians. But returning to the Prickle-palm, I shall only tell you that this palm-tree is in this only different from the Latanier, that the leaves are like those of the Frank-palm. Its seed is like that of the other palm-trees, only much bigger and rounder, almost as a farthing, and inwardly full of little kernels, which are as pleasing to the taste as our walnuts in Europe. This tree grows for the most part in the marshes and low grounds of the sea coast.

The Wine-palm is so called from the abundance of wine which is gathered from it. This palm grows in high and rocky mountains, not exceeding in tallness the height of forty or fifty foot, but yet of an extraordinary shape or form. For from the root to the half of its proportion, it is only three or four inches thick. But upwards, something above the two-thirds of its height, it is as big and as thick as an ordinary bucket or milk-pail. Within, it is full of a certain matter, very like the tender stalk of a white cabbage, which is very juicy of a liquor that is much pleasing to the palate. This liquor after fermentation and settling of the grounds reduces itself into a very good and clear wine, which is purchased with no great industry. For having wounded the tree with an ordinary hatchet, they make a square incision or orifice in it, through which they bruise the said matter until it be capable of being squeezed out, or expressed with the hands, they needing no other instrument than this. With the leaves they make certain vessels, not only to settle and purify the afore-mentioned liquor, but also to drink in. It bears its fruit like other palms, but of a very small shape, being not unlike cherries. The taste hereof is very good, but of dangerous consequence to the throat, where it causes huge and extreme pains, that produce malignant quinsies in them that eat it.

The Palma à Chapelet, or Rosary-palm, was thus called both by the French and Spaniards, because its seed is very fit to make rosaries or beads to say prayers upon, the beads being small, hard and capable of being easily bored for that use. This fourth species grows on the tops of the highest mountains, and is of an excessive tallness, but withal very straight, and adorned with very few leaves.

Here grows also in this island a certain sort of Apricot trees, whose fruit equals in bigness that of our ordinary melons. The colour is like ashes, and the taste the very same as that of our apricots in Europe, the inward stones of this fruit being of the bigness of a hen's egg. On these the wild boars feed very deliciously, and fatten even to admiration.

The trees called caremites are very like our pear-trees, whose fruits resemble much our Damascene plums or pruants of Europe, being of a very pleasant and agreeable taste and almost as sweet as milk. This fruit is black on the inside, and the kernels thereof, sometimes only two in number, sometimes three, others five, of the bigness of a lupin. This plum affords no less pleasant food to the wild boars than the apricots above-mentioned, only that it is not so commonly to be found upon the island, nor in such quantity as those are.

The Genipa-trees are seen everywhere all over this island, being very like our cherry-trees, although its branches are more dilated. The fruit hereof is of an ash colour, of the bigness of two fists, which interiorly is full of many prickles or points that are involved under a thin membrane or skin, the which, if not taken away at the time of eating, causes great obstructions and gripings of the belly. Before this fruit grows ripe, if pressed, it affords a juice as black as ink, being fit to write with upon paper. But the letters disappear within the space of nine days, the paper remaining as white as if it never had been written upon. The wood of this tree is very strong, solid and hard, good to build ships with, seeing it is observed to last many years in the water without putrefaction.

Besides these, divers other sorts of trees are natives of this delicious island, that produce very excellent and pleasant fruits. Of these I shall omit to name several, knowing there are entire volumes of learned authors that have both described and searched them with greater attention and curiosity than my own. Notwithstanding, I shall continue to make mention of some few more in particular. Such are the Cedars, which trees this part of the world produces in prodigious quantity. The French nation calls them *Acajou;* and they find them very useful for the building of ships and canoes.[1] These canoes are like little wherry-boats, being made of one tree only, excavated, and fitted for the sea. They are withal so swift as for that very property they may be called "Neptune's post-horses." The Indians make these canoes without the use of any iron instruments, by only burning the trees at the bottom near the root, and afterwards governing the fire with such industry that nothing is burnt more than what they would have. Some of them have hatchets, made of flint, wherewith they scrape or pare off whatsoever was burnt too far. And thus, by the sole instrument of fire, they know how to give them that shape which renders them capable of navigating threescore or fourscore leagues with ordinary security.

As to medicinal productions, here is to be found the tree that affords the *gum elemi*, used in our apothecaries' shops. Likewise *guaiacum*, or *lignum sanctum, lignum aloes*, or aloe-wood, *cassia lignea*, China-roots, with several others. The tree called *mapou*, besides that it is medicinal, is also used for making of canoes, as being very thick ; yet is it much inferior to the *acajou* or cedar, as being somewhat spongy, whereby it sucks in much water, rendering it dangerous in navigation. The tree called *acoma* has its wood very hard and heavy, of the colour of palm. These qualities render it very fit to make oars for the sugar mills. Here are also in great quantities *brasilete*, or brazil-wood, and that which the Spaniards call *mançanilla*.

Brazil-wood is now very well known in the provinces of Holland and the Low Countries. By another name it is called by the Spaniards *Lenna de Peje palo*. It

---

[1] The French term "Acajou" seems to be applied by the buccaneers to cedar wood; it is now, however, almost entirely confined to mahogany.

serves only, or chiefly, for dyeing, and what belongs to that trade. It grows abundantly along the sea coasts of this island, especially in two places called Jacmel and Jaquina. These are two commodious ports or bays, capable of receiving ships of the greatest bulk.

The tree called *mançanilla*, or dwarf-apple-tree,[1] grows near the sea shore, being naturally so low that its branches, though never so short, always touch the water. It bears a fruit something like our sweet-scented apples, which notwithstanding is of a very venomous quality. For these apples being eaten by any person, he instantly changes colour, and such a huge thirst seizes him as all the water of the Thames cannot extinguish, he dying raving mad within a little while after. But what is more, the fish that eat, as it often happens, of this fruit are also poisonous. This tree affords also a liquor, both thick and white, like the fig-tree, which, if touched by the hand, raises blisters upon the skin, and these are so red in colour as if it had been deeply scalded with hot water. One day being hugely tormented with mosquitos or gnats, and as yet unacquainted with the nature of this tree, I cut a branch thereof, to serve me instead of a fan, but all my face swelled the next day and filled with blisters, as if it were burnt to such a degree that I was blind for three days.

Ycao is the name of another sort of tree, so called by the Spaniards, which grows by the sides of rivers. This bears a certain fruit, not unlike our bullace or damson plums. And this food is extremely coveted by the wild boar, when at its perfect maturity, with which they fatten as much as our hogs with the sweetest acorns of Spain. These trees love sandy ground, yet are so low that, their branches being very large, they take up a great circumference, almost couched upon the ground. The trees named Abelcoses bear fruit of like colour with

---

[1] The well-known manchineel, erroneously supposed to be the upas-tree, which latter owes its reputation to a Malay legend.

the Ycaos above-mentioned, but of the bigness of melons, the seeds or kernels being as big as eggs. The substance of this fruit is yellow, and of a pleasant taste, which the poorest among the French eat instead of bread, the wild boar not caring at all for this fruit. These trees grow very tall and thick, being somewhat like our largest sort of pear-trees.

As to the insects which this island produces, I shall only take notice of three sorts of flies, which excessively torment all human bodies, but more especially such as never before, or but a little while, were acquainted with these countries. The first sort of these flies are as big as our common horse-flies in Europe. And these, darting themselves upon men's bodies, there stick and suck their blood till they can no longer fly. Their importunity obliges to make almost continual use of branches of trees wherewith to fan them away. The Spaniards in those parts call them mosquitos or gnats, but the French give them the name of *maranguines.* The second sort of these insects is no bigger than a grain of sand. These make no buzzing noise, as the preceding species does, for which reason it is less avoidable, as being able also through its smallness to penetrate the finest linen or cloth. The hunters are forced to anoint their faces with hogs'-grease, thereby to defend themselves from the stings of these little animals. By night, in their huts or cottages, they constantly for the same purpose burn the leaves of tobacco, without which smoke they were not able to rest. True it is that in the daytime they are not very troublesome, if any wind be stirring ; for this, though never so little, causes them to dissipate. The gnats of the third species exceed not the bigness of a grain of mustard.[1] Their colour is red. These sting not at all, but bite so sharply upon the flesh as to create little ulcers therein. Whence it often

[1] This is the Bête rouge, one of the greatest plagues of the West Indies.

comes that the face swells and is rendered hideous to the view, through this inconvenience.   These are chiefly troublesome by day, even from the beginning of the morning until sun-setting, after which time they take their rest, and permit human bodies to do the same. The Spaniards gave these insects the name of *rojados*, and the French that of *calarodes*.

The insects which the Spaniards call *cochinillas* and the English glow-worms are also to be found in these parts.   These are very like such as we have in Europe, unless that they are somewhat bigger and longer than ours.   They have two little specks on their heads, which by night give so much light that three or four of those animals, being together upon a tree, it is not discernible at a distance from a bright shining fire.   I had on a certain time at once three of these cochinillas in my cottage, which there continued until past midnight, shining so brightly that without any other light I could easily read in any book, although of never so small a print.   I attempted to bring some of these insects into Europe, when I came from those parts, but as soon as they came into a colder climate they died by the way. They lost also their shining on the change of air, even before their death.   This shining is so great, according to what I have related, that the Spaniards with great reason may well call them from their luminous quality *moscas de fuego*, that is to say fire-flies.

There be also in Hispaniola an excessive number of *grillones* or crickets.   These are of an extraordinary magnitude, if compared to ours, and so full of noise that they are ready to burst themselves with singing, if any person comes near them.   Here is no lesser number of reptiles, such as serpents and others, but by a particular providence of the Creator these have no poison. Neither do they any other harm than to what fowl they can catch, but more especially to pullets, pigeons and others of this kind.   Ofttimes these serpents or

snakes are useful in houses to cleanse them of rats and
mice. For with great cunning they counterfeit their
shrieks, and hereby both deceive and catch them at their
pleasure. Having taken them, they in no wise eat the
guts of these vermin, but only suck their blood at first.
Afterwards throwing away the guts, they swallow almost
entire the rest of the body, which, as it should seem,
they readily digest into soft excrements, of which they
discharge their bellies. Another sort of reptiles belonging to this island is called by the name of *caçadores de
moscas*, or fly-catchers. This name was given to this
 eptile by the Spaniards, by reason they never could
experience it lived upon any other food than flies.
Hence it cannot be said this creature causes any harm
to the inhabitants, but rather benefit, seeing it consumes
by its continual exercise of hunting the vexatious and
troublesome flies.

Land-tortoises here are also in great quantities.
They mostly breed in mud, and fields that are overflown
with water. The inhabitants eat them, and testify they
are very good food. But a sort of spider which is here
found is very hideous. These are as big as an ordinary
egg, and their feet as long as those of the biggest sea-
crabs. Withal, they are very hairy, and have four black
teeth, like those of a rabbit, both in bigness and shape.
Notwithstanding, their bites are not venomous, although
they can bite very sharply, and do use it very commonly.
They breed for the most part in the roofs of houses. This
island also is not free from the insect called in Latin
millepes, and in Greek *scolopendria*, or " Many-feet ":
neither is it void of scorpions. Yet, by the providence of
nature, neither the one nor the other bears the least
suspicion of poison. For although they cease not to
bite, yet their wounds require not the application of any
medicament for their cure. And although their bites
cause some inflammation and swelling at the beginning,
however these symptoms disappear of their own accord.

Thus in the whole circumference of Hispaniola, no animal is found that produces the least harm with its venom.

After the insects above-mentioned, I shall not omit to say something of that terrible beast called cayman. This is a certain species of crocodile, wherewith this island very plentifully abounds. Among these caymans some are found to be of a corpulency very horrible to the sight. Certain it is, that such have been seen as had no less than threescore and ten foot in length, and twelve in breadth. Yet more marvellous than their bulk is their cunning and subtlety wherewith they purchase their food. Being hungry, they place themselves near the sides of rivers, more especially at the fords, where cattle come to drink or wade over. Here they lie without any motion, nor stirring any part of their body, resembling an old tree fallen into the river, only floating upon the waters, whither these will carry them. Yet they recede not far from the bank-sides, but continually lurk in the same place, waiting till some wild boar or salvage cow comes to drink or refresh themselves at that place. At which point of time, with huge activity, they assault them, and seizing on them with no less fierceness, they drag the prey into the water and there stifle it. But what is more worthy admiration is, that three or four days before the caymans go upon this design, they eat nothing at all. But, diving into the river, they swallow one or two hundred-weight of stones, such as they can find. With these they render themselves more heavy than before, and make addition to their natural strength (which in this animal is very great), thereby to render their assault the more terrible and secure. The prey being thus stifled, they suffer it to lie four or five days under water untouched. For they could not eat the least bit thereof, unless half rotten. But when it is arrived at such a degree of putrefaction as is most pleasing to their palate, they devour it with great appetite and voracity. If they can lay hold on any hides

of beasts, such as the inhabitants ofttimes place in the
fields for drying in the sun, they drag them into the
water.   Here they leave them for some days, well
loaden with stones, till the hair falls off.   Then they eat
them with no less appetite than they would the animals
themselves, could they catch them.   I have seen myself,
many times, like things to these I have related.   But
besides my own experience, many writers of natural things
have made entire treatises of these animals, describing
not only their shape, magnitude and other qualities, but
also their voracity and brutish inclinations ; which, as I
have told you, are very strange.   A certain person of
good reputation and credit told me that one day he was
by the river-side, washing his *baraca*, or tent, wherein he
used to lie in the fields.   As soon as he began his work,
a cayman fastened upon the tent, and with incredible fury
dragged it under water.   The man, desirous to see if he
could save his tent, pulled on the contrary side with all
his strength, having in his mouth a butcher's knife
(wherewith as it happened he was scraping the canvas)
to defend himself in case of urgent necessity.   The
cayman, being angry at this opposition, vaulted upon his
body, out of the river, and drew him with great celerity
into the water, endeavouring with the weight of his bulk
to stifle him under the banks.   Thus finding himself in
the greatest extremity, almost crushed to death by that
huge and formidable animal, with his knife he gave the
cayman several wounds in the belly, wherewith he suddenly
expired.   Being thus delivered from the hands of imminent fate, he drew the cayman out of the water, and with
the same knife opened the body, to satisfy his curiosity.
In his stomach he found nearly one hundred-weight of
stones, each of them being almost of the bigness of his fist.
    The caymans are ordinarily busied in hunting and
catching of flies, which they eagerly devour.   The
occasion is, because close to their skin they have certain
little scales, which smell with a sweet scent, something

like musk. This aromatic odour is coveted by the flies, and here they come to repose themselves and sting. Thus they both persecute each other continually, with an incredible hatred and antipathy. Their manner of procreating and hatching their young ones is as follows. They approach the sandy banks of some river that lies exposed to the rays of the south sun. Among these sands they lay their eggs, which afterwards they cover with their feet; and here they find them hatched, and with young generation, by the heat only of the sun. These, as soon as they are out of the shell, by natural instinct run to the water. Many times those eggs are destroyed by birds that find them out, as they scrape among the sands. Hereupon the females of the caymans, at such times as they fear the coming of any flocks of birds, ofttimes by night swallow their eggs, and keep them in their stomach till the danger is over. And, from time to time, they bury them again in the sand, as I have told you, bringing them forth again out of their belly till the season is come of being excluded the shell. At this time, if the mother be near at hand, they run to her and play with her as little whelps would do with their dams, sporting themselves according to their own custom. In this sort of sport they will oftentimes run in and out of their mother's belly, even as rabbits into their holes. This I have seen them do many times, as I have spied them at play with their dam over the water upon the contrary banks of some river. At which time I have often disturbed their sport by throwing a stone that way, causing them on a sudden to creep into the mother's bowels, for fear of some imminent danger. The manner of procreating of those animals is always the same as I have related, and at the same time of the year, for they neither meddle nor make with one another but in the month of May. They give them in this country the name of crocodiles, though in other places of the West Indies they go under the name of caymans.

CHAPTER V.

*Of all sorts of quadruped Animals and Birds that are found in
this Island. As also a relation of the French Buccaneers.*

BESIDES the fruits which this island produces, whose
plenty, as is held for certain, surpasses all the islands of
America, it abounds also very plentifully in all sorts of
quadruped animals, such as horses, bulls, cows, wild
boars, and others very useful to human kind, not only for
common sustenance of life, but also for cultivating the
ground and the management of a sufficient commerce.

In this island therefore are still remaining a huge number of wild dogs. These destroy yearly multitudes of all
sorts of cattle. For no sooner has a cow brought forth
her calf, or a mare foaled, than these wild mastiffs come
to devour the young breed, if they find not some resistance from keepers and other domestic dogs. They run
up and down the woods and fields commonly in whole
troops of fifty, threescore or more, together, being
withal so fierce that they ofttimes will assault an entire
herd of wild boars, not ceasing to persecute them till they
have at last overcome and torn in pieces two or three.
One day a French buccaneer caused me to see a strange
action of this kind. Being in the fields hunting together, we heard a great noise of dogs, which had surrounded a wild boar. Having tame dogs with us, we left
them to the custody of our servants, desirous to see the
sport, if possible. Hence my companion and I, each of us,
climbed up into several trees, both for security and prospect. The wild boar was all alone, and standing against
a tree ; with his tusks he endeavoured to defend himself

from a great number of dogs that had enclosed him, having with his teeth killed and wounded several of them. This bloody fight continued about an hour, the wild boar meanwhile attempting many times to escape. At last, being upon the flight, one of those dogs leaped on his back, and the rest of the dogs, perceiving the courage of their companion, fastened likewise upon the boar, and presently after killed him. This being done, all of them the first only excepted, laid themselves down upon the ground about the prey, and there peaceably continued till he, the first and most courageous of the troop, had eaten as much as he could devour. When this dog had ended his repast and left the dead beast, all the rest fell in to take their share, till nothing was left that they could devour. What ought we to infer from this notable action, performed by the brutish sense of wild animals? Only this, that even beasts themselves are not destitute of knowledge, and that they give us documents how to honour such as have well deserved, seeing these, being irrational animals as they were, did reverence and respect him that exposed his life to the greatest danger, in vanquishing courageously the common enemy.

The Governor of Tortuga, Monsieur Ogeron, understanding that the wild dogs killed too many of the wild boars, and that the hunters of that island had much-a-do to find any, fearing lest that common sustenance of the isle should fail, caused a great quantity of poison to be brought from France, therewith to destroy the wild mastiffs. This was performed in the year 1668, by commanding certain horses to be killed and envenomed, and laid open in the woods and fields, at certain places where mostly wild dogs used to resort. This being continued for the space of six months, there were killed an incredible number in the said time. And yet all this industry was not sufficient to exterminate and destroy the race; yea, scarce to make any diminution thereof, their number appearing to be almost as entire as before. These wild

dogs are easily rendered tame among people, even as
tame as the ordinary dogs we breed in houses.   Moreover, the hunters of those parts, whensoever they find a
wild bitch with young whelps, commonly take away the
puppies, and bring them to their houses, where they find
them, being grown up, to hunt much better than other
dogs.

But here the curious reader may peradventure enquire
whence or by what accident came so many wild dogs into
those islands ?   The occasion was that the Spaniards,
having possessed themselves of these isles, found them
much peopled with Indians.   These were a barbarous
sort of people, totally given to sensuality and a brutish
custom of life, hating all manner of labour, and only in-
clined to run from place to place, killing and making war
against their neighbours, not out of any ambition to reign,
but only because they agreed not with themselves in
some common terms of language.   Hence perceiving
the dominion of the Spaniards laid a great restriction
upon their lazy and brutish customs, they conceived an
incredible odium against them, such as never was to be
reconciled.   But more especially, because they saw them
take possession of their kingdoms and dominions.   Hereupon they made against them all the resistance they were
capable of, opposing everywhere their designs to the
utmost of their power, until the Spaniards, finding themselves to be cruelly hated by those Indians, and no-
where secure from their treacheries, resolved to extirpate
and ruin them every one ; especially seeing they could
neither tame them by the civilities of their customs, nor
conquer them with the sword.   But the Indians, it being
their ancient custom to make their woods their chiefest
places of defence, at present made these their refuge
whenever they fled from the Spaniards that pursued them.
Hereupon those first conquerors of the New World made
use of dogs to range and search the intricatest thickets
of woods and forests for those their implacable and un-

conquerable enemies.   By this means they forced them
to leave their ancient refuge and submit to the sword,
seeing no milder usage would serve turn.   Hereupon
they killed some of them, and, quartering their bodies,
placed them in the highways, to the intent that others
might take warning from such a punishment, not to incur
the like danger.   But this severity proved to be of ill
consequence.   For, instead of frighting them and reducing
their minds to a civil society, they conceived such horror
of the Spaniards and their proceedings, that they resolved
to detest and fly their sight for ever.   And hence the
greatest part died in caves and subterraneous places of
the woods and mountains ; in which places I myself have
seen many times great numbers of human bones.   The
Spaniards afterwards, finding no more Indians to appear
about the woods, endeavoured to rid themselves of the
great number of dogs they had in their houses, whence
these animals, finding no masters to keep them, betook
themselves to the woods and fields, there to hunt for food
to preserve their lives.   Thus by degrees they became
unacquainted with the houses of their ancient masters,
and at last grew wild.   This is the truest account I can
give of the multitudes of wild dogs which are seen to this
day in these parts.

But besides the wild mastiffs above-mentioned, here
are also huge numbers of wild horses to be seen everywhere.   These run up and down in whole herds or flocks
all over the Island of Hispaniola.   They are but low of
stature, short-bodied, with great heads, long necks, and
big or thick legs.   In a word, they have nothing that is
handsome in all their shape.   They are seen to run up
and down commonly in troops of two or three hundred
together, one of them going always before, to lead the
multitude.   When they meet any person that travels
through the woods or fields, they stand still, suffering him
to approach till he can almost touch them, and then,
suddenly starting, they betake themselves to flight,

running away disorderly, as fast as they are able. The
hunters catch them with industry, only for the benefit of
their skins, although sometimes they preserve their flesh
likewise, which they harden with smoke, using it for provisions when they go to sea.

Here would be also wild bulls and cows, in greater
number than at present, if by continuation of hunting their
race were not much diminished. Yet considerable profit
is made even to this day by such as make it their business to kill them. The wild bulls are of a vast corpulency, or bigness of body ; and yet they do no hurt to
any person if they be not exasperated, but left to their
own repose. The hides which are taken from them are
from eleven to thirteen foot long.

The diversity of birds inhabiting the air of this island
is so great that I should be troublesome, as well to the
reader as myself, if I should attempt to muster up their
species. Hence, leaving aside the prolix catalogue of
their multitude, I shall content myself only to mention
some few of the chiefest. Here is a certain species of
pullets in the woods, which the Spaniards call by the
name of *pintadas*, which the inhabitants find without any
distinction to be as good as those which are bred in
houses. It is already known to everybody that the
parrots which we have in Europe are transported to us
from these parts of the world. Whence may be inferred
that, seeing such a number of these talkative birds are
preserved among us, notwithstanding the diversity of
climates, much greater multitudes are to be found where
the air and temperament is natural to them. The parrots make their nests in holes of palmetto-trees, which
holes are before made to their hand by other birds.
The reason is, forasmuch as they are not capable of
excavating any wood, though never so soft, as having
their own bills too crooked and blunt. Hence provident
nature has supplied them with the labour and industry of
another sort of small birds called *carpinteros*, or carpenters.

These are no bigger than sparrows, yet notwithstanding of such hard and piercing bills, that no iron instrument can be made more apt to excavate any tree, though never so solid and hard. In the holes therefore fabricated beforehand by these birds, the parrots get possession, and build their nests, as has been said.

Pigeons of all sorts are also here abundantly provided to the inhabitants by Him that created in the beginning and provided all things. For eating of them, those of this island observe the same seasons as we said before, speaking of the Isle of Tortuga. Betwixt the pigeons of both islands little or no difference is observable, only that these of Hispaniola are something fatter and bigger than those. Another sort of small birds here are called *cabreros*, or goat-keepers. These are very like others called *heronsetas*, and chiefly feed upon crabs of the sea. In these birds are found seven distinct bladders of gall, and hence their flesh is as bitter to the taste as aloes. Crows or ravens, more troublesome to the inhabitants than useful, here make a hideous noise through the whole circumference of the island. Their ordinary food is the flesh of wild dogs, or the carcases of those beasts the buccaneers kill and throw away. These clamorous birds no sooner hear the report of a fowling-piece or musket than they gather from all sides into whole flocks, and fill the air and woods with their unpleasant notes. They are in nothing different from those we see in Europe.

It is now high time to speak of the French nation, who inhabit a great part of this island. We have told, at the beginning of this book, after what manner they came at first into these parts. At present, therefore, we shall only describe their manner of living, customs and ordinary employments. The different callings or professions they follow are generally but three : either to hunt, or plant, or else to rove on the sea in quality of pirates. It is a general and solemn custom amongst them all to seek out for a comrade or companion, whom we may call partner, in their fortunes, with whom they join the whole stock of what they possess, towards a mutual and recip-rocal gain. This is done also by articles drawn and signed on both sides, according to what has been agreed between them. Some of these constitute their surviving companion absolute heir to what is left by the death of the first of the two. Others, if they be married, leave their estates to their wives and children; others to other relations. This being done, every one applies himself to his calling, which is always one of the three afore-mentioned.

The hunters are again sub-divided into two several sorts. For some of these are only given to hunt wild bulls and cows ; others hunt only wild boars. The first of these two sorts of hunters are called buccaneers. These not long ago were about the number of six hun-dred upon this island ; but at present there are not reckoned to be above three hundred, more or less. The cause has been the great decrease of wild cattle through the dominions of the French in Hispaniola, which has appeared to be so notable that, far from getting any con-siderable gain, they at present are but poor in this exer-cise. When the buccaneers go into the woods to hunt for wild bulls and cows, they commonly remain there the space of a whole twelvemonth or two years, without returning home. After the hunt is over and the spoil divided among them, they commonly sail to the Isle of Tortuga, there to provide themselves with guns, powder, bullets and small shot, with all other necessaries against another going out or hunting. The rest of their gains they spend with great liberality, giving themselves freely to all manner of vices and debauchery, among which the first is that of drunkenness, which they exercise for the most part with brandy. This they drink as liberally as the Spaniards do clear fountain water. Sometimes they buy together a pipe of wine ; this they stave at the one

end, and never cease drinking till they have made an end
of it Thus they celebrate the festivals of Bacchus so
long as they have any money left. For all the tavern-
keepers wait for the coming of these lewd buccaneers,
even after the same manner that they do at Amsterdam
for the arrival of the East India fleet at the Texel.
The said buccaneers are hugely cruel and tyrannical
towards their servants ; insomuch that commonly these
had rather be galley slaves in the Straits, or saw brazil-
wood in the rasp-houses of Holland, than serve such
barbarous masters.

The second sort of hunters hunt nothing else but wild
boars. The flesh of these they salt, and, being thus preserved from corruption, they sell it to the planters. These
hunters have also the same vicious customs of life, and
are as much addicted to all manner of debauchery as the
former. But their manner of hunting is quite different
from what is practised in Europe. For these buccaneers
have certain places, designed for hunting, where they live
for the space of three or four months, and sometimes,
though not often, a whole year. Such places are called
Deza Boulan ; and in these, with only the company of five
or six friends, who go along with them, they continue all
the time above-mentioned, in mutual friendship. The
first buccaneers we spoke of many times make an agreement with certain planters to furnish them with meat all
the whole year at a certain price. The payment hereof is often made with two or three hundred-weight of
tobacco, in the leaf. But the planters commonly into the
bargain furnish them likewise with a servant, whom they
send to help. To the servant they afford a sufficient
quantity of all necessaries for that purpose, especially of
powder, bullets and small shot, to hunt with.

The planters began to cultivate and plant the Isle of
Tortuga in the year 1598. The first plantation was of
tobacco, which grew to admiration, being likewise of very
good quality. Notwithstanding, by reason of the small

circumference of the island, they were then able to plant
but little; especially there being many pieces of land in
that isle that were not fit to produce tobacco. They
attempted likewise to make sugar, but by reason of the
great expenses necessary to defray the charges, they
could not bring it to any effect. So that the greatest part
of the inhabitants, as we said before, betook themselves
to the exercise of hunting, and the remaining part to that
of piracy. At last the hunters, finding themselves scarce
able to subsist by their first profession, began likewise to
seek out lands that might be rendered fit for culture; and
in these they also planted tobacco. The first land that
they chose for this purpose was Cul de Sac, whose territory extends towards the Southern part of the island.
This piece of ground they divided into several quarters,
which were called the Great Amea, Niep, Rochelois, the
Little Grave, the Great Grave, and the Augame. Here,
by little and little, they increased so much, that at present
there are above two thousand planters in those fields.
At the beginning they endured very much hardship,
seeing that while they were busied about their husbandry,
they could not go out of the island to seek provisions.
This hardship was also increased by the necessity of
grubbing, cutting down, burning and digging, whereby to
extirpate the innumerable roots of shrubs and trees. For
when the French possessed themselves of that island, it
was wholly overgrown with woods extremely thick, these
being only inhabited by an extraordinary number of wild
boars. The method they took to clear the ground was
to divide themselves into small companies of two or three
persons together, and these companies to separate far
enough from each other, provided with a few hatchets
and some quantity of coarse provision. With these things
they used to go into the woods, and there to build huts
for their habitation, of only a few rafters and boughs of
trees. Their first endeavour was to root up the shrubs
and little trees; afterwards to cut down the great ones.

These they gathered into heaps, with their branches, and then set them on fire, excepting the roots, which, last of all, they were constrained. to grub and dig up after the best manner they could. The first seed they committed to the ground was beans. These in those countries both ripen and dry away in the space of six weeks.

The second fruit, necessary to human life, which here they tried, was potatoes. These do not come to perfection in less time than four or five months. On these they most commonly make their breakfasts every morning. They dress them no otherwise than by boiling them in a kettle with fair water. Afterwards they cover them with a cloth for the space of half an hour, by which manner of dressing they become as soft as boiled chestnuts. Of the said potatoes also they make a drink called Maiz. They cut them into small slices, and cover them with hot water. When they are well imbibed with water, they press them through a coarse cloth, and the liquor that comes out, although somewhat thick, they keep in vessels made for that purpose. Here, after settling two or three days, it begins to work; and, having thrown off its lees, is fit for drink. They use it with great delight, and although the taste is somewhat sour, yet it is very pleasant, substantial and wholesome. The industry of this composition is owing to the Indians, as well as of many others, which the ingenuity of those barbarians caused them to invent both for the preservation and the pleasure of their own life.

The third fruit the newly cultivated land afforded was Mandioca, which the Indians by another name call Cassava. This is a certain root which they plant, but comes not to perfection till after eight or nine months, sometimes a whole year. Being thoroughly ripe, it may be left in the ground the space of eleven or twelve months, without the least suspicion of corruption. But this time being past, the said roots must be converted to use some way or another, otherwise they conceive a total

putrefaction. Of these roots of Cassava, in those countries,
is made a sort of granulous flour or meal, extremely dry
and white, which supplies the want of common bread
made of wheat, whereof the fields are altogether barren
in that island. For this purpose they have in their houses
certain graters made either of copper or tin, wherewith they grate the afore-mentioned roots, just as they
do Mirick in Holland. By the by, let me tell you,
Mirick is a certain root of a very biting taste, not unlike
to strong mustard, wherewith they usually make sauces
for some sorts of fish. When they have grated as much
Cassava root as will serve turn, they put the gratings
into bags or sacks, made of coarse linen, and press out all
the moisture, until they remain very dry. Afterwards
they pass the gratings through a sieve, leaving them,
after sifting, very like sawdust. The meal being thus
prepared, they lay it upon planches of iron, which are
made very hot, upon which it is converted into a sort of
cakes, very thin. These cakes are afterwards placed
in the sun, upon the tops of houses, where they are
thoroughly and perfectly dried. And lest they should
lose any part of their meal, what did not pass the sieve is
made up into rolls, five or six inches thick. These are
placed one upon another, and left in this posture until
they begin to corrupt. Of this corrupted matter they
make a liquor, by them called Veycou, which they find
very excellent, and certainly is not inferior to our English
beer.

Bananas are likewise another sort of fruit, of which is
made another excellent liquor, which, both in strength
and pleasantness of taste, may be compared with the best
wines of Spain. But this liquor of Bananas, as it easily
causes drunkenness in such as use it immoderately, so it
likewise very frequently inflames the throat, and produces
dangerous diseases in that part. Guines agudos is also
another fruit whereof they make drink. But this sort of
liquor is not so strong as the preceding. Howbeit, both

the one and the other are frequently mingled with water, thereby to quench thirst.

After they had cultivated these plantations, and filled them with all sorts of roots and fruits necessary for human life, they began to plant tobacco, for trading. The manner of planting this frequent commodity is as follows. They make certain beds of earth in the field, no larger than twelve foot square. These beds they cover very well with palmetto leaves, to the intent that the rays of the sun may not touch the earth wherein tobacco is sowed. They water them, likewise, when it does not rain, as we do our gardens in Europe. When it is grown about the bigness of young lettuce, they transplant it into straight lines which they make in other spacious fields, setting every plant at the distance of three foot from each other. They observe, likewise, the fittest seasons of the year for these things, which are commonly from January until the end of March, these being the months wherein most rains fall in those countries. Tobacco ought to be weeded very carefully, seeing that the least root of any other herb, coming near it, is sufficient to hinder its growth. When it is grown to the height of one foot and a half or there-abouts, they cut off the tops, thereby to hinder the stalks and leaves from shooting too high upwards, to the intent that the whole plant may receive greater strength from the earth, which affords it all its vigour and taste. While it ripens and comes to full perfection, they prepare in their houses certain apartments of fifty or threescore foot in length, and thirty or forty in breadth. These they fill with branches of trees and rafters, and upon them lay the green tobacco to dry. When it is thoroughly dried, they strip off the leaf from the stalks, and cause it to be rolled up by certain people who are employed in this work and no other. To these they afford for their labour the tenth part of what they make up into rolls. This property is peculiar to tobacco, which therefore I shall not omit, that if, while it is yet in the ground, the leaf be pulled off from

the stalk, it sprouts again, no less than four times in one
year.   Here I should be glad to give an account also of
the manner of making sugar, indigo, and gimbes [1]; but
seeing these things are not planted in those parts whereof we now speak, I have thought fit to pass them over in
silence.

The French planters of the Isle of Hispaniola have
always to this present time been subject to the Governors of Tortuga.   Yet this obedience has not been rendered without much reluctance and grudging on their
side.   In the year 1664 the West India Company of
France laid the foundations of a colony in Tortuga, under
which colony the planters of Hispaniola were compre-
hended and named, as subjects thereto.   This decree
disgusted the said planters very much, they taking it very
ill to be reputed subjects to a private Company of men
who had no authority to make them so ; especially being
in a country which did not belong to the dominions of
the King of France.   Hereupon they resolved to work
no longer for the said Company.   And this resolution of
theirs was sufficient to compel the Company to a total
dissolution of the Colony.   But at last the Governor of
Tortuga, who was pretty well stocked with planters, conceiving he could more easily force them than the West
India Company, found an invention whereby to draw
them to his obedience.   He promised them he would put
off their several sorts of merchandise, and cause such
returns to be made, in lieu of their goods from France,
as they should best like.   Withal, he dealt with the merchants under hand, that all ships whatsoever should come
consigned to him, and no persons should entertain any
correspondence with those planters of Hispaniola ; thinking thereby to avoid many inconveniences, and compel
them through necessity and want of all things to obey.
By this means he not only obtained the obedience he
designed from those people, but also that some merchants

[1] Probably gambier.

who had promised to deal with them and visit them now and then, no longer did it.

Notwithstanding what has been said, in the year 1669 two ships from Holland happened to arrive at the Isle of Hispaniola with all sorts of merchandise necessary in those parts. With these ships presently the planters aforesaid resolved to deal, and with the Dutch nation for the future, thinking hereby to withdraw their obedience from the Governor of Tortuga, and, by frustrating his designs, revenge themselves of what they had endured under his government. Not long after the arrival of the Hollanders, the Governor of Tortuga came to visit the plantation of Hispaniola, in a vessel very well armed. But the planters not only forbade him to come ashore, but with their guns also forced him to weigh anchor, and retire faster than he came. Thus the Hollanders began to trade with these people for all manner of things. But such relations and friends as the Governor had in Hispaniola used all the endeavours they were capable of to impede the commerce. This being understood by the planters, they sent them word that *in case they laid not aside their artifices, for the hindrance of the commerce which was begun with the Hollanders, they should every one assuredly be torn in pieces.* Moreover, to oblige farther the Hollanders and contemn the Governor and his party, they gave greater ladings to the two ships than they could desire, with many gifts and presents to the officers and mariners, whereby they sent them very well contented to their own country. The Hollanders came again very punctually, according to their promise, and found the planters under a greater indignation than before against the Governor; either because of the great satisfaction they had already conceived of this commerce with the Dutch, or that by their means they hoped to subsist by themselves without any further dependence upon the French nation. However, it was suddenly after, they set up another resolution something more strange than the preceding. The tenour hereof was, that they would go to the Island of Tortuga, and cut the Governor in pieces. Hereupon they gathered together as many canoes as they could, and set sail from Hispaniola, with design not only to kill the Governor, but also to possess themselves of the whole island. This they thought they could more easily perform, by reason of all necessary assistance which they believed would at any time be sent them from Holland. By which means they were already determined in their minds to erect themselves into a new Commonwealth, independent of the Crown of France. But no sooner had they begun this great revolution of their little State, when they received news of a war declared between the two nations in Europe. This wrought such a consternation in their minds as caused them to give over that enterprize, and retire without attempting anything.

In the meanwhile the Governor of Tortuga sent into France for aid towards his own security, and the reduction of those people to their former obedience. This was granted him, and two men-of-war were sent to Tortuga, with orders to be at his commands. Having received such a considerable support, he sent them very well equipped to the Isle of Hispaniola. Being arrived at the place, they landed part of their forces, with a design to force the people to the obedience of those whom they much hated in their hearts. But the planters, seeing the arrival of those two frigates, and not being ignorant of their design, fled into the woods, abandoning their houses and many of their goods, which they left behind. These were immediately rifled and burnt by the French without any compassion, not sparing the least cottage they found. Afterwards the Governor began to relent in his anger, and let them know by some messengers that *in case they would return to his obedience, he would give ear to some accommodation between them.* Hereupon the planters finding themselves destitute of all human relief and that they could expect no help from any side, surrendered to the Governor upon Articles, which were made and signed on both sides. But these were not too strictly observed, for he commanded two of the chief among them to be hanged. The residue were pardoned, and, moreover, he gave them free leave *to trade with any nation whatsoever they found most fit for their purpose.* With the grant of this liberty they began to recultivate their plantations, which gave them a huge quantity of very good tobacco; they selling yearly to the sum of twenty or thirty thousand rolls.

In this country the planters have but very few slaves, for want of which they themselves, and some servants they have, are constrained to do all the drudgery. These servants commonly oblige and bind themselves to their masters for the space of three years. But their masters, forsaking all conscience and justice, oftentimes traffic with their bodies, as with horses at a fair; selling them to other masters, just as they sell negroes brought from the coast of Guinea. Yea, to advance this trade, some persons there are who go purposely into France (the same happens in England and other countries), and travelling through the cities, towns and villages, endeavour to pick up young men or boys, whom they transport, by making them great promises. These, being once allured and conveyed into the islands I speak of, they force to work like horses, the toil they impose upon them being much harder than what they usually enjoin on the negroes, their slaves. For these they endeavour in some manner to preserve, as being their perpetual bond-men; but as for their white servants, they care not whether they live or die, seeing that they are to continue no longer than three years in their service. These miserable kidnapped people are frequently subject to a certain disease, which in those parts is called coma, being a total privation of all their senses. And this distemper is judged to proceed from their hard usage, together with

VOL. I.   E

the change from their native climate into that which is
directly opposite. Oftentimes it happens that, among
these transported people, such are found as are persons
of good quality and tender education. And these, being
of a softer constitution, are more suddenly surprised with
the disease above-mentioned and with several others
belonging to those countries, than those who have harder
bodies and have been brought up to all manner of
fatigue. Besides the hard usage they endure in their
diet, apparel and repose, many times they beat them so
cruelly that some of them fall down dead under the
hands of their cruel masters. This I have often seen
with my own eyes, not without great grief and regret.
Of many instances of this nature I shall only give you
the following history, as being somewhat remarkable in
its circumstances.

It happened that a certain planter of those countries
exercised such cruelty towards one of his servants as
caused him to run away. Having absconded for some
days in the woods from the fury of his tyrannical master,
at last he was taken, and brought back to the dominion
of this wicked Pharaoh. No sooner had he got him into
his hands than he commanded him to be tied to a tree.
Here he gave him so many lashes upon his naked back
as made his body run an entire stream of gore blood,
embruing therewith the ground about the tree. Afterwards, to make the smart of his wounds the greater, he
anointed them with juice of lemon mingled with salt
and pepper, being ground small together. In this
miserable posture he left him tied to the tree for the
space of four and twenty hours. These being past, he
commenced his punishment again, lashing him as before,
with so much cruelty that the miserable wretch, under
this torture, gave up the ghost, with these dying words
in his mouth: *I beseech the Almighty God, Creator of
heaven and earth, that he permit the wicked Spirit to
make thee feel as many torments, before thy death, as*

thou hast caused me to feel before mine. A strange thing
and worthy all astonishment and admiration! Scarce
three or four days were past after this horrible fact, when
the Almighty Judge, who had heard the clamours of that
tormented wretch, gave permission to the Author of
Wickedness suddenly to possess the body of that barbarous and inhuman *Amirricide*, who tormented him to
death. Insomuch that those tyrannical hands, wherewith he had punished to death his innocent servant, were
the tormentors of his own body. For with them, after a
miserable manner, he beat himself and lacerated his own
flesh, till he lost the very shape of man which nature had
given him; not ceasing to howl and cry, without any
rest either by day or night. Thus he continued to do
until he died, in that condition of raving madness wherein he surrendered his ghost to the same Spirit of Darkness who had tormented his body. Many other examples
of this kind I could rehearse, but these, not belonging to
our present discourse, I shall therefore omit.

The planters that inhabit the Caribbee Islands are
rather worse and more cruel to their servants than the
preceding. In the Isle of Saint Christopher dwells one,
whose name is Bettesa, very well known among the
Dutch merchants, who has killed above a hundred of his
servants with blows and stripes. The English do the
same with their servants. And the mildest cruelty they
exercise towards them is that, when they have served six
years of their time (the years they are bound for among
the English being seven complete), they use them with
such cruel hardship as forces them to beg of their masters
to sell them to others, although it be to begin another
servitude of seven years, or at least three or four. I
have known many who after this manner served fifteen
and twenty years before they could obtain their freedom.
Another thing very rigorous among that nation is a law
in those islands, whereby if any man owes to another
above five and twenty shillings, English money, in case

he cannot pay, he is liable to be sold for the space of six or eight months. I shall not trouble the patience of my reader any longer with relations of this kind, as belonging to another subject, different from what I have proposed to myself in this history. Whereupon I shall take my beginning hence to describe the famous actions and exploits of the greatest Pirates of my time, during my residence in those parts. These I shall endeavour to relate without the least note of passion or partiality ; yea, with that candour which is peculiar both to my mind and style : withal assuring my reader I shall give him no stories taken from others upon trust or hearsay, but only those enterprizes to which I was myself an eye-witness.

CHAPTER VI.

Of the Origin of the most famous Pirates of the coasts of America.
A notable exploit of Pierre le Grand.

I HAVE told you in the preceding chapters of this book, after what manner I was compelled to adventure my life among the Pirates of America—to which sort of men I think myself obliged to give this name, for no other reason than that they are not maintained or upheld in their actions by any Sovereign Prince. For this is certain, that the Kings of Spain have upon several occasions sent, by their Ambassadors, to the Kings of France and England, *complaining of the molestations and troubles those Pirates often caused upon the coasts of America, even in the calm of peace.* To whose Ambassadors it has always been answered: *That such men did not commit those acts of hostility and piracy as subjects of their Majesties; and therefore his Catholic Majesty might proceed against them according as he should find fit.* The King of France, besides what has been said, added to this answer: *That he had no fortress nor castle upon the Isle of Hispaniola, neither did he receive one farthing of tribute thence.* Moreover, the King of England adjoined: *That he had never given any patents or commissions to those of Jamaica, for committing any hostility against the subjects of his Catholic Majesty.* Neither did he only give this bare answer, but also, out of his Royal desire to pleasure the Court of Spain, recalled the Governor of Jamaica, placing another in his room. All this was not sufficient to prevent the Pirates of those parts from acting what mischief they could to the contrary. But before I commence the relation of their bold and insolent actions, I shall say something of their origin and most common exercises, as also of the chief among them, and their manner of arming before they go out to sea.

The first Pirate that was known upon the Island of Tortuga was named Pierre le Grand, or Peter the Great. He was born at the town of Dieppe, in Normandy. The action which rendered him famous was his taking of the Vice-Admiral of the Spanish flota, near the Cape of Tiburon, upon the Western side of the Island of Hispaniola. This bold exploit he performed alone with only one boat, wherein he had eight and twenty persons, no more, to help him. What gave occasion to this enterprize was that until that time the Spaniards had passed and repassed with all security, and without finding the least opposition, through the Bahama Channel. So that Pierre le Grand set out to sea by the Caicos, where he took this great ship with almost all facility imaginable. The Spaniards they found aboard were all set on shore, and the vessel presently sent into France. The manner how this undaunted spirit attempted and took such an huge ship, I shall give you out of the Journal of a true and faithful author, in the same words as I read. *The Boat*, he says, *wherein Pierre le Grand was with his companions, had now been at sea a long time, without finding anything, according to his intent of piracy, suitable to make a prey. And now their provisions beginning to fail, they could keep themselves no longer upon the ocean, or they must of necessity starve. Being almost reduced to despair, they espied a great ship belonging to the Spanish flota, which had separated from the rest. This bulky vessel they resolved to set upon and take, or die in the attempt. Hereupon they made sail towards her, with design to view her strength. And although they judged the vessel to be far above their forces, yet the covetousness of such a prey, and the extremity of fortune they were reduced to, made them adventure on such an enterprize. Being now come so near that they could not escape without danger of being all killed, the Pirates jointly made an oath to their captain, Pierre le Grand, to behave themselves courageously in this attempt, without the least fear or fainting. True it is, that these rovers had conceived an opinion that they should find the ship unprovided to fight, and that through this occasion they should master her by degrees. It was in the dusk of the evening, or soon after, when this great action was performed. But before it was begun, they gave orders to the surgeon of the boat to bore a hole in the sides thereof, to the intent that, their own vessel sinking under them, they might be compelled to attack more vigorously, and endeavour more hastily to run aboard the great ship. This was performed accordingly; and without any other arms than a pistol in one of their hands and a sword in the other, they immediately climbed up the sides of the ship, and ran altogether into the great cabin, where they found the Captain, with several of his companions, playing at cards. Here they set a pistol to his breast, commanding him to deliver up the ship to their obedience. The Spaniards seeing the Pirates aboard their ship, without scarce having seen them at sea, cried out, "Jesus bless us! Are these devils, or what are they?" In the meanwhile some of them took possession of the gun-room, and seized the arms and military affairs they found there, killing as many of the ship as made any opposition. By which means the Spaniards presently were compelled to surrender. That very day the Captain of the ship had been told by some of the Seamen that the boat, which was in view cruizing, was a boat of Pirates. To whom the Captain, slighting their advice, made answer:* "What then? Must I be afraid of such a pitiful thing as that is? No, nor though she were a ship as big and as strong as mine is." *As soon as Pierre le Grand had taken this magnificent prize, he detained in his service as many of the common seamen as he had need of, and the rest he set on shore. This being done, he immediately set sail for France, carrying with him all the riches he found in that huge vessel: here he continued without ever returning to the parts of America.*

The planters and hunters of the Isle of Tortuga had no sooner understood this happy event, and the rich prize those Pirates had obtained, than they resolved to follow their example. Hereupon many of them left their ordinary exercises and common employments, and used what means they could to get either boats or small vessels, wherein to exercise piracy. But not being able either to purchase or build them at Tortuga, at last they resolved to set forth in their canoes and seek them elsewhere. With these, therefore, they cruized at first upon Cape d'Alvarez, whereabouts the Spaniards used much to trade from one city to another in small boats. In these they carry hides, tobacco and other commodities to the port of Havana, which is the metropolis of that island, and to which the Spaniards from Europe frequently resort.

Hereabouts it was that those Pirates at the beginning took a great number of boats, laden with the aforesaid commodities. These boats they used to carry to the Isle of Tortuga, and there sell the whole purchase to the ships that waited in the port for their return, or accidentally happened to be there. With the gain of these prizes they provided themselves with necessaries, wherewithal to undertake other voyages. Some of these voyages were made towards the coast of Campeche, and others towards that of New Spain; in both which places the Spaniards at that time frequently exercised much commerce and trade. Upon those coasts they commonly found a great number of trading vessels and many times ships of great burden. Two of the biggest of these vessels, and two great ships which the Spaniards had laden with plate in the port of Campeche to go to Caracas, they took in less than a month's time, by cruizing to and fro. Being arrived at Tortuga with these prizes, and the whole people of the island admiring their progresses, especially that within the space of two years the riches of the country were much increased, the number also of Pirates augmented so fast, that from these beginnings, within a little space of time, there were to be numbered in that small island and port above twenty ships of this sort of people. Hereupon the Spaniards, not able to bear their robberies any longer, were constrained to put forth to sea two great men-of-war, both for the defence of their own coasts, and to cruize upon the enemies

CHAPTER VII.

After what manner the Pirates arm their vessels, and how they regulate their voyages.

BEFORE the Pirates go out to sea, they give notice to every one that goes upon the voyage, of the day on which they ought precisely to embark, intimating also to them their obligation of bringing each man in particular so many pounds of powder and bullets as they think necessary for that expedition. Being all come on board, they join together in council, concerning what place they ought first to go to wherein to get provisions—especially of flesh, seeing they scarce eat anything else. And of this the most common sort among them is pork. The next food is tortoises, which they are accustomed to salt a little. Sometimes they resolve to rob such or such hog-yards, wherein the Spaniards often have a thousand heads of swine together. They come to these places in the dark of the night, and having beset the keeper's lodge, they force him to rise, and give them as many heads as they desire, threatening withal to kill him in case he disobeys their commands or makes any noise. Yea, these menaces are oftentimes put in execution, without giving any quarter to the miserable swine-keepers, or any other person that endeavours to hinder their robberies.

Having got provisions of flesh sufficient for their voyage, they return to their ship. Here their allowance, twice a day to every one, is as much as he can eat, without either weight or measure. Neither does the steward of the vessel give any greater proportion of flesh, or anything else to the captain than to the meanest mariner.

The ship being well victualled, they call another council, to deliberate towards what place they shall go, to seek their desperate fortunes. In this council, likewise, they agree upon certain Articles, which are put in writing,. by way of bond or obligation, which every one is bound to observe, and all of them, or the chief, set their hands to it. Herein they specify, and set down very distinctly, what sums of money each particular person ought to have for that voyage, the fund of all the payments being the common stock of what is gotten by the whole expedition; for otherwise it is the same law, among these people, as with other Pirates, *No prey, no pay.* In the first place, therefore, they mention how much the Captain ought to have for his ship. Next the salary of the carpenter, or shipwright, who careened, mended and rigged the vessel. This commonly amounts to one hundred or an hundred and fifty pieces of eight,[1] being, according to the agreement, more or less. Afterwards for provisions and victualling they draw out of the same common stock about two hundred pieces of eight. Also a competent salary for the surgeon and his chest of medicaments, which usually is rated at two hundred or two hundred and fifty pieces of eight. Lastly they stipulate in writing what recompense or reward each one ought to have, that is either wounded or maimed in his body, suffering the loss of any limb, by that voyage. Thus they order for the loss of a right arm six hundred pieces of eight, or six slaves; for the loss of a left arm five hundred pieces of eight, or five slaves; for a right leg five hundred pieces of eight, or five slaves; for the left leg four hundred pieces of eight, or four slaves; for an eye one hundred pieces of eight, or one slave; for a finger of the hand the same reward as for the eye. All which sums of money, as I have said before, are taken out of the capital sum or common stock of what is got by their piracy. For a very exact and equal

[1] A piece of eight is equivalent to about five shillings.

dividend is made of the remainder among them all.
Yet herein they have also regard to qualities and places.
Thus the Captain, or chief Commander, is allotted five
or six portions to what the ordinary seamen have; the
Master's Mate only two; and other Officers proportionate
to their employment. After whom they draw equal parts
from the highest even to the lowest mariner, the boys
not being omitted. For even these draw half a share, by
reason that, when they happen to take a better vessel
than their own, it is the duty of the boys to set fire to
the ship or boat wherein they are, and then retire to the
prize which they have taken.

They observe among themselves very good orders.
For in the prizes they take, it is severely prohibited to
every one to usurp anything in particular to themselves.
Hence all they take is equally divided, according to what
has been said before. Yea, they make a solemn oath to
each other not to abscond, or conceal the least thing
they find amongst the prey. If afterwards any one is
found unfaithful, who has contravened the said oath,
immediately he is separated and turned out of the society.
Among themselves they are very civil and charitable to
each other. Insomuch that if any wants what another
has, with great liberality they give it one to another.
As soon as these Pirates have taken any prize of ship or
boat, the first thing they endeavour is to set on shore the
prisoners, detaining only some few for their own help
and service, to whom also they give their liberty after
the space of two or three years. They put in very frequently for refreshment at one island or another; but
more especially into those which lie on the Southern side
of the Isle of Cuba. Here they careen their vessels, and
in the meanwhile some of them go to hunt, others to
cruize upon the seas in canoes, seeking their fortune.
Many times they take the poor fishermen of tortoises,
and, carrying them to their habitations, they make them
work so long as the Pirates are pleased.

In the several parts of America are found four distinct species of tortoises. The first hereof are so great that every one reaches the weight of two or three thousand pounds. The scales of the species are so soft that they may easily be cut with a knife. Yet these tortoises are not good to be eaten. The second species is of an indifferent bigness, and are green in colour. The scales of these are harder than the first, and this sort is of a very pleasant taste. The third is very little different in size and bigness from the second, unless that it has the head something bigger. This third species is called by the French *cavana*, and is not good for food. The fourth is named *caret*, being very like the tortoises we have in Europe. This sort keeps most commonly among the rocks, whence they crawl out to seek their food, which is for the greatest part nothing but apples of the sea. These other species above-mentioned feed upon grass, which grows in the water upon the banks of sand. These banks or shelves, for their pleasant green, resemble the delightful meadows of the United Provinces. Their eggs are almost like those of the crocodile, but without any shell, being only covered with a thin membrane or film. They are found in such prodigious quantities along the sandy shores of those countries, that, were they not frequently destroyed by birds, the sea would infinitely abound with tortoises.

These creatures have certain customary places whither they repair every year to lay their eggs. The chief of these places are the three islands called Caymanes, situated in the latitude of twenty degrees and fifteen minutes North, being at the distance of five and forty leagues from the Isle of Cuba, on the Northern side thereof.

It is a thing much deserving consideration how the tortoises can find out these islands. For the greatest part of them come from the Gulf of Honduras, distant thence the whole space of one hundred and fifty leagues. Certain it is, that many times the ships, having lost their

latitude through the darkness of the weather, have steered
their course only by the noise of the tortoises swimming
that way, and have arrived at those isles.   When their
season of hatching is past, they retire towards the Island
of Cuba, where are many good places that afford them
food.   But while they are at the Islands of Caymanes,
they eat very little or nothing.   When they have been
about the space of one month in the seas of Cuba, and
are grown fat, the Spaniards go out to fish for them,
they being then to be taken in such abundance that they
provide with them sufficiently their cities, towns and
villages.   Their manner of taking them is by making
with a great nail a certain kind of dart.   This they fix
at the end of a long stick or pole, with which they wound
the tortoises, as with a dagger, whensoever they appear
above water to breathe fresh air.

The inhabitants of New Spain and Campeche lade
their principal sorts of merchandises in ships of great
bulk ; and with these they exercise their commerce to
and fro.   The vessels from Campeche in winter time
set out towards Caracas, Trinity Isles and Margarita.
For in summer the winds are contrary, though very
favourable to return to Campeche, as they are accustomed
to do at the beginning of that season.   The Pirates are
not ignorant of these times, being very dextrous in
searching out all places and circumstances most suitable
to their designs.   Hence in the places and seasons aforementioned, they cruize upon the said ships for some
while.   But in case they can perform nothing, and that
fortune does not favour them with some prize or other,
after holding a council thereupon, they commonly enterprize things very desperate.   Of these their resolutions
I shall give you one instance very remarkable.   One
certain Pirate, whose name was Pierre François, or Peter
Francis, happened to be a long time at sea with his boat
and six and twenty persons, waiting for the ships that
were to return from Maracaibo towards Campeche.   Not

being able to find anything, nor get any prey, at last he
resolved to direct his course to Rancherias, which is near
the river called De la Plata, in the latitude of twelve
degrees and a half North.   In this place lies a rich
bank of pearl, to the fishery whereof they yearly send
from Cartagena a fleet of a dozen vessels, with a man-of-
war for their defence.   Every vessel has at least a couple
of negroes in it, who are very dextrous in diving, even
to the depth of six fathoms within the sea, whereabouts
they find good store of pearls.   Upon this fleet of
vessels, though small, called the Pearl Fleet, Pierre
François resolved to adventure, rather than go home
with empty hands.   They rode at anchor, at that time,
at the mouth of the river De la Hacha, the man-of-war
being scarce half a league distant from the small ships,
and the wind very calm.   Having espied them in this
posture, he presently pulled down his sails and rowed
along the coast, dissembling to be a Spanish vessel that
came from Maracaibo, and only passed that way.   But
no sooner was he come to the Pearl Bank, than suddenly
he assaulted the Vice-Admiral of the said fleet, mounted
with eight guns and threescore men well armed, commanding them to surrender.   But the Spaniards, running
to their arms, did what they could to defend themselves, fighting for some while ; till at last they were
constrained to submit to the Pirate.   Being thus possessed of the Vice-Admiral, he resolved next to adventure with some other stratagem upon the man-of-war,
thinking thereby to get strength sufficient to master the
rest of the fleet.   With this intent he presently sank his
own boat in the river, and, putting forth the Spanish
colours, weighed anchor, with a little wind, which then
began to stir, having with promises and menaces compelled most of the Spaniards to assist him in his design.
But no sooner did the man-of-war perceive one of his
fleet to set sail than he did so too, fearing lest the
mariners should have any design to run away with the

vessel and riches they had on board. This caused the
Pirates immediately to give over that dangerous enterprize, thinking themselves unable to encounter force to
force with the said man-of-war that now came against
them. Hereupon they attempted to get out of the
river and gain the open seas with the riches they had
taken, by making as much sail as possibly the vessel
would bear. This being perceived by the man-of-war,
he presently gave them chase. But the Pirates, having
laid on too much sail, and a gust of wind suddenly arising,
had their main-mast blown down by the board, which
disabled them from prosecuting their escape.

This unhappy event much encouraged those that were
in the man-of-war, they advancing and gaining upon the
Pirates every moment ; by which means at last they were
overtaken. But these notwithstanding, finding themselves still with two and twenty persons sound, the rest
being either killed or wounded, resolved to defend themselves so long as it were possible. This they performed
very courageously for some while, until being thereunto
forced by the man-of-war, they were compelled to surrender. Yet this was not done without Articles, which
the Spaniards were glad to allow them, as follows : That
they should not use them as slaves, forcing them to carry
or bring stones, or employing them in other labours, for
three or four years, as they commonly employ their
negroes. But that they should set them on shore, upon
free land, without doing them any harm in their bodies.
Upon these Articles they delivered themselves, with all
that they had taken, which was worth only in pearls to
the value of above one hundred thousand pieces of eight,
besides the vessel, provisions, goods and other things.
All which, being put together, would have made to this
Pirate one of the greatest prizes he could desire ; which
he would certainly have obtained, had it not been for the
loss of his main-mast, as was said before.

Another bold attempt, not unlike that which I have

BARTOLOMEW PORTUGUES.

related, nor less remarkable, I shall also give you at present. A certain Pirate, born in Portugal, and from the name of his country called Bartholomew Portugues, was cruizing in his boat from Jamaica (wherein he had only thirty men and four small guns) upon the Cape de Corrientes, in the Island of Cuba. In this place he met with a great ship, that came from Maracaibo and Cartegena, bound for the Havana, well provided with twenty great guns and threescore and ten men, between passengers and mariners. This ship he presently assaulted, but found as strongly defended by them that were on board. The Pirate escaped the first encounter, resolving to attack her more vigorously than before, seeing he had sustained no great damage hitherto. This resolution he boldly performed, renewing his assaults so often that after a long and dangerous fight he became master of the great vessel. The Portuguese lost only ten men and had four wounded, so that he had still remaining twenty fighting men, whereas the Spaniards had double that number. Having possessed themselves of such a ship, and the wind being contrary to return to Jamaica, they resolved to steer their course towards the Cape of Saint Antony (which lies on the Western side of the Isle of Cuba), there to repair themselves and take in fresh water, of which they had great necessity at that time.

Being now very near the cape above-mentioned, they unexpectedly met with three great ships that were coming from New Spain and bound for the Havana. By these, as not being able to escape, they were easily retaken, both ship and Pirates. Thus they were all made prisoners, through the sudden change of fortune, and found themselves poor, oppressed, and stripped of all the riches they had pillaged so little before. The cargo of this ship consisted of one hundred and twenty thousand weight of cacao-nuts, the chief ingredient of that rich liquor called chocolate, and threescore and ten thousand pieces

of eight. Two days after this misfortune, there happened
to arise a huge and dangerous tempest, which largely
separated the ships from one another. The great vessel
wherein the Pirates were, arrived at Campeche, where
many considerable merchants came to salute and welcome
the Captain thereof. These presently knew the Portuguese Pirate, as being him who had committed innumerable excessive insolences upon those coasts, not only
infinite murders and robberies, but also lamentable
incendiums (*i.e.*, fires), which the people of Campeche
still preserved very fresh in their memory.

Hereupon, the next day after their arrival, the magistrates of the city sent several of their officers to demand
and take into custody the criminal prisoners from on
board the ship, with intent to punish them according to
their deserts. Yet fearing lest the Captain of those
Pirates should escape out of their hands on shore (as he
had formerly done, being once their prisoner in the city
before), they judged it more convenient to leave him
safely guarded on board the ship for the present. In
the meanwhile they caused a gibbet to be erected, whereupon to hang him the very next day, without any other
form of process than to lead him from the ship to the
place of punishment. The rumour of this future tragedy
was presently brought to Bartholomew Portugues' ears,
whereby he sought all the means he could to escape that
night. With this design he took two earthen jars,
wherein the Spaniards usually carry wine from Spain
to the West Indies, and stopped them very well, intending to use them for swimming, as those who are unskilful
in that art do calabashes, a sort of pumpkins, in Spain,
and in other places empty bladders. Having made this
necessary preparation, he waited for the night, when all
should be asleep, even the sentry that guarded him.
But seeing he could not escape his vigilancy, he secretly
secured a knife, and with the same gave him such a
mortal stab as suddenly deprived him of life and the

possibility of making any noise. At that instant he committed himself to sea, with those two earthen jars before-
mentioned, and by their help and support, though never
having learned to swim, he reached the shore. Being
arrived upon land, without any delay he took refuge in
the woods, where he hid himself for three days, without
daring to appear nor eating any other food than wild herbs.

Those of the city failed not the next day to make a
diligent search for him in the woods, where they concluded him to be. This strict enquiry Portugues had
the convenience to espy from the hollow of a tree, wherein he lay absconded. Hence perceiving them to return
without finding what they sought for, he adventured to
sally forth towards the coasts called Del Golfo Triste, forty
leagues distant from the city of Campeche. Hither he
arrived within a fortnight after his escape from the ship.
In which space of time, as also afterwards, he endured
extreme hunger, thirst, and fears of falling again into the
hands of the Spaniards. For during all this journey he
had no other provision with him than a small calabash,
with a little water ; neither did he eat anything else than
a few shell-fish, which he found among the rocks near
the sea-shore. Besides that, he was compelled to pass
some rivers, not knowing well to swim. Being in this
distress, he found an old board, which the waves had
thrown upon the shore, wherein stuck a few great nails.
These he took, and with no small labour whetted against
a stone, until he had made them capable of cutting like
knives, though very imperfectly. With these, and no
better instruments, he cut down some branches of trees,
which with twigs and osiers he joined together, and
made as well as he could a boat, or rather a raft,
wherewith he rafted over the rivers. Thus he arrived
finally at the Cape of Golfo Triste, as was said before,
where he happened to find a certain vessel of Pirates,
who were great comrades of his own, and were lately
come from Jamaica.

To these Pirates he instantly related all his adversities and misfortunes, and withal demanded of them that they would fit him with a boat and twenty men. With which company alone he promised to return to Campeche and assault the ship that was in the river, which he had been taken by and escaped from fourteen days before. They readily granted his request, and equipped him a boat with the said number of men. With this small company he set forth towards the execution of his design, which he bravely performed eight days after he separated from his comrades at the Cape of Golfo Triste. For being arrived at the river of Campeche, with undaunted courage and without any rumour of noise he assaulted the ship before-mentioned. Those that were on board were persuaded this was a boat from land, that came to bring contraband goods ; and hereupon were not in any posture of defence. Thus the Pirates, laying hold on this occasion, assaulted them without any fear of ill success, and in short space of time compelled the Spaniards to surrender.

Being now masters of the ship, they immediately weighed anchor and set sail, determining to fly from the port, lest they should be pursued by other vessels. This they did with extremity of joy, seeing themselves possessors of such a brave ship. Especially Portugues, their captain, who now by a second turn of Fortune's wheel was become rich and powerful again, who had been so lately in that same vessel a poor miserable prisoner and condemned to the gallows. With this great booty he designed in his mind greater things ; which he might well hope to obtain, seeing he had found in the vessel great quantity of rich merchandise still remaining on board, although the plate had been transported into the city. Thus he continued his voyage towards Jamaica for some days. But coming near the Isle of Pinos, on the South side of the Island of Cuba, Fortune suddenly turned her back upon him once more, never to show him her countenance again. For a horrible storm arising at

ROCK . BRASILIANO

sea occasioned the ship to split against the rocks or banks called Jardines. Insomuch that the vessel was totally lost, and Portugues, with his companions, escaped in a canoe. After this manner he arrived at Jamaica, where he remained no long time, being only there till he could prepare himself to seek his fortune anew, which from that time proved always adverse to him.

Nothing less rare and admirable than the preceding are the actions of another Pirate, who at present lives at Jamaica, and who has on sundry occasions enterprized and achieved things very strange. The place of his birth was the city of Groningen, in the United Provinces; but his own proper name is not known : the Pirates, his companions, having only given him that of Roche Brasiliano by reason of his long residence in the country of Brazil, whence he was forced to flee, when the Portuguese retook those countries from the West India Company of Amsterdam, several nations then inhabiting at Brazil (as English, French, Dutch and others) being constrained to seek new fortunes.

This fellow at that conjuncture of time retired to Jamaica, where being at a stand how to get a livelihood, he entered the Society of Pirates. Under these he served in quality of a private mariner for some while, in which degree he behaved himself so well that he was both beloved and respected by all, as one that deserved to be their Commander for the future. One day certain mariners happened to engage in a dissension with their Captain ; the effect whereof was that they left the boat. Brasiliano followed the rest, and by these was chosen for their conductor and leader, who also fitted him out a boat or small vessel, wherein he received the title of Captain.

Few days were past from his being chosen Captain, when he took a great ship that was coming from New Spain, on board of which he found great quantity of plate, and both one and the other he carried to Jamaica.

This action gave him renown, and caused him to be both esteemed and feared, every one apprehending him much abroad. Howbeit, in his domestic and private affairs he had no good behaviour nor government over himself; for in these he would oftentimes shew himself either brutish or foolish. Many times being in drink, he would run up and down the streets, beating or wounding whom he met, no person daring to oppose him or make any resistance.

To the Spaniards he always showed himself very barbarous and cruel, only out of an inveterate hatred he had against that nation. Of these he commanded several to be roasted alive upon wooden spits, for no other crime than that they would not shew him the places or hogyards, where he might steal swine. After many of these cruelties, it happened as he was cruizing upon the coasts of Campeche, that a dismal tempest suddenly surprised him. This proved to be so violent that at last his ship was wrecked upon the coasts, the mariners only escaping with their muskets and some few bullets and powder, which were the only things they could save of all that was in the vessel. The place where the ship was lost was precisely between Campeche and the Golfo Triste. Here they got on shore in a canoe, and marching along the coast with all the speed they could, they directed their course towards Golfo Triste, as being a place where the Pirates commonly used to repair and refresh themselves. Being upon this journey and all very hungry and thirsty, as is usual in desert places, they were pursued by some Spaniards, being a whole troop of a hundred horsemen. Brasiliano no sooner perceived this imminent danger than he animated his companions, telling them : " *We had better, fellow soldiers, choose to die under our arms fighting, as becomes men of courage, than surrender to the Spaniards, who, in case they overcome us, will take away our lives with cruel torments.*" The Pirates were no more than thirty in number, who, notwithstanding, seeing their brave Commander oppose himself with courage to the enemy, resolved to do the like. Hereupon they faced the troop of Spaniards, and discharged their muskets against them with such dexterity, that they killed one horseman with almost every shot. The fight continued for the space of an hour, till at last the Spaniards were put to flight by the Pirates. They stripped the dead, and took from them what they thought most convenient for their use. But such as were not already dead, they helped to quit the miseries of life with the ends of their muskets.

Having vanquished the enemy, they all mounted on several horses they found in the field, and continued the journey aforementioned, Brasiliano having lost but two of his companions in this bloody fight, and had two others wounded. As they prosecuted their way, before they came to the port, they espied a boat from Campeche, well manned, that rode at anchor, protecting a small number of canoes that were lading wood. Hereupon they sent a detachment of six of their men to watch them; and these the next morning possessed themselves of the canoes. Having given notice to their companions, they went all on board, and with no great difficulty took also the boat, or little man-of-war, their convoy. Thus having rendered themselves masters of the whole fleet, they wanted only provisions, which they found but very small aboard those vessels. But this defect was supplied by the horses, which they instantly killed and salted with salt which by good fortune the wood-cutters had brought with them. Upon which victuals they made shift to keep themselves, until such time as they could procure better.

These very same Pirates, I mean Brasiliano and his companions, took also another ship that was going from New Spain to Maracaibo, laden with divers sorts of merchandise, and a very considerable number of pieces of eight, which were designed to buy cacao-nuts for their lading home. All these prizes they carried into Jamaica, where they safely arrived, and, according to their custom, wasted in a few days in taverns all they had gained, by giving themselves to all manner of debauchery. Such of these Pirates are found who will spend two or three thousand pieces of eight in one night, not leaving themselves peradventure a good shirt to wear on their backs in the morning. My own master would buy, on like occasions, a whole pipe of wine, and, placing it in the street, would force every one that passed by to drink with him; threatening also to pistol them, in case they would not do it. At other times he would do the same with barrels of ale or beer. And, very often, with both his hands, he would throw these liquors about the streets, and wet the clothes of such as walked by, without regarding whether he spoiled their apparel or not, were they men or women.

Among themselves, and to each other, these Pirates are extremely liberal and free. If any one of them has lost all his goods, which often happens in their manner of life, they freely give him, and make him partaker of what they have. In taverns and ale-houses they always have great credit; but in such houses at Jamaica they ought not to run very deep in debt, seeing the inhabitants of that island easily sell one another for debt. Thus it happened to my patron, or master, to be sold for a debt of a tavern, wherein he had spent the greatest part of his money. This man had, within the space of three months before, three thousand pieces of eight in ready cash, all which he wasted in that short space of time, and became as poor as I have told you.

But now to return to our discourse, I must let my reader know that Brasiliano, after having spent all that he had robbed, was constrained to go to sea again, to seek his fortune once more. Thus he set forth towards the coast of Campeche, his common place of rendezvous. Fifteen days after his arrival there, he put himself into a canoe, with intent to espy the port of that city, and see if he could rob any Spanish vessel. But his fortune was so bad, that both he and all his men were taken prisoners, and carried into the presence of the Governor. This man immediately cast them into a dungeon, with full intention to hang them every person. And doubtless he had performed his intent, were it not for a stratagem that Brasiliano used, which proved sufficient to save their lives. He wrote therefore a letter to the Governor, making him believe it came from other Pirates that were abroad at sea, and withal telling him : *He should have a care how he used those persons he had in his custody. For in case he caused them any harm, they did swear unto him they would never give quarter to any person of the Spanish nation that should fall into their hands.*

Because these Pirates had been many times at Campeche, and in many other towns and villages of the West Indies belonging to the Spanish dominions, the Governor began to fear what mischief they might cause by means of their companions abroad, in case he should punish them. Hereupon he released them out of prison, exacting only an oath of them beforehand, that they would leave their exercise of piracy for ever. And withal he sent them as common mariners, or passengers in the galleons to Spain. They got in this voyage altogether five hundred pieces of eight, whereby they tarried not long there after their arrival. But providing themselves with some few necessaries, they all returned to Jamaica within a little while. Whence they set forth again to sea, committing greater robberies and cruelties than ever they had done before ; but more especially abusing the poor Spaniards that happened to fall into their hands, with all sorts of cruelty imaginable.

The Spaniards perceiving they could gain nothing upon this sort of people, nor diminish their number, which rather increased daily, resolved to diminish the number of their ships wherein they exercised trading to

and fro.   But neither was this resolution of any effect, or
did them any good service.   For the Pirates, finding not
so many ships at sea as before, began to gather into
greater companies, and land upon the Spanish dominions,
ruining whole cities, towns and villages; and withal
pillaging, burning and carrying away as much as they
could find possible.

The first Pirate who gave a beginning to these invasions by land, was named Lewis Scot, who sacked and
pillaged the city of Campeche.   He almost ruined the
town, robbing and destroying all he could; and, after he
had put it to the ransom of an excessive sum of money,
he left it.   After Scot came another named Mansvelt,
who enterprized to set footing in Granada, and penetrate
with his piracies even to the South Sea.   Both which
things he effected, till at last, for want of provision,
he was constrained to go back.   He assaulted the Isle
of Saint Catharine, which was the first land he took, and
upon it some few prisoners.   These showed him the way
towards Cartagena, which is a principal city situate in
the kingdom of New Granada.   But the bold attempts
and actions of John Davis, born at Jamaica, ought not
to be forgotten in this history, as being some of the most
remarkable thereof, especially his rare prudence and
valour, wherewith he behaved himself in the aforementioned kingdom of Granada.   This Pirate having cruized
a long time in the Gulf of Pocatauro upon the ships that
were expected from Cartagena bound for Nicaragua, and
not being able to meet any of the said ships, resolved at
last to land in Nicaragua, leaving his ship concealed
about the coast.

This design he presently put in execution.   For taking
fourscore men, out of fourscore and ten which he had in
all (the rest being left to keep the ship), he divided them
equally into three canoes.   His intent was to rob the
churches, and rifle the houses of the chief citizens of the
aforesaid town of Nicaragua.   Thus, in the obscurity of

the night, they mounted the river which leads to that
city, rowing with oars in their canoes. By day they
concealed themselves and boats under the branches of
trees that were upon the banks. These grow very thick
and intricate along the sides of the rivers in those coun
tries, as also along the sea-coast. Under which, likewise,
those who remained behind absconded from their vessel,
lest they should be seen either by fishermen or Indians.
After this manner they arrived at the city the third night,
where the sentry, who kept the post of the river, thought
them to be fishermen that had been fishing in the lake.
And as the greatest part of the Pirates are skilful in the
Spanish tongue, so he never doubted thereof as soon as
he heard them speak. They had in their company an
Indian, who had run away from his master because he
would make him a slave after having served him a long
time. This Indian went first on shore, and, rushing at
the sentry, he instantly killed him. Being animated
with this success, they entered into the city, and went
directly to three or four houses of the chief citizens,
where they knocked with dissimulation. These believing
them to be friends opened the doors, and the Pirates
suddenly possessing themselves of the houses, robbed all
the money and plate they could find. Neither did they
spare the churches and most sacred things, all which
were pillaged and profaned without any respect or vene-
ration.

In the meanwhile great cries and lamentation were
heard about the town, of some who had escaped their
hands ; by which means the whole city was brought into
an uproar and alarm. Hence the whole number of
citizens rallied together, intending to put themselves in
defence. This being perceived by the Pirates, they
instantly put themselves to flight, carrying with them
all that they had robbed, and likewise some prisoners.
These they led away, to the intent that, if any of them
should happen to be taken by the Spaniards, they might

make use of them for ransom. Thus they got to their
ship, and with all speed imaginable put out to sea, forcing
the prisoners, before they would let them go, to procure
them as much flesh as they thought necessary for their
voyage to Jamaica. But no sooner had they weighed
anchor, than they saw on shore a troop of about five
hundred Spaniards, all being very well armed, at the
sea-side. Against these they let fly several guns, wherewith they forced them to quit the sands and retire towards home, with no small regret to see those Pirates
carry away so much plate of their churches and houses,
though distant at least forty leagues from the sea.

These Pirates robbed on this occasion above four
thousand pieces of eight in ready money, besides great
quantities of plate uncoined and many jewels. All which
was computed to be worth the sum of fifty thousand
pieces of eight, or more. With this great booty they
arrived at Jamaica, soon after the exploit. But as this
sort of people are never masters of their money but a
very little while, so were they soon constrained to seek
more, by the same means they had used before. This
adventure caused Captain John Davis, presently after
his return, to be chosen Admiral of seven or eight boats
of Pirates ; he being now esteemed by common consent
an able conductor for such enterprizes as these were.
He began the exercise of this new command by directing
his fleet towards the coasts of the North of Cuba, there
to wait for the fleet which was to pass from New Spain.
But, not being able to find anything by this design, they
determined to go towards the coasts of Florida. Being
arrived there, they landed part of their men, and sacked
a small city, named Saint Augustine of Florida, the
castle of which place had a garrison of two hundred men,
which, notwithstanding, could not prevent the pillage of
the city, they effecting it without receiving the least
damage from either soldiers or townsmen.

Hitherto we have spoken in the first part of this book

of the constitution of the Islands of Hispaniola and Tortuga, their peculiarities and inhabitants, as also of the fruits to be found in those countries. In the second part of this work we shall bend our discourse to describe the actions of two of the most famous Pirates, who committed many horrible crimes and inhuman cruelties against the Spanish nation.

The End of the First Part.

FRANCIS LOLONOIS.

PART II.

CHAPTER I.

Origin of Francis L'Ollonais, and beginning of his robberies.

FRANCIS L'OLLONAIS was a native of that territory in France which is called Les Sables d'Ollone, or the Sands of Ollone. In his youth he was transported to the Caribbee Islands, in quality of a servant or slave, according to the custom of France and other countries; of which we have already spoken in the first part of this book. Being out of his time, when he had obtained his freedom, he came to the Isle of Hispaniola. Here he placed himself for some while among the hunters, before he began his robberies against the Spaniards; whereof I shall make mention at present, until his unfortunate death.

At first he made two or three voyages in quality of a common mariner, wherein he behaved himself so courageously as to deserve the favour and esteem of the Governor of Tortuga, who was then Monsieur de la Place. Insomuch that this gentleman gave him a ship, and made him captain thereof, to the intent he might seek his fortune. This Dame shewed herself very favourable to him at the beginning, for in a short while he pillaged great riches. But, withal, his cruelties against the Spaniards were such that the very fame of them made him known through the whole Indies. For which reason the Spaniards, in his time, whensoever they

were attacked by sea, would choose rather to die or sink
fighting than surrender, knowing they should have no
mercy nor quarter at his hands.   But as Fortune is seldom constant, so after some time she turned her back
upon him.   The beginning of whose disasters was, that in
a huge storm he lost his ship upon the coasts of Campeche.   The men were all saved ; but coming upon dry
land, the Spaniards pursued them, and killed the greatest
part of them, wounding also L'Ollonais, their captain.
Not knowing how to escape, he thought to save his life
by a stratagem.   Hereupon he took several handfuls of
sand and mingled them with the blood of his own
wounds, with which he besmeared his face and other
parts of his body.   Then hiding himself dextrously
among the dead, he continued there till the Spaniards
had quitted the field.

After they were gone, he retired into the woods, and
bound up his wounds as well as he could.   These being
by the help of Nature pretty well healed, he took his
way to the city of Campeche, having perfectly disguised
himself in Spanish habit.   Here he spoke with certain
slaves, to whom he promised their liberty, in case they
would obey him and trust in his conduct.   They accepted
his promises, and stealing one night a canoe from one of
their masters, they went to sea with the Pirate.   The
Spaniards in the meanwhile had made prisoner several
of his companions, whom they kept in close dungeons in
the city, while L'Ollonais went about the town and saw all
that passed.   These were often asked by the Spaniards,
" *What is become of your Captain ?* " to whom they
constantly answered, " *He is dead.*"   With which news
the Spaniards were hugely gladdened, and made great
demonstrations of joy, kindling bonfires, and, like those
that knew nothing to the contrary, giving thanks to God
Almighty for their deliverance from such a cruel Pirate.
L'Ollonais, having seen these joys for his death, made
haste to escape with the slaves above-mentioned, and

came safe to Tortuga, the common place of refuge of all sorts of wickedness, and the seminary, as it were, of all manner of Pirates and thieves. Though now his fortune was but low, yet he failed not of means to get another ship, which with craft and subtlety he obtained, and in it one and twenty persons. Being well provided with arms and other necessaries, he set forth towards the Isle of Cuba, on the South side whereof lies a small village, which is called De los Cayos. The inhabitants of this town drive a great trade in tobacco, sugar and hides; and all in boats, as not being able to make use of ships by reason of the little depth of that sea.

L'Ollonais was greatly persuaded he should get here some considerable prey; but by the good fortune of some fishermen who saw him, and the mercy of the Almighty, they escaped his tyrannical hands. For the inhabitants of the town of Cayos dispatched immediately a messenger overland to Havana, complaining to the Governor that L'Ollonais was come to destroy them, with two canoes. The Governor could very hardly be persuaded of the truth of this story, seeing he had received letters from Campeche that he was dead. Notwithstanding, at the importunity of the petitioners he sent a ship to their relief, with ten guns and fourscore and ten persons, well armed; giving them withal this express command: *They should not return unto his presence without having totally destroyed those Pirates.* To this effect he gave them also a negro, who might serve them for a hangman; his orders being that *They should immediately hang every one of the said Pirates, excepting L'Ollonais their Captain, whom they should bring alive to Havana.* This ship arrived at Cayos; of whose coming the Pirates were advertised beforehand; and, instead of flying, went to seek the said vessel in the river Estera, where she rode at anchor. The Pirates apprehended some fishermen, and forced them, by night, to shew the entry of the port, hoping soon to obtain a greater vessel than their two canoes, and thereby to mend their fortune. They arrived, after two o'clock in the morning, very near the ship. And the watch on board the ship asking them : *Whence they came, and if they had seen any Pirates abroad,* they caused one of the prisoners to answer : *They had seen no Pirates, nor anything else.* Which answer brought them into persuasion that they were fled away, having heard of their coming.

But they experienced very soon the contrary; for about break of day the Pirates bega . to assault the vessel on both sides with their two canoes. This attack they performed with such vigour that, although the Spaniards behaved themselves as they ought and made as good defence as they could, shooting against them likewise some great guns, yet they were forced to surrender, after being beaten by the Pirates, with swords in hand, down under the hatches. Hence L'Ollonais commanded them to be brought up one by one, and in this order caused their heads to be struck off. Among the rest came up the negro, designed to be the Pirates' executioner by the Governor of Havana. This fellow implored mercy at his hands very dolefully, desiring not to be killed, and telling L'Ollonais he was constituted hangman of that ship; and that, in case he would spare him, he would tell him faithfully all that he should desire to know. L'Ollonais made him confess as many things as he thought fit to ask him ; and, having done, commanded him to be murdered with the rest. Thus he cruelly and barbarously put them all to death, reserving of the whole number only one alive, whom he sent back to the Governor of Havana, with this message given him in writing : *I shall never henceforward give quarter to any Spaniard whatsoever ; and I have great hopes I shall execute on your own person the very same punishment I have done upon them you sent against me. Thus I have retaliated the kindness you designed to me and my companions.* The Governor was much troubled. to understand these sad and withal insolent news ; which occasioned him to swear, in the presence of many, he would never grant quarter to any Pirate that should fall into his hands. But the citizens of Havana desired him not to persist in the execution of that rash and rigorous oath, *seeing the Pirates would certainly take occasion thence to do the same ; and they had an hundred times more opportunity of revenge than he : that, being necessitated to get their livelihood by fishery, they should hereafter always be in danger of losing their lives.* By these reasons he was persuaded to bridle his anger, and remit the severity of his oath aforementioned.

Now L'Ollonais had got himself a good ship, but withal very few provisions and people in it. Hereupon, to secure both the one and the other, he resolved to use his customary means of cruizing from one port to another. This he did for some while, till at last not being able to procure anything, he determined to go to the port of Maracaibo. Here he took by surprize a ship that was laden with plate and other merchandize, being outward bound to buy cacao-nuts. With these prizes he returned to Tortuga, where he was received with no small joy by the inhabitants, they congratulating his happy success and their own private interest. He continued not long there, but pitched upon new designs of equipping a whole fleet, sufficient to transport five hundred men, with all other necessaries. With these preparations he resolved to go to the Spanish dominions, and pillage both cities, towns and villages, and finally take Maracaibo itself. For this purpose, he knew the Island of Tortuga would afford him many resolute and courageous men, very fit for such enterprizes. Besides that, he had in his service several prisoners, who were exactly acquainted with the ways and places he designed upon.

CHAPTER II.

L'Ollonais equips a fleet to land upon the Spanish islands of America, with intent to rob, sack and burn whatever he met.

OF this his design L'Ollonais gave notice to all the Pirates who at that conjuncture of time were either at home or abroad. By which means he got together in a little while above four hundred men. Besides which, there was at that present in the Isle of Tortuga another Pirate, whose name was Michael de Basco. This man by his piracy had got riches sufficient to live at ease, and go no more abroad to sea ; having withal the office of Major of the Island. Yet seeing the great preparations that L'Ollonais made for this expedition, he entered into a straight league of friendship with him, and proffered him that, in case he would make him his chief captain by land (seeing he knew the country very well and all its avenues), he would take part in his fortunes, and go along with him. They both agreed upon articles, with great joy of L'Ollonais, as knowing that Basco had performed great actions in Europe, and had gained the repute of a good soldier. He gave him therefore the command he desired, and the conduct of all his people by land. Thus they all embarked in eight vessels, that of L'Ollonais being the greatest, as having ten guns of various carriage.

All things being in readiness, and the whole company on board, they set sail together about the end of April, having a considerable number of men for those parts, that is in all six hundred and threescore persons. They directed their course towards that part which is

called Bayala, situated on the North side of the Island of
Hispaniola. Here they also took into their company a
certain number of French hunters, who voluntarily offered
themselves to go along with them. And here likewise
they provided themselves with victuals and other necessaries for that voyage.

Hence they set sail again the last day of July, and
steered directly towards the Eastern Cape of the Isle,
called Punta d' Espada. Hereabouts they suddenly
espied a ship that was coming from Porto Rico, and
bound for New Spain, being laden with cacao-nuts.
L'Ollonais, the Admiral, presently commanded the rest of
the fleet they should wait for him near the Isle of Savona,
situate on the Eastern side of Cape Punta d' Espada,
forasmuch as he alone intended to go and take the said
vessel. The Spaniards, although they had been in sight
now fully two hours, and knew them to be Pirates, yet
they would not flee, but rather prepared to fight ; as
being well armed, and provided of all things necessary
thereto. Thus the combat began between L'Ollonais and
the Spanish vessel, which lasted three hours ; and these
being past, they surrendered to him. This ship was
mounted with sixteen guns, and had fifty fighting men
on board. They found in her *one hundred and twenty
thousand weight of cacao, forty thousand pieces of eight,
and the value of ten thousand more in jewels.* L'Ollonais
sent the vessel presently to Tortuga to be unladed, with
orders to return with the said ship as soon as possible to
the Isle of Savona, where he would wait for their coming.
In the meanwhile the rest of the fleet, being arrived at the
said Island of Savona, met with another Spanish vessel
that was coming from Comana with military provisions to
the Isle of Hispaniola ; and also with money to pay the
garrisons of the said island. This vessel also they took
without any resistance, although mounted with eight
guns. Here were found seven thousand weight of powder, great number of muskets and other things of this

kind, together with twelve thousand pieces of eight in
ready money.

These forementioned events gave good encouragement
to the Pirates, as judging them very good beginnings to
the business they had in hand, especially finding their
fleet pretty well recruited within a little while. For the
first ship that was taken being arrived at Tortuga, the
Governor ordered to be instantly unladen, and soon after
sent her back with fresh provisions and other necessaries
to L'Ollonais. This ship he chose for his own, and gave
that which he commanded to his comrade Antony du
Puis. Thus having received new recruits of men, in lieu
of them he had lost in taking the prizes above-mentioned
and by sickness, he found himself in a good condition to
prosecute his voyage. All being well animated and full
of courage, they set sail for Maracaibo, which port is
situated in the province of New Venezuela, in the latitude of twelve degrees and some minutes North. This
island is in length twenty leagues, and twelve in breadth.
To this port also belong the Islands of Onega and
Monges. The East side thereof is called Cape St.
Roman, and the Western side Cape of Caquibacoa.
The gulf is called by some the Gulf of Venezuela ; but
the Pirates usually call it the Bay of Maracaibo.

At the beginning of this gulf are two islands, which
extend for the greatest part from East to West. That
which lies towards the East is called Isla de las Vigilias,
or the Watch Isle, because in the middle thereof is to be
seen a high hill, upon which stands a house wherein
dwells perpetually a watchman. The other is called Isla
de las Palomas, or the Isle of Pigeons. Between these
two islands runs a little sea, or rather a lake, of fresh
water, being threescore leagues in length and thirty in
breadth ; which disgorges into the ocean, and dilates itself about the two islands afore-mentioned. Between them
is found the best passage for ships, the channel of this
passage being no broader than the flight of a great gun

of eight pound carriage, more or less. Upon the Isle of Pigeons stands a castle, to impede the entry of any vessels; all such as come in being necessitated to approach very near the castle, by reason of two banks of sand that lie on the other side, with only fourteen foot water. Many other banks of sand are also found in this lake, as that which is called El Tablazo, or The Great Table, which is no deeper than ten foot; but this lies forty leagues within the lake. Others there are that are no more than six, seven or eight foot in depth. All of them are very dangerous, especially to such mariners as are little acquainted with this lake. On the West side hereof is situated the city of Maracaibo, being very pleasant to the view, by reason its houses are built along the shore, having delicate prospects everywhere round about. The city may possibly contain three or four thousand persons, the slaves being included in this number; all which make a town of reasonable bigness. Among these are judged to be eight hundred persons, more or less, able to bear arms, all of them Spaniards. Here are also one Parish Church, of very good fabric and well adorned, four monasteries and one hospital. The city is governed by a Deputy-Governor, who is substituted here by the Governor of Caracas, as being his dependency. The commerce or trading here exercised consists for the greatest part in hides and tobacco. The inhabitants possess great numbers of cattle, and many plantations, which extend for the space of thirty leagues within the country; especially on that side that looks towards the great and populous town of Gibraltar. At which place are gathered huge quantities of cacao-nuts, and all other sorts of garden fruits; which greatly serve for the regalement and sustenance of the inhabitants of Maracaibo, whose territories are much drier than those of Gibraltar. To this place those of Maracaibo send great quantities of flesh; they making returns in oranges, lemons, and several other fruits. For the in-

habitants of Gibraltar have great scarcity of provisions
of flesh, their fields being not capable of feeding cows
or sheep.

Before the city of Maracaibo lies a very spacious and
secure port, wherein may be built all sort of vessels ; as
having great convenience of timber, which may be transported thither at very little charge. Near the town lies
also a small island called Borrica, which serves them to
feed great numbers of goats, of which cattle the inhabitants of Maracaibo make greater use of their skins than
their flesh or milk ; they making no great account of
these two, unless while they are as yet but tender and
young kids. In the fields about the town are fed some
numbers of sheep, but of a very small size. In some of
the islands that belong to the lake, and in other places
hereabouts, inhabit many savage Indians, whom the
Spaniards call Bravos, or Wild. These Indians could
never agree as yet, nor be reduced to any accord with
the Spaniards, by reason of their brutish and untamable
nature. They dwell for the most part towards the
Western side of the lake, in little huts that are built upon
trees which grow in the water, the cause hereof being
only to exempt themselves as much as possible from the
innumerable quantity of mosquitos or gnats which infest
those parts, and by which they are tormented night and
day. Towards the East side of the said lake are also to
be seen whole towns of fishermen, who likewise are constrained to live in huts, built upon trees, like the former.
Another reason of thus dwelling is the frequent inundations of waters : for after great rains, the land is often
overflowed for the space of two or three leagues, there
being no less than five and twenty great rivers that feed
this lake. The town of Gibraltar is also frequently
drowned by these inundations, insomuch that the inhabitants are constrained to leave their houses and retire to
their plantations.

Gibraltar is situated at the side of the lake, forty

leagues or thereabouts within it, and receives its necessary provisions of flesh, as has been said, from Maracaibo.
The town is inhabited by fifteen hundred persons, more
or less, whereof four hundred may be capable of bearing
arms. The greatest part of the inhabitants keep open
shops, wherein they exercise one mechanic trade or other.
All the adjacent fields about this town are cultivated with
numerous plantations of sugar and cacao, in which are
many tall and beautiful trees, of whose timber houses
may be built, and also ships. Among these trees are
found great store of handsome and proportionable cedars,
being seven or eight foot in circumference, which serve
there very commonly to build boats and ships. These
they build after such manner as to bear only one great
sail ; and such vessels are called Piraguas. The whole
country round about is sufficiently furnished with rivers
and brooks, which are very useful to the inhabitants in
time of droughts, they opening in that occasion many
little channels, through which they lead the rivulets to
water their fields and plantations. They plant in like
manner great quantity of tobacco, which is much
esteemed in Europe ; and for its goodness, is called
there Tabaco de Sacerdotes, or Priest's Tobacco. They
enjoy nigh twenty leagues of jurisdiction, which is
bounded and defended by very high mountains that are
perpetually covered with snow. On the other side of
these mountains is situated a great city called Merida, to
which the town of Gibraltar is subject. All sort of merchandize is carried from this town to the aforesaid city,
upon mules ; and that but at one season of the year, by
reason of the excessive cold endured in those high mountains. Upon the said mules great returns are made in
flour of meal, which comes from towards Peru by the
way of Estaffe.

Thus far I thought it convenient to make a short
description of the aforesaid lake of Maracaibo, and its
situation ; to the intent my reader might the better be

enabled to comprehend what I shall say concerning what
was acted by the Pirates in this place, the history
whereof I shall presently begin.

As soon as L'Ollonais arrived at the Gulf of Venezuela,
he cast anchor with his whole fleet, out of sight of the
watch-tower of the Island of Vigilias, or Watch-Isle. The
next day, very early, he set sail hence, with all his ships,
for the lake of Maracaibo ; where being arrived, they
cast anchor the second time.   Soon after, they landed all
their men, with design to attack in the first place the
castle or fortress that commanded the bar, and is therefore called De la Barra.   This fort consists only of
several great baskets of earth, placed upon a rising
ground, upon which are planted sixteen great guns, with
several other heaps of earth round about, for covering
the men within.   The Pirates having landed at the
distance of a league from this fort, began to advance
by degrees towards it.   But the Governor thereof,
having espied their landing, had placed an ambuscade
of some of his men, with design to cut them off behind,
while he meant to attack them in the front.   This
ambuscade was found out by the Pirates ; and, hereupon
getting before, they assaulted and defeated it so entirely
that not one man could retreat to the castle.   This
obstacle being removed, L'Ollonais with all his companions advanced in great haste towards the fort.   And
after a fight of almost three hours, wherein they behaved
themselves with desperate courage, such as this sort
of people are used to show, they became masters
thereof, having made use of no other arms than their
swords and pistols.   And while they were fighting,
those who were routed in the ambuscade, not being
able to get into the castle, retired towards the city of
Maracaibo in great confusion and disorder, crying : *The
Pirates will presently be here with two thousand men and
more.*   This city having formerly been taken by such
kind of people as these were, and sacked even to the

remotest corners thereof, preserved still in its memory a
fresh *Idea* of that misery.   Hereupon, as soon as they
heard this dismal news, they endeavoured to escape as
fast as they could towards Gibraltar in their boats and
canoes, carrying with them all the goods and money they
could.   Being come to Gibraltar, they dispersed the
rumour that the fortress was taken, and that nothing had
been saved, nor any persons able to escape the fury of
the Pirates.

The castle being taken by the Pirates, as was said
before, they presently made sign to the ships of the
victory they had obtained ; to the end they should come
farther in, without apprehension of any danger.   The
rest of that day was spent in ruining and demolishing
the said castle.   They nailed the guns, and burnt as
much as they could not carry away ; burying also the
dead, and sending on board the fleet such as were
wounded.   The next day very early in the morning
they weighed anchor, and directed their course all together towards the city of Maracaibo, distant only six
leagues more or less from the fort.   But the wind being
very scarce, that day they could advance but little, as
being forced to expect the flowing of the tide.   The
next morning they came within sight of the town, and
began to make preparations for landing under the pro-
tection of their own guns; being persuaded the Spaniards
might have laid an ambuscade among the trees and
woods.   Thus they put their men into canoes, which for
that purpose they brought with them, and landed where
they thought most convenient, shooting in the meanwhile
very furiously with their great guns.   Of the people that
were in the canoes, half only went on shore, the other
half remained on board the said canoes.   They fired
with their guns from the ships as fast as was possible
towards the woody part of the shore ; but could see, and
were answered by, nobody.   Thus they marched in good
order into the town, whose inhabitants, as I told you

before, were all retired into the woods, and towards Gibraltar, with their wives, children and families. Their houses they left well provided with all sort of victuals, such as flour, bread, pork, brandy, wines and good store of poultry. With these things the Pirates fell to banqueting and making good cheer ; for in four weeks before they had had no opportunity of filling their stomachs with such plenty.

They instantly possessed themselves of the best houses in the town, and placed sentries everywhere they thought convenient. The great church served them for their main *corps du garde.* The next day they sent a body of one hundred and sixty men to find out some of the inhabitants of the town, whom they understood were hidden in the woods not far thence. These returned that very night, bringing with them twenty thousand pieces of eight, several mules laden with household goods and merchandize, and twenty prisoners, between men, women and children. Some of these prisoners were put to the rack, only to make them confess where they had hidden the rest of their goods ; but they could extort very little from them. L'Ollonais, who never used to make any great account of murdering, though in cold blood, ten or twelve Spaniards, drew his cutlass and hacked one to pieces in the presence of all the rest, saying : *If you do not confess and declare where you have hidden the rest of your goods, I will do the like to all your companions.* At last, amongst these horrible cruelties and inhuman threats, one was found who promised to conduct him and show the place where the rest of the Spaniards were hidden. But those that were fled, having intelligence that one had discovered their lurking holes to the Pirates, changed place, and buried all the remnant of their riches under ground ; insomuch that the Pirates could not find them out, unless some other person of their own party should reveal them. Besides that the Spaniards, flying from one place to another every day and often changing woods, were jealous even of each other; insomuch as the father scarce presumed to trust his own son.

Finally, after that the Pirates had been fifteen days in Maracaibo, they resolved to go towards Gibraltar. But the inhabitants of this place, having received intelligence thereof beforehand, as also that they intended afterwards to go to Merida, gave notice of this design to the Governor thereof, who was a valiant soldier and had served his king in Flanders in many military offices. His answer was: *He would have them take no care; for he hoped in a little while to exterminate the said Pirates.* Whereupon he transferred himself immediately to Gibraltar, with four hundred men well armed, ordering at the same time the inhabitants of the said town to put themselves in arms; so that in all he made a body of eight hundred fighting men. With the same speed he commanded a battery to be raised towards the sea, whereon he mounted twenty guns, covering them all with great baskets of earth. Another battery likewise he placed in another place, mounted with eight guns. After this was done, he barricaded a highway or narrow passage into the town, through which the Pirates of necessity ought to pass; opening at the same time another, through much dirt and mud, in the wood, which was totally unknown to the Pirates.

The Pirates, not knowing anything of these preparations, having embarked all their prisoners and what they had robbed, took their way towards Gibraltar. Being come within sight of the place, they perceived the Royal standard hanging forth, and that those of the town had a mind to fight and defend their houses. L'Ollonais, seeing this resolution, called a council of war, to deliberate what he ought to do in such case; propounding withal to his officers and mariners, that the difficulty of such an enterprize was very great, seeing the Spaniards had had so much time to put themselves in a posture of defence, and had got a good body of men together, with many martial provisions. *But notwithstanding,* said he, *have a good courage. We must either defend ourselves like good soldiers, or lose our lives with all the riches we have got. Do as I shall do, who am your Captain. At other times we have fought with fewer men than we have in our company at present, and yet we have overcome greater numbers than there possibly can be in this town. The more they are, the more glory we shall attribute unto our fortune, and the greater riches we shall increase unto it.* The Pirates were under this suspicion, that all those riches which the inhabitants of Maracaibo had absconded, were transported to Gibraltar, or at least the greatest part thereof. After this speech they all promised to follow him and obey very exactly his commands. To whom L'Ollonais made answer : *'Tis well; but know ye withal that the first man who shall show any fear, or the least apprehension thereof, I will pistol him with my own hands.*

With this resolution they cast anchor near the shore, at the distance of one quarter of a league from the town. The next day, before sunrise, they were all landed, being to the number of three hundred and fourscore men, well provided, and armed every one with a cutlass and one or two pistols ; and withal sufficient powder and bullet for thirty charges. Here, upon the shore, they all shook hands with one another in testimony of good courage, and began their march, L'Ollonais speaking these words to them : *Come, my brothers, follow me, and have a good courage.* They followed their way with a guide they had provided. But he, believing he led them well, brought them to the way which the Governor had obstructed with barricades. Through this not being able to pass, they went to the other, which was newly made in the wood among the mire, to which the Spaniards could shoot at pleasure. Notwithstanding, the Pirates being full of courage, cut down multitude of branches of trees, and threw them in the dirt upon the way, to the end they might not stick so fast in it. In the meanwhile, those of Gibraltar fired at them with their great guns so furiously that they could scarce hear or see one another through the noise and smoke. Being now past the wood, they came upon firm ground, where they met with a battery of six guns, which immediately the Spaniards discharged against them, all being loaded with small bullets and pieces of iron. After this, the Spaniards sallying forth set upon them with such fury, as caused the Pirates to give way and retire; very few of them daring to advance towards the fort. They continued still firing against the Pirates, of whom they had already killed and wounded many. This made them go back to seek some other way through the middle of the wood; but the Spaniards having cut down many trees to hinder the passage, they could find none, and thus were forced to return to that they had left. Here the Spaniards continued to fire as before; neither would they sally out of their batteries to attack the Pirates any more. Hereby L'Ollonais and his companions, not being able to grimp up the baskets of earth, were compelled to make use of an old stratagem; wherewith at last they deceived and overcame the Spaniards.

L'Ollonais retired suddenly with all his men, making show as if he fled. Hereupon the Spaniards, crying out, *They flee, they flee; let us follow them,* sallied forth with great disorder, to pursue the fugitive Pirates. After they had drawn them some distance from their batteries, which was their only design, they turned upon them unexpectedly with swords in hand, and killed above two hundred men. And thus fighting their way through those who remained alive, they possessed themselves of the batteries. The Spaniards that remained abroad gave themselves up for lost, and consequently took their flight to the woods. The other part that was in the battery of eight guns surrendered themselves upon conditions of

obtaining quarter for their lives.   The Pirates, being now
become masters of the whole town, pulled down the
Spanish colours, and set up their own, taking prisoners
at the same time as many as they could find.   These
they carried to the great church, whither also they transferred many great guns, wherewith they raised a battery
to defend themselves, fearing lest the Spaniards that
were fled should rally more of their own party and come
upon them again.   But the next day, after they were all
fortified, all their fears disappeared.   They gathered all
the dead, with intent to allow them burial, finding the
number of above five hundred Spaniards killed, besides
those that were wounded within the town and those that
died of their wounds in the woods, where they sought
for refuge.   Besides which, the Pirates had in their
custody above one hundred and fifty prisoners, and nigh
five hundred slaves, many women and children.

Of their own companions the Pirates found only forty
dead, and almost as many more wounded.   Whereof the
greatest part died afterwards, through the constitution of
the air, which brought fevers and other accidents upon
them.   They put all the Spaniards that were slain into
two great boats, and carrying them one quarter of a
league within the sea, they sank the boats.   These things
being done, they gathered all the plate, household stuff
and merchandize they could rob or thought convenient
to carry away.   But the Spaniards who had anything as
yet left to them, hid it very carefully.   Soon after, the
Pirates, as if they were unsatisfied with the great riches
they had got, began to seek for more goods and merchandize, not sparing those who lived in the fields, such
as hunters and planters.   They had scarce been eighteen
days upon the place, when the greatest part of the
prisoners they had taken died of hunger.   For in the
town very few provisions, especially of flesh, were to be
found.   Howbeit, they had some quantity of flour of
meal although perhaps something less than what was

sufficient. But this the Pirates had taken into their custody to make bread for themselves. As to the swine, cows, sheep and poultry that were found upon the place, they took them likewise for their own sustenance, without allowing any share thereof to the poor prisoners. For these they only provided some small quantity of mules' and asses' flesh, which they killed for that purpose. And such as could not eat of that loathsome provision were constrained to die of hunger, as many did, their stomachs not being accustomed to such unusual sustenance. Only some women were found, who were allowed better cheer by the Pirates, because they served them in their sensual delights, to which those robbers are hugely given. Among those women, some had been forced, others were volunteers; though almost all had rather taken up that vice through poverty and hunger, more than any other cause. Of the prisoners many also died under the torments they sustained, to make them confess where they had hidden their money or jewels. And of these, some because they had none nor knew of any, and others for denying what they knew, endured such horrible deaths.

Finally, after having been in possession of the town four entire weeks, they sent four of the prisoners, remaining alive, to the Spaniards that were fled into the woods, demanding of them a ransom for not burning the town. The sum hereof they constituted *ten thousand pieces of eight*, which, unless it were sent to them, they threatened to fire and reduce into ashes the whole village. For bringing in of this money they allowed them only the space of two days. These being past, and the Spaniards not having been able to gather so punctually such a sum, the Pirates began to set fire to many places of the town. Thus the inhabitants, perceiving the Pirates to be in earnest, begged of them to help to extinguish the fire; and withal promised the ransom should be readily paid. The Pirates condescended to

their petition, helping as much as they could to stop the
progress of the fire.   Yet, though they used the best
endeavours they possibly could, one part of the town
was ruined, especially the church belonging to the mon-
astery, which was burnt even to dust.   After they had
received the sum above-mentioned, they carried on board
their ships all the riches they had robbed, together with
a great number of slaves which had not as yet paid their
ransom.   For all the prisoners had sums of money set
upon them, and the slaves were also commanded to be
redeemed.   Hence they returned to Maracaibo, where
being arrived they found a general consternation in the
whole city.   To which they sent three or four prisoners
to tell the governor and inhabitants : *They should bring
them thirty thousand pieces of eight on board their ships,
for a ransom of their houses ; otherwise they should be
entirely sacked anew and burnt.*

Among these debates a certain party of Pirates came
on shore to rob, and these carried away the images, the
pictures and bells of the great church, on board the fleet.
The Spaniards, who were sent to demand of those that
were fled the sum afore-mentioned, returned with orders
to make some agreement with the Pirates.   This they performed, and concluded with the Pirates they would give
for their ransom and liberty the sum of twenty thousand
pieces of eight and five hundred cows.   The condition
hereof being that they should commit no farther acts
of hostility against any person, but should depart thence
presently after payment of the money and cattle.   The
one and the other being delivered, they set sail with
the whole fleet, causing great joy to the inhabitants of
Maracaibo to see themselves quit of this sort of people.
Notwithstanding, three days after they resumed their
fears and admiration, seeing the Pirates to appear again
and re-enter the port they had left with all their ships.
But these apprehensions soon vanished, by only hearing
the errand of one of the Pirates, who came on shore

to tell them from L'Ollonais: *They should send him a skilful Pilot to conduct one of his greatest ships over the dangerous bank that lies at the entry of the lake.* Which petition, or rather command, was instantly granted.

The Pirates had now been full two months in those towns, wherein they committed those cruel and insolent actions we have told you of. Departing therefore thence, they took their course towards the island Hispaniola, and arrived thither in eight days, casting anchor in a port called Isla de la Vaca, or Cow Island. This isle is inhabited by French buccaneers, who most commonly sell the flesh they hunt to Pirates and others who now and then put in there with intent of victualling or trading with them. Here they unladed the whole cargo of riches they had robbed ; the usual storehouse of the Pirates being commonly under the shelter of the buccaneers. Here also they made a dividend amongst them of all their prizes and gains, according to that order and degree which belonged to every one, as hath been mentioned above. Having cast up the account and made exact calculation of all they had purchased, they found in ready money two hundred and threescore thousand pieces of eight. Whereupon, this being divided, every one received to his share in money, and also in pieces of silk, linen and other commodities, the value of above one hundred pieces of eight. Those who had been wounded in this expedition received their part before all the rest ; I mean, such recompences as I spoke of in the first Book, for the loss of their limbs which many sustained. Afterwards they weighed all the plate that was uncoined, reckoning after the rate of ten pieces of eight for every pound. The jewels were prized with much variety, either at too high or too low rates ; being thus occasioned by their own ignorance. This being done, every one was put to his oath again, that he had not concealed anything nor subtracted from the common stock. Hence they proceeded to the dividend of what shares belonged to such as were dead amongst them, either in battle or otherwise. These shares were given to their friends to be kept entire for them, and to be delivered in due time to their nearest relations, or whomsoever should appear to be their lawful heirs.

The whole dividend being entirely finished, they set sail thence for the Isle of Tortuga. Here they arrived one month after, to the great joy of most that were upon the island. For as to the common Pirates, in three weeks they had scarce any money left them; having spent it all in things of little value, or at play either at cards or dice. Here also arrived, not long before them, two French ships laden with wine and brandy and other things of this kind; whereby these liquors, at the arrival of the Pirates, were sold indifferent cheap. But this lasted not long; for soon after they were enhanced extremely, a gallon of brandy being sold for four pieces of eight. The Governor of the island bought of the Pirates the whole cargo of the ship laden with cacao, giving them for that rich commodity scarce the twentieth part of what it was worth. Thus they made shift to lose and spend the riches they had got in much less time than they were purchased by robbing. The taverns, according to the custom of Pirates, got the greatest part thereof; insomuch that soon after they were constrained to seek more by the same unlawful means they had obtained the preceding.

CHAPTER III.

L'Ollonais makes new preparations to take the city of St. James de Leon; as also that of Nicaragua, where he miserably perishes.

L'OLLONAIS had got himself very great esteem and repute at Tortuga by this last voyage, by reason he brought them home such considerable profit. And now he needed take no great care how to gather men to serve under his colours, seeing more came in voluntarily to proffer their service to him than he could employ, every one reposing such great confidence in his conduct for seeking their fortunes, that they judged it a matter of the greatest security imaginable to expose themselves in his company to the hugest dangers that might possibly occur. He resolved therefore for a second voyage, to go with his officers and soldiers towards the parts of Nicaragua, and pillage there as many towns as he could meet.

Having published his new preparations, he had all his men together at the time appointed, being about the number of seven hundred, more or less. Of these he put three hundred on board the ship he took at Maracaibo, and the rest in other vessels of lesser burden, which were five more : so that the whole number were in all six ships. The first port they went to was in the Island of Hispaniola, to a place called Bayaha, where they determined to victual the fleet and take in provisions. This being done, they set sail thence, and steered their course to a port called Matamana, lying on the South side of the Isle of Cuba. Their intent was to take here all the canoes they could meet, these coasts

being frequented by an huge number of fishermen of
tortoises, who carry them thence to Havana. They
took as many of the said canoes, to the great grief of
those miserable people, as they thought necessary for
their designs. For they had great necessity of these
small bottoms, by reason the port whither they designed
to go was not of depth sufficient to bear ships of any
burden. Hence they took their course towards the cape
called Gracias à Dios, situate upon the continent in
latitude fifteen degrees North, at the distance of one
hundred leagues from the island De los Pinos. But
being out at sea they were taken with a sad and
tedious calm, and by the agitation of the waves alone
were thrown into the Gulf of Honduras. Here they
laboured very much to regain what they had lost, but all
in vain ; both the waters in their course, and the winds,
being contrary to their endeavours. Besides that the
ship wherein L'Ollonais was embarked could not follow
the rest ; and what was worse, they wanted already provisions. Hereupon they were forced to put into the
first port or bay they could reach, to revictual their fleet.
Thus they entered with their canoes into a river called
Xagua, inhabited by Indians, whom they totally robbed
and destroyed ; they finding amongst their goods great
quantity of millet, many hogs and hens. Not contented
with what they had done, they determined to remain
there until the bad weather was over, and to pillage all
the towns and villages lying along the coast of the gulf.
Thus they passed from one place to another, seeking as
yet more provisions, by reason they had not what they
wanted for the accomplishment of their designs. Having
searched and rifled many villages, where they found no
great matter, they came at last to Puerto Cavallo. In
this port the Spaniards have two several storehouses,
which serve to keep the merchandizes that are brought
from the inner parts of the country until the arrival of
the ships. There was in the port at that occasion a

Spanish ship mounted with four and twenty guns and
sixteen pateraras or mortar-pieces.   This ship was
immediately seized by the Pirates ; and then, drawing
near the shore, they landed and burnt the two store-
houses, with all the rest of the houses belonging to the
place.   Many inhabitants likewise they took prisoners,
and committed upon them the most insolent and inhuman cruelties that ever heathens invented, putting
them to the cruellest tortures they could imagine or
devise.   It was the custom of L'Ollonais that, having
tormented any persons and they not confessing, he would
instantly cut them in pieces with his hanger, and pull out
their tongues ; desiring to do the same, if possible, to
every Spaniard in the world.   Oftentimes it happened
that some of these miserable prisoners, being forced
thereunto by the rack, would promise to discover the
places where the fugitive Spaniards lay hidden ; which
being not able afterwards to perform, they were put to
more enormous and cruel deaths than they who were
dead before.

The prisoners being all dead and annihilated (excepting only two, whom they reserved to show them what
they desired), they marched hence to the town of San
Pedro, or St. Peter, distant ten or twelve leagues from
Puerto Cavallo, having in their company three hundred
men, whom L'Ollonais led, and leaving behind him Moses
van Vin for his lieutenant to govern the rest in his
absence.   Being come three leagues upon their way,
they met with a troop of Spaniards, who lay in ambuscade for their coming.   These they set upon with all the
courage imaginable, and at last totally defeated, howbeit
they behaved themselves very manfully at the beginning
of the fight.   But not being able to resist the fury of the
Pirates, they were forced to give way and save themselves by flight, leaving many Pirates dead upon the
place and wounded, as also some of their own party
maimed by the way.   These L'Ollonais put to death with-

out mercy, having asked them what questions he thought fit for his purpose.

There were still remaining some few prisoners who were not wounded. These were asked by L'Ollonais if any more Spaniards did lie farther on in ambuscade? To whom they answered, there were. Then he commanded them to be brought before him, one by one, and asked if there was no other way to be found to the town but that? This he did out of a design to excuse, if possible, those ambuscades. But they all constantly answered him, they knew none. Having asked them all, and finding they could show him no other way, L'Ollonais grew outrageously passionate; insomuch that he drew his cutlass, and with it cut open the breast of one of those poor Spaniards, and pulling out his heart with his sacrilegious hands, began to bite and gnaw it with his teeth, like a ravenous wolf, saying to the rest: *I will serve you all alike, if you show me not another way.*

Hereupon those miserable wretches promised to show him another way; but withal they told him, it was extremely difficult and laborious. Thus, to satisfy that cruel tyrant, they began to lead him and his army. But finding it not for his purpose, even as they told him, he was constrained to return to the former way, swearing with great choler and indignation: *Mort Dieu, les Espagnols me le payeront* (*By God's death the Spaniards shall pay me for this*).

The next day he fell into another ambuscade; the which he assaulted with such horrible fury that in less than an hour's time he routed the Spaniards, and killed the greatest part of them. The Spaniards were persuaded that by these ambuscades they should better be able to destroy the Pirates, assaulting them by degrees; and for this reason had posted themselves in several places. At last he met with a third ambuscade, where was placed a party of Spaniards both stronger and to

The Cruelty of Lolonois
LOLONOIS

greater advantage than the former. Yet, notwithstanding, the Pirates, by throwing with their hands little fireballs in great number, and continuing to do so for some time, forced this party, as well as the preceding, to flee. And this with such great loss of men as that, before they could reach the town, the greatest part of the Spaniards were either killed or wounded. There was but one path which led to the town. This path was very well barricaded with good defences; and the rest of the town round about was planted with certain shrubs or trees named Raqueltes, very full of thorns and these very sharp-pointed. This sort of fortification seemed stronger than the triangles which are used in Europe, when an army is of necessity to pass by the place of an enemy, it being almost impossible for the Pirates to traverse those shrubs. The Spaniards that were posted behind the said defences, seeing the Pirates come, began to shoot at them with their great guns. But these, perceiving them ready to fire, used to stoop down, and when the shot was made, fall upon the defendants with fireballs in hands and naked swords, killing with these weapons many of the town. Yet, notwithstanding, not being able to advance any farther, they were constrained to retire for the first time. Afterwards they returned to the attack again, with fewer men than before; and observing not to shoot till they were very near, they gave the Spaniards a charge so dexterously, that with every shot they killed an enemy.

The attack continuing thus eager on both sides till night, the Spaniards were compelled to hang forth a white flag, in token of truce and that they desired to come to a parley. The only conditions they required for delivering the town were : *That the Pirates should give the inhabitants quarter for two hours.* This short space of time they demanded, with intent to carry away and abscond as much of their goods and riches as they could, as also to flee to some other neighbouring town. Upon the agreement of this article they entered the town, and continued there the two hours above-mentioned, without committing the least act of hostility, or causing any trouble to the inhabitants. But no sooner that time was passed, than L'Ollonais ordered the inhabitants should be followed and robbed of all they had carried away ; and not only goods, but their persons likewise to be made all prisoners. Notwithstanding, the greatest part of their merchandize and goods were in such manner absconded as the Pirates could not find them ; they meeting only a few leathern sacks that were filled with anil or indigo.

Having stayed at this town some few days, and according to their usual customs committed there most horrid insolencies, they at last quitted the place, carrying away with them all that they possibly could, and reducing the town totally into ashes. Being come to the seaside, where they left a party of their own comrades, they found these had busied themselves in cruizing upon the fishermen that lived thereabouts or came that way from the river of Guatemala. In this river also was expected a ship that was to come from Spain. Finally they resolved to go towards the islands that lie on the other side of the gulf, there to cleanse and careen their vessels. But in the meanwhile they left two canoes before the coast, or rather the mouth of the river of Guatemala, to the intent they should take the ship which, as I said before, was expected from Spain.

But their chief intention of going to those islands was to seek provisions, as knowing the tortoises of those places are very excellent and pleasant food. As soon as they arrived there, they divided into troops, each party choosing a fit post for that fishery. Every one of them undertook to knit a net with the rinds of certain trees, called in those parts Macoa. Of these rinds they make also ropes and cables for the service of ships : insomuch that no vessel can be in need of such things whensoever they can but find the said trees. There are also in those parts many places where they find pitch,[1] which is gathered thereabouts in great abundance. The quantity hereof is so great that, running down the sea-coasts, being melted by the heat of the sun, it congeals in the water into great heaps, and represents the shape of small islands. ΄ This pitch is not like that we have in the countries of Europe, but is hugely like, both in colour and shape, that froth of the sea which is called by the naturalists bitumen. But in my judgment this matter is nothing else but wax, which stormy weather has cast into the sea, being part of that huge quantity which in the neighbouring territories is made by the bees. Thus from places far distant from the sea it is also brought to the sea-coast by the winds and rolling waves of great rivers ; being likewise mingled with sand, and having the smell of black amber, such as is sent us from the Orient. In those parts are found great quantities of the said bees, who make their honey in trees ; whence it happens that the honey-combs being fixed to the bodies of the trees, when tempests arise they are torn away, and by the fury of the winds carried into the sea, as has been said before. Some naturalists are willing to say that between the honey and the wax is made a separation by means of the salt water, whence proceeds also the good amber. This opinion is rendered the more probable because the said amber being found and tasted, it affords the like taste as wax does.

But now, returning to my discourse, I shall let you know that the Pirates made in those islands all the haste to equip their vessels they could possibly, by reason they had news the Spanish ship which they expected was come. They spent some time in cruizing upon the coasts of Yucatan, whereabouts inhabit many Indians, who seek for the amber above-mentioned in those seas.

---

[1] One of the largest pitch or asphalt lakes is to be seen in the British island of Trinidad, a very good description of which is to be found in C. Kingsley's "At Last." Similar deposits on a small scale are not uncommon in the West Indian Islands, which are mostly of volcanic origin.

But seeing we are come to this place, I shall here, by
the by, make some short remarks on the manner of
living of these Indians, and the divine worship which
they practise.

The Indians of the coasts of Yucatan have now been
above one hundred years under the dominion of the
Spaniards. To this nation they performed all manner
of service ; for, whensoever any of them had need of a
slave or servant, they sent to seek one of these Indians
to serve them as long as they pleased. By the Spaniards
they were initiated at first in the principles of Christian
faith and religion. Being thus made a part of Christi-
anity, they used to send them every Sunday and holiday
through the whole year a priest to perform divine service
among them. Afterwards, for what reasons are not
known, but certainly through evil temptations of the
Father of Idolatry, the Devil, they suddenly cast off
Christian religion again, and abandoned the true divine
worship, beating withal and abusing the priest was sent
them. This provoked the Spaniards to punish them
according to their deserts, which they did by casting
many of the chief of these Indians into prison. Every
one of those barbarians had, and has still, a god to himself, whom he serves and worships. It is a thing that
deserves all admiration, to consider how they use in this
particular a child that is newly born into the world. As
soon as this is issued from the womb of the mother, they
carry it to the temple. Here they make a circle or hole,
which they fill with ashes, without mingling anything
else with them. Upon this heap of ashes they place
the child naked, leaving it there a whole night alone,
not without great danger ; nobody daring to come near
it. In the meanwhile the temple is open on all sides, to
the intent all sorts of beasts may freely come in and out.
The next day the father and relations of the infant return
thither, to see if the track or step of any animal appears
to be printed in the ashes. Not finding any, they leave

the child there until some beast hath approached the
infant, and left behind him the mark of his feet.   To
this animal, whatsoever it be, they consecrate the creature newly born, as unto its god ; which he is bound to
worship and serve all his life, esteeming the said beast
as his patron and protector in all cases of danger or
necessity.   They offer to their gods sacrifices of fire,
wherein they burn a certain gum called by them copal,
whose smoke affords a very delicious smell.   When the
infant is grown up, the parents thereof tell him and show
him whom he ought to worship, serve and honour as his
own proper god.   This being known, he goes to the
temple, where he makes offerings to the said beast.
Afterwards, if in the course of his life any one has injured
him, or any evil happens to him, he complains thereof to
that beast, and sacrifices to it for revenge.   Whence
many times comes that those who have done the injury
of which he complains are found to be bitten, killed, or
otherwise hurt by such animals.

After this superstitious and idolatrous manner do live
those miserable and ignorant Indians, that inhabit all the
islands of the Gulf of Honduras, as also many of them
that dwell upon the continent of Yucatan.   In the territories of which country are found most excellent ports
for the safety of ships, where those Indians most commonly love to build their houses.   These people are not
very faithful one to another, and likewise use strange
ceremonies at their marriages.   Whensoever any one
pretends to marry a young damsel, he first applies himself to her father or nearest relation.   He then examines
him very exactly concerning the manner of cultivating
their plantations and other things at his pleasure.
Having satisfied the questions that were put to him by
the father-in-law, he gives the young man a bow and
arrow.   With these things he repairs to the young maid,
and presents her with a garland of green leaves, inter-
weaved with sweet-smelling flowers.   This she is obliged

to put upon her head, and lay aside that which she wore before that time ; it being the custom of the country that all virgins go perpetually crowned with flowers. This garland being received and put upon the head, every one of the relations and friends go to advise with others, among themselves, whether that marriage will be useful and of likely happiness, or not. Afterwards the aforesaid relations and friends meet together at the house of the damsel's father, and there they drink of a certain liquor made of maize, or Indian wheat. And here before the whole company the father gives his daughter in marriage to the bridegroom. The next day the newly-married bride comes to her mother, and in her presence pulls off the garland and tears it in pieces, with great cries and bitter lamentations, according to the custom of the country. Many other things I could relate at large of the manner of living and customs of those Indians ; but these I shall omit, thereby to follow my discourse.

Our Pirates therefore had many canoes of the Indians in the Isle of Sambale, five leagues distant from the coasts of Yucatan. In the aforesaid island is found great quantity of amber, but more especially when any storm arises from towards the East, whence the waves bring many things and very different. Through this sea no vessels can pass, unless very small, the waters being too shallow. In the lands that are surrounded by this sea is found huge quantity of Campeche wood (*i.e.* logwood), and other things of this kind, that serve for the art of dyeing, which occasions them to be much esteemed in Europe, and doubtless would be much more, in case we had the skill and science of the Indians, who are so industrious as to make a dye or tincture that never changes its colour nor fades away.

After that the Pirates had been in that gulf three entire months, they received advice that the Spanish ship was come. Hereupon they hastened to the port, where the ship lay at anchor unlading the merchandize it brought, with design to assault her as soon as it were possible. But before this attempt they thought it convenient to send away some of their boats from the mouth of the river, to seek for a small vessel which was expected; having notice that she was very richly laden, the greatest part of the cargo being plate, indigo and cochineal. In the meanwhile the people of the ship that was in the port had notice given that the Pirates designed upon them. Hereupon they prepared all things very well for the defence of the said vessel, which was mounted with forty-two guns, had many arms on board and other necessaries, together with one hundred and thirty fighting men. To L'Ollonais all this seemed but little; and thus he assaulted her with great courage, his own ship carrying only twenty-two guns, and having no more than a small saëtia, or flyboat, for help. But the Spaniards defended themselves after such manner as they forced the Pirates to retire. Notwithstanding, while the smoke of the powder continued very thick, as amidst a dark fog or mist, they sent four canoes very well manned, and boarded the ship with great agility, whereby they compelled the Spaniards to surrender.

The ship being taken, they found not in her what they thought, as being already almost wholly unladed. All the treasure they here got consisted only in fifty bars of iron, a small parcel of paper, some earthen jars full of wine, and other things of this kind; all of small importance.

Presently after, L'Ollonais called a council of the whole fleet, wherein he told them he intended to go to Guatemala. Upon this point they divided into several sentiments; some of them liking the proposal very well ,and others disliking it as much—especially a certain party of them, who were but new in those exercises of piracy, and who had imagined at their setting forth from Tortuga that pieces of eight were gathered as easily as pears from a tree. But having found at last most things contrary to their expectation, they quitted the fleet, and returned whence they set out.   Others, on the contrary, affirmed they had rather die of hunger, than return home without a great deal of money.

But the major part of the company, judging the propounded voyage little fit for their purpose, separated from L'Ollonais and the rest.   Among these was ringleader one Moses Vanclein, who was captain of the ship taken at Puerto Cavallo.   This fellow took his course towards Tortuga, designing to cruize to and fro in those seas. With him also joined another comrade of his own, by name Pierre le Picard, who, seeing the rest to leave L'Ollonais, thought fit to do the same.   These runaways having thus parted company, steered their course homewards, coasting along the continent, till they came at last to Costa Rica.   Here they landed a strong party of men near the river of Veraguas, and marched in good order to the town of the same name.   This place they took and totally pillaged, notwithstanding that the Spaniards made a strong and warlike resistance.   They brought away some of the inhabitants as prisoners, with all that they had robbed, which was of no great importance, the reason hereof being the poverty of the place, which exercises no manner of trade than only working in the mines, where some of the inhabitants constantly attend. Yet no other persons seek for the gold than only slaves.   These they compel to dig, whether they live or die, and wash the earth that is taken out in the neighbouring rivers; where oftentimes they find pieces of gold as big as peas.   Finally, the Pirates found in this robbery no greater value than seven or eight pounds weight of gold.   Hereupon they returned back, giving over the design they had to go farther on to the town of Nata, situated upon the coasts of the South sea. Hitherto they designed to march, knowing the inhabitants to be rich merchants, who had their slaves at work in the mines of Veraguas.   But from this enterprize they were deterred by the multitude of Spaniards whom they saw gather on all sides to fall upon them; whereof they had timely advice beforehand.

L'Ollonais, thus abandoned by his companions, remained alone in the Gulf of Honduras, by reason his ship was too great to get out at the time of the reflux of those seas, which the smaller vessels could more easily do. There he sustained great want of all sorts of provisions; insomuch as they were constrained to go ashore every day, to seek wherewithal to maintain themselves. And not finding anything else, they were forced to kill monkeys and other animals such as they could find, for their sustenance.

At last having found, in the latitude of the Cape of Gracias à Dios, certain little islands called De las Pertas, here, near these isles, his ship fell upon a bank of sand, where it stuck so fast that no art could be found to get her off into deep water again, notwithstanding they unladed all the guns, iron and other weighty things as much as possibly they could: but all they could do was to little or no effect. Hereupon they were necessitated to break the ship in pieces, and with some of the planks and nails build themselves a boat, wherewith to get away from those islands. Thus they began their work; and while they are employed about it, I shall pass to describe succinctly the isles aforementioned and their inhabitants.

The islands called De las Pertas are inhabited by Indians, who are properly savages, not having at any time known or conversed with any civil people. They are tall in stature and very nimble in running, which they perform almost as fast as horses. At diving also in the sea they are very dexterous and hardy. From the bottom of the sea I saw them take up an anchor that weighed six hundred pound, by tying a cable to it with great dexterity, and pulling it from a rock. They use no other arms than such as are made of wood, without any iron, unless that some instead thereof fix a crocodile

tooth, which serves for a point. They have neither bows
nor arrows among them, as other Indians have ; but their
common weapon is a sort of lances, that are long a fathom
and a half. In these islands there are many plantations
surrounded with woods, whence they gather great abundance of fruits. Such are potatoes, bananas, racoven,
ananas and many others, which the constitution of the
soil affords. Near these plantations they have no houses
to dwell in, as in other places of the Indies. Some are
of opinion that these Indians eat human flesh, which seems
to be confirmed by what happened when L'Ollonais was
there. Two of his companions, the one being a Frenchman and the other a Spaniard, went into the woods,
where having straggled up and down some while, they
met with a troop of Indians that began to pursue them.
They defended themselves as well as they could with
their swords ; but at last were forced to flee. This the
Frenchman performed with great agility; but the Spaniard,
being not so swift as his companion, was taken by those
barbarians, and heard of no more. Some days after, they
attempted to go into the woods to see what was become
of their companion. To this effect twelve Pirates set
forth very well armed, amongst whom was the Frenchman, who conducted them, and shewed them the place
where he left his companion. Here they found, near the
place, that the Indians had kindled a fire ; and, at a small
distance thence, they found the bones of the said Spaniard
very well roasted. Hence they inferred that they had
roasted the miserable Spaniard, of whom they found
more, some pieces of flesh ill scraped off from the bones,
and one hand, which had only two fingers remaining.

They marched farther on, seeking for Indians. Of
these they found a great number together, who endeavoured to escape, seeing the Pirates so strong and well
armed. But they overtook some of them, and brought
on board their ships five men and four women. With
these they used all the means they could invent to make

themselves be understood and gain their affections; giving them certain small trifles, as knives, beads and the like things. They gave them also victuals and drink; but nothing of either would they taste. It was also observable that all the while they were prisoners on board the ships, they spoke not one word to each other among themselves. Thus the Pirates, seeing these poor Indians were much afraid of them, presented them again with some small things, and let them go. When they departed, they made signs, giving them to understand they would come again. But they soon forgot their benefactors, and were never heard nor seen more. Neither could any notice afterwards be had of these Indians or any others in the whole island after that time. Which occasioned the Pirates to suspect that both those that were taken, and all the rest of the island, did all swim away by night to some other little neighbouring islands, especially considering they could never set eyes on any Indian more; neither was there ever seen any boat or other vessel in the whole circumference of the island.

In the meanwhile the Pirates were very desirous to see their long-boat finished, which they were building with the timber of the ship that struck upon the sands. Yet, considering their work would be but long, they began to cultivate some pieces of ground. Here they sowed French beans, which came to maturity in six weeks' time, and many other fruits. They had good provision of Spanish wheat, bananas, racoven and other things. With the wheat they made bread, and baked it in portable ovens, which they had brought with them to this effect. Thus they feared not hunger in those desert places. After this manner they employed themselves for the space of five or six months. Which time being passed, and the long-boat finished, they determined to go to the river of Nicaragua, to see if they could take some few canoes, and herewith return to the said islands and fetch away their companions that remained behind, by reason the boat they had built was not capable of transporting so many men together.   Hereupon, to avoid any disputes that might arise, they cast lots among themselves, determining thereby who should go, or stay, in the island.

The lot fell only upon one half of the people of the lost vessel ; who embarked upon the long-boat they had built, and also the skiff which they had before ; the other half remaining on shore.   L'Ollonais having set sail, arrived in a few days at the mouth of the river of Nicaragua.   Here suddenly his ill-fortune assailed him, which of long time had been reserved for him, as a punishment due to the multitude of horrible crimes, which in his licentious and wicked life he had committed. Here he met with both Spaniards and Indians, who jointly together set upon him and his companions, and used them so roughly that the greatest part of the Pirates were killed upon the place.   L'Ollonais, with those that remained alive, had much ado to escape on board their boats aforementioned.   Yet notwithstanding this great loss of men, he resolved not to return to seek those he had left at the Isle of Pertas, without taking some boats, such as he looked for.   To this effect he determined to go farther on to the coasts of Cartagena, with design to seek for canoes.   But God Almighty, the time of His Divine justice being now already come, had appointed the Indians of Darien to be the instruments and executioners thereof.   The Indians of Darien are esteemed as bravos, or wild savage Indians, by the neighbouring Spaniards, who never could reduce them to civility.   Hither L'Ollonais came (being rather brought by his evil conscience that cried for punishment of his crimes), thinking to act in that country his former cruelties.   But the Indians within a few days after his arrival took him prisoner and tore him in pieces alive, throwing his body limb by limb into the fire. and his ashes into the air ; to the intent no trace nor memory might remain of such an infamous, inhuman creature. One of his companions gave me an exact account of the aforesaid tragedy ; affirming withal that he himself had escaped the same punishment, not without the greatest of difficulties. He believed also that many of his comrades who were taken prisoners in that encounter by the Indians of Darien were after the same manner as their cruel captain torn in pieces and burned alive. Thus ends the history of the life and miserable death of that infernal wretch L'Ollonais, who, full of horrid, execrable and enormous deeds, and also debtor to so much innocent blood, died by cruel and butcherly hands, such as his own were in the course of his life.

Those that remained in the island De las Pertas, waiting for the return of them who got away, only to their great misfortune, hearing no news of their captain nor companions, at last embarked themselves upon the ship of a certain Pirate who happened to pass that way. This fellow was come from Jamaica with intent to land at the Cape of Gracias à Dios, and hence to mount the river with his canoes, and take the city of Cartagena. These two parcels of Pirates being now joined together were infinitely gladdened at the presence and society of one another. Those because they found themselves delivered from their miseries, poverty and necessities, wherein now they had lived the space of ten entire months—these, because they were now considerably strengthened, whereby to effect with greater satisfaction their intended designs. Hereupon, as soon as they were arrived at the aforesaid Cape of Gracias à Dios, they all put themselves into canoes, and with these vessels mounted the river, being in number five hundred men ; leaving only five or six persons in every ship to keep them. They took no provisions with them, as being persuaded they should find everywhere sufficient. But these their own hopes were found totally vain,

as not being grounded in God Almighty. For He
ordained it so that the Indians having perceived
their coming, were all fled before them, not leaving in
their houses nor plantations, which for the most part
border upon the sides of rivers, anything of necessary
provisions or victuals. Hereby, in few days after they
had quitted their ships, they were reduced to such necessity and hunger as nothing could be more extreme.
Notwithstanding, the hopes they had conceived of
making their fortunes very soon animated them for the
present, being contented in this affliction with a few
green herbs, such as they could gather as they went upon
the banks of the river.

Yet all this courage and vigour of mind could not last
above a fortnight. After which, their hearts, as well as
their bodies, began to fail for hunger; insomuch as they
found themselves constrained to quit the river and betake
themselves to the woods, seeking out some small villages
where they might find relief for their necessity. But all
was in vain : for, having ranged up and down the woods
for some days without finding the least comfort to their
hungry desires, they were forced to return again to the
river. Where being come, they thought it convenient to
descend to the sea-coasts where they had left their ships,
not being able to find in the present enterprize what they
sought for. In this laborious journey they were reduced
to such extremity that many of them devoured their own
shoes, the sheaths of their swords, knives and other
things of this kind, being almost ravenous, and fully
desirous to meet some Indians, intending to sacrifice
them unto their teeth. At last they arrived at the coast
of the sea, where they found some comfort and relief to
their former miseries, and also means to seek more. Yet
notwithstanding, the greatest part of them perished
through faintness and other diseases contracted by
hunger; which occasioned also the remaining part to
disperse. Till at last by degrees many or most of them

fell into the same pit that L'Ollonais did. Of him, and of his companions I have hitherto given my reader a compendious narrative ; which now I shall continue with the actions and exploits of Captain Henry Morgan, who may not undeservedly be called the second L'Ollonais, as not being unlike or inferior to him either in achievements against the Spaniards or in robberies of many innocent people.

CHAPTER IV.

Of the Origin and Descent of Captain Henry Morgan—his Exploits and a continuation of the most remarkable actions of his life.

CAPTAIN HENRY MORGAN was born in the Kingdom of England, and there in the principality of Wales. His father was a rich yeoman, or farmer, and of good quality in that country, even as most who bear that name in Wales are known to be. Morgan, being as yet young, had no inclinations to follow the calling of his father; and therefore left his country, and came towards the sea-coasts to seek some other employ more suitable to his humour, that aspired to something else. There he found entertainment in a certain port where several ships lay at anchor, that were bound for the Isle of Barbados. With these ships he resolved to go in the service of one, who, according to what is commonly practised in those parts by the English and other nations, sold him as soon as he came on shore. He served his time at Barbados, and when he had obtained his liberty, thence transferred himself to the Island of Jamaica, there to seek new fortunes. Here he found two vessels of Pirates that were ready to go to sea. Being destitute of employ, he put himself into one of these ships, with intent to follow the exercises of that sort of people. He learned in a little while their manner of living; and so exactly, that having performed three or four voyages with some profit and good success, he agreed with some of his comrades, who had gotten by the same voyages a small parcel of money, to join stocks and buy a ship. The vessel being bought

they unanimously chose him to be the captain and com-
·mander thereof.

With this ship, soon after, he set forth from Jamaica
to cruize upon the coasts of Campeche ; in which voyage
he had the fortune to take several ships, with which
he returned triumphant to the same island. Here he
found at the same time an old Pirate, named Mansvelt
(of whom we have already made mention in the first
part of this book), who was then busied in equipping
a considerable fleet of ships with design to land upon
the Continent, and pillage whatever came in his way.
Mansvelt, seeing Captain Morgan return with so many
prizes, judged him, from his actions, to be of undaunted
courage ; and hereupon was moved to choose him for
his Vice-Admiral in that expedition. Thus having fitted
out fifteen ships, between great and small, they set sail
from Jamaica with five hundred men, both Walloons and
French. With this fleet they arrived not long after at
the Isle of St. Catharine, situated near the Continent of
Costa Rica, in the latitude of twelve degrees and a
half North, and distant thirty-five leagues from the
river of Chagre, between North and South. Here they
made their first descent, landing most of their men presently after.

Being now come to try their arms and fortune, they
in a short while forced the garrison that kept the island
to surrender and deliver into their hands all the forts and
castles belonging thereunto. All these they instantly
demolished, reserving only one, wherein they placed one
hundred men of their own party, and all the slaves they
had taken from the Spaniards. With the rest of their
men they marched to another small island near that of
St. Catharine, and adjoining so near to it, that with a
bridge they could get over. In few days they made a
bridge, and passed thither, conveying also over it all the
pieces of ordnance which they had taken upon the great
island. Having ruined and destroyed, with sword and

fire, both the islands, leaving what orders were necessary
at the castle above-mentioned, they put forth to sea again
with the Spaniards they had taken prisoners. Yet these
they set on shore, not long after, upon the firm land,
near a place called Porto Bello. After this they began
to cruize upon the coasts of Costa Rica, till finally they
came to the river of Colla, designing to rob and pillage
all the towns they could find in those parts, and afterwards to pass to the village of Nata, to do the same.

The President or Governor of Panama, having had
advice of the arrival of these Pirates and the hostilities
they committed everywhere, thought it his duty to set
forth to their encounter with a body of men. His
coming caused the Pirates to retire suddenly with all
speed and care, especially seeing the whole country
alarmed at their arrival, and that their designs were
known and consequently could be of no great effect at
that present. Hereupon they returned to the Isle of
St. Catharine, to visit the hundred men they had left in
garrison there. The Governor of these men was a
certain Frenchman named Le Sieur Simon, who behaved
himself very well in that charge, while Mansvelt was
absent. Insomuch that he had put the great island in a
very good posture of defence ; and the little one he had
caused to be cultivated with many fertile plantations,
which were sufficient to revictual the whole fleet with
provisions and fruits, not only for present refreshment,
but also in case of a new voyage. Mansvelt's inclinations
were very much bent to keep these two islands in perpetual possession, as being very commodious, and profit-
ably situated for the use of the Pirates, chiefly because
they were so near the Spanish dominions, and easily to
be defended against them ; as I shall represent in the
third part of this history more at large, in a copper
plate, delineated for this purpose.

Hereupon Mansvelt determined to return to Jamaica,
with design to send some recruit to the Isle of St.

Catharine, that in case of any invasion of the Spaniards, the Pirates might be provided for a defence. As soon as he arrived, he propounded his mind and intentions to the Governor of that island ; but he liked not the propositions of Mansvelt, fearing lest by granting such things he should displease his Master, . the King of England, besides, that giving him the men he desired, and other necessaries for that purpose, he must of necessity diminish and weaken the forces of that island whereof he was Governor. Mansvelt seeing the unwillingness of the Governor of Jamaica, and that of his own accord he could not compass what he desired, with the same intent and designs went to the Isle of Tortuga. But there, before he could accomplish his desires, or put in execution what was intended, death suddenly surprised him, and put a period to his wicked life ; all things hereby remaining in suspense, until the occasion which I shall hereafter relate.

Le Sieur Simon, who remained at the Isle of St. Catharine in quality of Governor thereof, receiving no news from Mansvelt, his Admiral, was greatly impatient, and desirous to know what might be the cause thereof. In the meanwhile Don John Perez de Guzman, being newly come to the government of Costa Rica, thought it no ways convenient for the interest of the King of Spain that that island should remain in the hands of the Pirates. And hereupon he equipped a considerable fleet, which he sent to the said island to retake it. But before he came to use any great violence, he wrote a letter to Le Sieur Simon, wherein he gave him to understand, if he would surrender the island to his Catholic Majesty, he should be very well rewarded ; but in case of refusal, severely punished when he had forced him to do it. Le Sieur Simon, seeing no appearance or probability of being able to defend it alone, nor any emolument that by so doing could accrue either to him or his people, after some small resistance delivered up the island into the hands of its true lord and master, under the same articles they had obtained it from the Spaniards. Few days after the surrender of the island, there arrived from Jamaica an English ship which the Governor of the said island had sent underhand, wherein was a good supply of people, both men and women. The Spaniards from the castle having espied this ship, put forth the English colours, and persuaded Le Sieur Simon to go on board, and conduct the said ship into a port they assigned him. This he performed immediately with dissimulation, whereby they were all made prisoners. A certain Spanish engineer has published, before me, an exact account and relation of the retaking of the Isle of St. Catharine by the Spaniards; which printed paper being fallen into my hands, I have thought it fit to be inserted here.

A true Relation and particular Account of the Victory obtained by the Arms of his Catholic Majesty against the English Pirates, by the direction and valour of Don John Perez de Guzman, *Knight of the Order of St. James, Governor and Captain-General of Terra Firma and the Province of Veraguas.*

THE Kingdom of Terra Firma, which of itself is sufficiently strong to repulse and extirpate great fleets, but more especially the Pirates of Jamaica, had several ways notice, under several hands, imparted to the Governor thereof, that fourteen English vessels did cruize upon the coasts belonging to his Catholic Majesty. The 14th day of July, 1665, news came to Panama, that the English Pirates of the said fleet were arrived at Puerto de Naos, and had forced the Spanish garrison of the Isle of St. Catharine, whose Governor was Don Estevan del Campo; and that they had possessed themselves of the said island, taking prisoners the inhabitants, and destroying all that ever they met. Moreover, about the same time Don John Perez de Guzman received particular information of these robberies from the relation of some Spaniards who escaped out of the island (and whom he ordered to be conveyed to Porto Bello), who more distinctly told him, that the aforementioned Pirates came into the island the 2nd day of May, by night, without being perceived by anybody ; and that the next day, after some disputes by arms, they had taken the fortresses and made prisoners all the inhabitants and soldiers, not one excepted, unless those that by good fortune had escaped their hands. This being heard by Don John, he called a council of war, wherein he declared the great progress the said Pirates had made in the dominions of his Catholic Majesty. Here likewise he propounded : *That it was absolutely necessary to send some forces to the Isle of St. Catharine, sufficient to retake it from the Pirates ; the honour and interest of his Majesty of Spain being very narrowly concerned herein. Otherwise the Pirates by such conquests might easily in course of time possess themselves of all the countries thereabouts.* To these reasons some were found who made answer : *That the Pirates, as not being able to subsist in the said island, would of necessity consume and waste themselves, and be forced to quit it, without any necessity of retaking it. That consequently it was not worth the while to engage in so many expenses and troubles as might be foreseen this would cost.* Notwithstanding these reasons to the contrary, Don John, as one who was an expert and valiant soldier, gave order that a quantity of provisions should be conveyed to Porto Bello, for the use and service of the militia. And neither to be idle nor negligent in his master's affairs, he transported himself thither, with no small danger to his life. Here he arrived the 7th day of July, with most things necessary to the expedition in hand ; where he found in the port a good ship, called *St. Vincent*, that belonged to the Company of the Negroes. This ship being of itself a strong vessel and well mounted with guns, he manned and victualled very well and sent to the Isle of St. Catharine, constituting Captain Joseph Sanchez Ximenez, mayor of the city of Porto Bello, commander thereof. The people he carried with him were two hundred threescore and ten soldiers, and thirty-seven prisoners of the same island, besides four-and-thirty Spaniards belonging to the garrison of Porto Bello, nine-and-twenty mulattos of Panama, twelve Indians very dexterous at shooting with bows and arrows, seven expert and able gunners, two lieutenants, two pilots, one surgeon, and one religious man of the Order of St. Francis for their chaplain.

Don John soon after gave his orders to every one of the officers, instructing them how they ought to behave themselves, telling them withal that the Governor of Cartagena would assist and supply them with more men, boats, and all things else they should find necessary for that enterprize; to which effect he had already written to the said Governor. On the 24th day of the said month Don John commanded the ship to weigh anchor, and sail out of the port. Then seeing a fair wind to blow, he called before him all the people designed for that expedition, and made them a speech, encouraging them to fight against the enemies of their country and religion, but more especially against those inhuman Pirates who had heretofore committed so many horrid and cruel actions against the subjects of his Catholic Majesty. Withal, promising to every one of them most liberal rewards; but especially to such as should behave themselves as they ought in the service of their king and country. Thus Don John bid them farewell; and immediately the ship weighed anchor, and set sail under a favourable gale of wind. The 22nd of the said month they arrived at Cartagena, and presented a letter to the Governor of the said city from the noble and valiant Don John; who received it, with testimonies of great affection to the person of Don John and his Majesty's service. And seeing their resolute courage to be conformable to his desires and expectation, he promised them his assistance, which should be with one frigate, one galleon, one boat, and one hundred and twenty-six men, the one half out of his own garrison, and the other half mulattos. Thus all of them being well provided with necessaries, they set forth from the port of Cartagena, the 2nd day of August; and the 10th of the said month they arrived within sight of the Isle of St. Catharine, towards the Western point thereof. And although the wind was contrary, yet they reached the port, and came to an anchor within it; having lost one of their boats, by foul weather, at the rock called Quita Signos.

The Pirates, seeing our ships come to an anchor, gave them presently three guns with bullets; the which were soon answered in the same coin. Hereupon the Mayor Joseph Sanchez Ximenez sent on shore to the Pirates one of his officers, to require them in the name of the Catholic King, his Master, to surrender the island, seeing they had taken it in the midst of peace between the two crowns of Spain and England; and that in case they would be obstinate, he would certainly put them all to the sword. The Pirates made answer, That island had once before belonged to the Government and dominions of the King of England; and that, instead of surrendering it, they preferred to lose their lives.

On Friday, the 13th of the said month, three negroes, from the enemy, came swimming aboard our Admiral. These brought intelligence, that all the Pirates that were upon the island were only threescore and twelve in number; and that they were under a great consternation, seeing such considerable forces come against them. With this intelligence the Spaniards resolved to land, and advance towards the fortresses, the which ceased not to fire as many great guns against them as they possibly could; which were corresponded in the same manner on our side till dark night. On Sunday, the 15th of the said month, which

was the day of the Assumption of Our Lady, the weather
being very calm and clear, the Spaniards began to
advance thus.   The ship named *St. Vincent*, which
rode Admiral, discharged two whole broadsides upon
the battery called the Conception.   The ship called
St. Peter, that was Vice-Admiral, discharged likewise her
guns against the other battery named St. James.   In
the meanwhile our people were landed in small boats,
directing their course towards the point of the battery
last mentioned, and thence they marched towards the
gate called Cortadura.   The lieutenant Frances de
Cazeres, being desirous to view the strength of the
enemy, with only fifteen men, was compelled to retreat
in all haste, by reason of the great guns which played so
furiously upon the place where he stood, they shooting
not only pieces of iron and small bullets, but also the
organs of the church, discharging in every shot threescore pipes at a time.

Notwithstanding this heat of the enemy, Captain Don
Joseph Ramirez de Leyva, with threescore men, made a
strong attack, wherein they fought on both sides very
desperately, till at last he overcame and forced the
Pirates to surrender the fort he had taken in hand.

On the other side, Captain John Galeno, with fourscore and ten men, passed over the hills, to advance that
way towards the castle of St. Teresa.   In the meanwhile
the Mayor Don Joseph Sanchez Ximenez, as com-
mander-in-chief, with the rest of his men set forth from
the battery of St. James, passing the fort with four boats,
and landing in despite of the enemy.   About this same
time Captain John Galeno began to advance with the
men he led to the forementioned fortress.   So that our
men made three attacks upon the enemy, on three several
sides, at one and the same time, with great courage and
valour.   Thus the Pirates, seeing many of their men
already killed and that they could in no manner subsist
any longer, retreated towards Cortadura, where they

surrendered themselves and likewise the whole island into our hands. Our people possessed themselves of all, and set up the Spanish colours, as soon as they had rendered thanks to God Almighty for the victory obtained on such a signalized day. The number of dead were six men of the enemy's, with many wounded, and threescore and ten prisoners. On our side was found only one man killed, and four wounded.

There was found upon the island eight hundred pound of powder, two hundred and fifty pound of small bullets, with many other military provisions. Among the prisoners were taken also two Spaniards, who had borne arms under the English against his Catholic Majesty. These were commanded to be shot to death the next day by order of the Mayor. The 10th day of September arrived at the isle an English vessel, which being seen at a great distance by the Mayor, he gave order to Le Sieur Simon, who was a Frenchman, to go and visit the said ship, and tell them that were on board the island belonged still to the English. He performed the commands, and found in the said ship only fourteen men, one woman and her daughter; who were all instantly made prisoners.

The English Pirates were all transported to Porto Bello; excepting only three, who by order of the Governor were carried to Panama, there to work in the castle of St. Jerome. This fortification is an excellent piece of workmanship, and very strong; being raised in the middle of the port, of quadrangular form, and of very hard stone. Its elevation or height is eightyeight geometrical feet, the walls being fourteen and the curtains seventy-five feet diameter. It was built at the expense of several private persons, the Governor of the city furnishing the greatest part of the money; so that it did not cost his Majesty any sum at all.

CHAPTER V.

Some account of the Island of Cuba. Capt. Morgan attempts to preserve the Isle of St. Catharine as a refuge and nest to Pirates; but fails of his designs. He arrives at and takes the village of El Puerto del Principe.

CAPTAIN MORGAN, seeing his predecessor and Admiral Mansvelt was dead, endeavoured as much as he could, and used all the means that were possible, to preserve and keep in perpetual possession the Isle of St. Catharine, seated near that of Cuba. His principal intent was to consecrate it as a refuge and sanctuary to the Pirates of those parts, putting it in a sufficient condition of being a convenient receptacle or storehouse of their preys and robberies. To this effect he left no stone unmoved whereby to compass his designs, writing for the same purpose to several merchants that lived in Virginia and New England, and persuading them to send him provisions and other necessary things towards the putting the said island in such a posture of defence as it might neither fear any external dangers nor be moved at any suspicions of invasion from any side that might attempt to disquiet it. At last all his thoughts and cares proved ineffectual by the Spaniards retaking the said island. Yet, notwithstanding, Captain Morgan retained his ancient courage, which instantly put him upon new designs. Thus he equipped at first a ship, with intention to gather an entire fleet, both as great and as strong as he could compass. By degrees he put the whole matter in execution, and gave order to every member of his fleet, they should meet at a certain port of Cuba. Here he determined to call a council, and deliberate concerning what were best to be done, and what place first they should fall upon. Leaving these new preparations in this condition, I shall here give my reader some small account of the aforementioned Isle of Cuba, in whose ports this expedition was hatched, seeing I omitted to do it in its proper place.

The Island of Cuba lies from East to West, in the latitude and situation of twenty to three and twenty degrees North, being in length one hundred and fifty German leagues and about forty in breadth. Its fertility is equal to that of the Island of Hispaniola. Besides which, it affords many things proper for trading and commerce, such as are hides of several beasts, particularly those that in Europe are called Hides of Havana. On all sides it is surrounded with a great number of small islands, which go altogether under the name of Cayos. Of these little islands the Pirates make great use, as of their own proper ports of refuge. Here most commonly they make their meetings and hold their councils, how to assault more easily the Spaniards. It is thoroughly irrigated on all sides with the streams of plentiful and pleasant rivers, whose entries form both secure and spacious ports, besides many other harbours for ships, which along the calm shores and coasts adorn many parts of this rich and beautiful island ; all which contribute very much to its happiness, by facilitating the exercise of trade, whereunto they invite both natives and aliens. The chief of these ports are Santiago, Bayame, Santa Maria, Espiritu Santo, Trinidad, Xagoa, Cabo de Corrientes and others, all which are seated on the south side of the island. On the northern side hereof are found the following : La Havana, Puerto Mariano, Santa Cruz, Mata Ricos and Barracoa.

This island has two principal cities, by which the whole country is governed, and to which all the towns and villages thereof give obedience. The first of these is named Santiago, or St. James, being seated on the south side, and having under its jurisdiction one half of the island. The chief magistrates hereof are a Bishop and a Governor, who command over the villages and towns belonging to the half above-mentioned. The chief of these are, on the southern side Espiritu Santo, Puerto del Principe and Bayame; on the north side it has Barracoa and the town called De los Cayos. The greatest part of the commerce driven at the aforementioned city of Santiago comes from the Canary Islands, whither they transport great quantity of tobacco, sugar, and hides : which sorts of merchandize are drawn to the head city from the subordinate towns and villages. In former times the city of Santiago was miserably sacked by the Pirates of Jamaica and Tortuga, notwithstanding that it is defended by a considerable castle.

The city and port De la Havana lies between the north and west side of the island. This is one of the most renowned and strongest places of all the West Indies. Its jurisdiction extends over the other half of the island, the chief places under it being Santa Cruz on the northern side and La Trinidad on the south. Hence is transported huge quantity of tobacco, which is sent in great plenty to New Spain and Costa Rica, even as far as the South Sea ; besides many ships laden with this commodity that are consigned to Spain and other parts of Europe, not only in the leaf but also in rolls. This city is defended by three castles, very great and strong ; two of which lie towards the port, and the other is seated upon a hill that commands the town. 'Tis esteemed to contain ten thousand families, more or less ; among which number of people the merchants of this place trade in New Spain, Campeche, Honduras and Florida. All the ships that come from the parts aforementioned, as also from Caracas, Cartagena and Costa Rica, are necessitated to take their provisions in at Havana, wherewith to make their voyage for Spain ;

this being the necessary and straight course they ought to steer for the South of Europe and other parts. The plate-fleet of Spain, which the Spaniards call Flôta, being homeward bound, touches here yearly, to take in the rest of their full cargo, as hides, tobacco and Campeche-wood.

Captain Morgan had been no longer than two months in the above-mentioned ports of the South of Cuba, when he had got together a fleet of twelve sail, between ships and great boats ; wherein he had seven hundred fighting men, part of which were English and part French. They called a council, and some were of opinion 'twere convenient to assault the city of Havana, under the obscurity of the night. Which enterprize, they said, might easily be performed, especially if they could but take a few of the ecclesiastics, and make them prisoners. Yca, that the city might be sacked, before the castles could put themselves in a posture of defence. Others propounded, according to their several opinions, other attempts. Notwithstanding, the former proposal was rejected, because many of the Pirates had been prisoners at other times in the said city ; and these affirmed nothing of consequence could be done, unless with fifteen hundred men. Moreover, that with all this number of people they ought first to go to the island De los Pinos, and land them in small boats about Matamano, fourteen leagues distant from the aforesaid city, whereby to accomplish by these means and order their designs.

Finally, they saw no possibility of gathering so great a fleet ; and hereupon, with that they had, they concluded to attempt some other place. Among the rest was found, at last, one who propounded they should go and assault the town of El Puerto del Principe. This proposition he endeavoured to persuade, by saying he knew that place very well, and that, being at a distance from the sea, it never was sacked by any Pirates ; where-

by the inhabitants were rich, as exercising their trade for
ready money with those of Havana, who kept here an
established commerce which consisted chiefly in hides.
This proposal was presently admitted by Captain Morgan
and the chief of his companions. And hereupon they
gave order to every captain to weigh anchor and set
sail, steering their course towards that coast that lies
nearest to El Puerto del Principe. Hereabouts is to
be seen a bay, named by the Spaniards El Puerto de
Santa Maria. Being arrived at this bay, a certain
Spaniard, who was prisoner on board the fleet, swam
ashore by night, and came to the town of Puerto
del Principe, giving account to the inhabitants of the
design the Pirates had against them. This he affirmed
to have overheard in their discourse, while they thought
he did not understand the English tongue. The
Spaniards, as soon as they received this fortunate advice,
began instantly to hide their riches, and carry away what
movables they could. The Governor also immediately
raised all the people of the town, both freemen and
slaves ; and with part of them took a post by which of
necessity the Pirates were to pass. He commanded
likewise many trees to be cut down and laid amidst the
ways to hinder their passage. In like manner he placed
several ambuscades, which were strengthened with some
pieces of cannon, to play upon them on their march. He
gathered in all about eight hundred men, of which he
distributed several into the aforementioned ambuscades,
and with the rest he begirt the town, displaying them upon
the plain of a spacious field, whence they could see the
coming of the Pirates at length.

Captain Morgan, with his men, being now upon the
march, found the avenues and passages to the town
impenetrable. Hereupon they took their way through
the wood, traversing it with great difficulty, whereby
they escaped divers ambuscades. Thus at last they
came into the plain aforementioned, which, from its

figure, is called by the Spaniards, La Savana, or the
Sheet. The Governor, seeing them come, made a detachment of a troop of horse, which he sent to charge
them in the front, thinking to disperse them, and, by
putting them to flight, pursue them with his main body.
But this design succeeded not as it was intended. For
the Pirates marched in very good rank and file, at the
sound of their drums and with flying colours. When
they came near the horse, they drew into the form of
a semicircle, and thus advanced towards the Spaniards,
who charged them like valiant and courageous soldiers
for some while. But seeing that the Pirates were very
dextrous at their arms, and their Governor, with many
of their companions, killed, they began to retreat towards
the wood. Here they designed to save themselves with
more advantage; but, before they could reach it, the
greatest part of them were unfortunately killed by the
hands of the Pirates. Thus they left the victory to
these new-come enemies, who had no considerable loss
of men in this battle, and but very few wounded, howbeit the skirmish continued for the space of four hours.
They entered the town, though not without great resistance of such as were within; who defended themselves as
long as was possible, thinking by their defence to hinder
the pillage. Hereupon many, seeing the enemy within
the town, shut themselves up in their own houses, and
thence made several shot against the Pirates, who, perceiving the mischief of this disadvantage, presently
began to threaten them, saying : *If you surrender not
voluntarily, you shall soon see the town in a flame, and
your wives and children torn in pieces before your faces.*
With these menaces the Spaniards submitted entirely to
the discretion of the Pirates, believing they could not
continue there long, and would soon be forced to dis-
lodge.

As soon as the Pirates had possessed themselves of
the town, they enclosed all the Spaniards, both men,

women, children and slaves, in several churches ; and
gathered all the goods they could find by way of pillage.
Afterwards they searched the whole country round about
the town, bringing in day by day many goods and
prisoners, with much provision. With this they fell to
banqueting among themselves and making great cheer
after their customary way, without remembering the poor
prisoners, whom they permitted to starve in the churches.
In the meanwhile they ceased not to torment them daily
after an inhuman manner, thereby to make them confess
where they had hid their goods, moneys and other
things, though little or nothing was left them. To this
effect they punished also the women and little children,
giving them nothing to eat ; whereby the greatest part
perished.

When they could find no more to rob, and that provisions began to grow scarce, they thought it convenient
to depart and seek new fortunes in other places. Hence
they intimated to the prisoners : *They should find
moneys to ransom themselves, else they should be all transported to Jamaica. Which being done, if they did not
pay a second ransom for the town, they would turn every
house into ashes.* The Spaniards, hearing these severe
menaces, nominated among themselves four fellow-
prisoners to go and seek for the above-mentioned con-
tributions. But the Pirates, to the intent they should
return speedily with the ransoms prescribed, tormented
several in their presence, before they departed, with all
rigour imaginable. After few days, the Spaniards returned from the fatigue of their unreasonable commissions, telling Captain Morgan : *We have run up and
down, and searched all the neighbouring woods and places
we most suspected, and yet have not been able to find any
of our own party, nor consequently any fruit of our
embassy. But if you are pleased to have a little longer
patience with us, we shall certainly cause all that you
demand to be paid within the space of fifteen days.* Cap-

tain Morgan was contented, as it should seem, to grant
them this petition. But, not long after, there came into
the town seven or eight Pirates, who had been ranging
in the woods and fields, and got thereabouts some considerable booty. These brought among other prisoners
a certain negro, whom they had taken with letters about
him. Captain Morgan having perused them, found they
were from the Governor of Santiago, being written to
some of the prisoners ; wherein he told them : *They
should not make too much haste to pay any ransom for
their town or persons, or any other pretext. But, on the
contrary, they should put off the Pirates as well as they
could with excuses and delays ; expecting to be relieved by
him within a short while, when he would certainly come
to their aid.* This intelligence being heard by Captain
Morgan, he immediately gave orders that all they had
robbed should be carried on board the ships. And,
withal, he intimated to the Spaniards that the very next
day they should pay their ransoms, forasmuch as he
would not wait one moment longer, but reduce the whole
town to ashes in case they failed to perform the sum he
demanded.

With this intimation Captain Morgan made no mention to the Spaniards of the letters he had intercepted.
Whereupon they made him answer, that it was totally
impossible for them to give such a sum of money in so
short a space of time ; seeing their fellow-townsmen
were not to be found in all the country thereabouts.
Captain Morgan knew full well their intentions, and,
withal, thought it not convenient to remain there any
longer time. Hence he demanded of them only five
hundred oxen or cows, together with sufficient salt
wherewith to salt them. Hereunto he added only this
condition, that they should carry them on board his
ships, which they promised to do. Thus he departed
with all his men, taking with him only six of the principal prisoners, as pledges of what he intended. The

next day the Spaniards brought the cattle and salt to
the ships, and required the prisoners. But Captain
Morgan refused to deliver them till such time as they
had helped his men to kill and salt the beeves. This
was likewise performed in great haste, he not caring
to stay there any longer, lest he should be surprised by
the forces that were gathering against him. Having
received all on board his vessels, he set at liberty the
prisoners he had kept as hostages of his demands.
While these things were in agitation, there happened
to arise some dissensions between the English and the
French. The occasion of their discord was as follows : A
certain Frenchman being employed in killing and salting
one of the beeves, an English Pirate came to him and
took away the marrow-bones he had taken out of the ox;
which sort of meat these people esteem very much.
Hereupon they challenged one another. Being come to
the place of duel, the Englishman drew his sword treacherously against the Frenchman, wounding him in the
back, before he had put himself into a just posture of
defence ; whereby he suddenly fell dead upon the place.
The other Frenchmen, desirous to revenge this base
action, made an insurrection against the English. But
Captain Morgan soon extinguished this flame, by commanding the criminal to be bound in chains, and thus
carried to Jamaica; promising to them all he would see
justice done upon him. For although it was permitted
him to challenge his adversary, yet it was not lawful
to kill him treacherously, as he did.

As soon as all things were in readiness, and on
board the ships, and likewise the prisoners set at liberty,
they sailed thence, directing their course to a certain
island, where Captain Morgan intended to make a dividend of what they had pillaged in that voyage. Being
arrived at the place assigned, they found near the value
of fifty thousand pieces of eight, both in money and
goods. The sum being known, it caused a general

resentment and grief, to see such a small booty; which was not sufficient to pay their debts at Jamaica. Hereupon Captain Morgan propounded to them, they should think upon some other enterprize and pillage before they returned home. But the Frenchmen not being able to agree with the English, separated from their company, leaving Captain Morgan alone with those of his own nation; notwithstanding all the persuasions he used to induce them to continue in his company. Thus they parted with all external signs of friendship; Captain Morgan reiterating his promises to them that he would see justice done upon the criminal. This he performed: for being arrived at Jamaica, he caused him to be hanged; which was all the satisfaction the French Pirates could expect.

CHAPTER VI.

Captain Morgan resolves to attack and plunder the city of Porto Bello. To this effect he equips a fleet, and, with little expense and small forces, takes the said place.

SOME nations may think that the French having deserted Captain Morgan, the English alone could not have sufficient courage to attempt such great actions as before. But Captain Morgan, who always communicated vigour with his words, infused such spirits into his men as were able to put every one of them instantly upon new designs; they being all persuaded by his reasons, that the sole execution of his orders would be a certain means of obtaining great riches. This persuasion had such influence upon their minds, that with inimitable courage they all resolved to follow him. The same likewise did a certain Pirate of Campeche, who in this occasion joined with Captain Morgan, to seek new fortunes under his conduct, and greater advantages than he had found before. Thus Captain Morgan in a few days gathered a fleet of nine sail, between ships and great boats, wherein he had four hundred and threescore military men.

After that all things were in a good posture of readiness, they put forth to sea, Captain Morgan imparting the design he had in his mind to nobody for that present. He only told them on several occasions, that he held as indubitable he should make a good fortune by that voyage, if strange occurrences altered not the course of his designs. They directed their course towards the continent, where they arrived in few days upon the coast of Costa Rica, with all their fleet entire. No sooner had they discovered land than Captain Morgan declared his intentions to the Captains, and presently after to all the rest of the company. He told them he intended in that expedition to plunder Porto Bello, and that he would perform it by night, being resolved to put the whole city to the sack, not the least corner escaping his diligence. Moreover, to encourage them, he added : This enterprize could not fail to succeed well, seeing he had kept it secret in his mind without revealing it to anybody ; whereby they could not have notice of his coming. To this proposition some made answer : They had not a sufficient number of men wherewith to assault so strong and great a city. But Captain Morgan replied : *If our number is small, our hearts are great. And the fewer persons we are, the more union and better shares we shall have in the spoil.* Hereupon, being stimulated with the ambition of those vast riches they promised themselves from their good success, they unanimously concluded to venture upon that design. But, now, to the intent my reader may better comprehend the incomparable boldness of this exploit, it may be necessary to say something beforehand of the city of Porto Bello.

The city which bears this name in America is seated in the Province of Costa Rica, under the latitude of ten degrees North, at the distance of fourteen leagues from the Gulf of Darien, and eight westwards from the port called Nombre de Dios. It is judged to be the strongest place that the King of Spain possesses in all the West Indies, excepting two, that is to say Havana and Cartagena. Here are two castles, almost inexpugnable, that defend the city, being situated at the entry of the port ; so that no ship or boat can pass without permission. The garrison consists of three hundred soldiers, and the town constantly inhabited by four hundred families, more or less. The merchants dwell not here, but only reside for awhile, when the galleons come or go from Spain; by reason of the unhealthiness of the air, occasioned by certain vapours that exhale from the mountains. Notwithstanding, their chief warehouses are at Porto Bello, howbeit their habitations be all the year long at Panama, whence they bring the plate upon mules at such times as the fair begins, and when the ships, belonging to the Company of Negroes, arrive here to sell slaves.

Captain Morgan, who knew very well all the avenues of this city, as also all the neighbouring coasts, arrived in the dusk of the evening at the place called Puerto de Naos, distant ten leagues towards the west of Porto Bello. Being come to this place, they mounted the river in their ships, as far as another harbour called Puerto Pontin; where they came to an anchor. Here they put themselves immediately into boats and canoes, leaving in the ships only a few men to keep them and conduct them the next day to the port. About midnight they came to a certain place called Estera longa Lemos, where they all went on shore, and marched by land to the first posts of the city. They had in their company a certain Englishman, who had been formerly a prisoner in those parts, and who now served them for a guide. To him, and three or four more, they gave commission to take the sentry, if possible, or kill him upon the place. But they laid hands on him and apprehended him with such cunning, that he had no time to give warning with his musket, or make any other noise. Thus they brought him, with his hands bound, to Captain Morgan, who asked him: *How things went in the city, and what forces they had*: with many other circumstances, which he was desirous to know. After every question, they made him a thousand menaces to kill him, in case he declared not the truth. Thus they began to advance towards the city, carrying always the said sentry bound before them. Having marched about one quarter of a league, they came to the castle that is near the city, which presently they closely surrounded, so that no person could get either in or out of the said fortress.

Being thus posted under the walls of the castle, Captain Morgan commanded the sentry whom they had taken prisoner, to speak to those that were within, charging them to surrender, and deliver themselves up to his discretion ; otherwise they should be all cut to pieces, without giving quarter to any one. But they would hearken to none of these threats, beginning instantly to fire ; which gave notice to the city, and this was suddenly alarmed. Yet, notwithstanding, although the Governor and soldiers of the said castle made as great resistance as could be performed, they were constrained to surrender to the Pirates. These no sooner had taken the castle, than they resolved to be as good as their words, in putting the Spaniards to the sword, thereby to strike a terror into the rest of the city. Hereupon, having shut up all the soldiers and officers as prisoners into one room, they instantly set fire to the powder (whereof they found great quantity), and blew up the whole castle into the air, with all the Spaniards that were within. This being done, they pursued the course of their victory, falling upon the city, which as yet was not in order to receive them. Many of the inhabitants cast their precious jewels and moneys into wells and cisterns or hid them in other places underground, to excuse, as much as were possible, their being totally robbed. One party of the Pirates being assigned to this purpose, ran immediately to the cloisters, and took as many religious men and women as they could find. The Governor of the city not being able to rally the citizens, through the huge confusion of the town, retired to one of the castles remaining, and thence began to fire incessantly at the Pirates. But these were not in the least negligent either to assault him or defend themselves with all the courage imaginable. Thus it was observable that, amidst the horror of the assault, they made very few shot in

vain. For aiming with great dexterity at the mouths of
the guns, the Spaniards were certain to lose one or two
men every time they charged each gun anew.

The assault of this castle where the Governor was continued very furious on both sides, from break of day until
noon. Yea, about this time of the day the case was very
dubious which party should conquer or be conquered. At
last the Pirates, perceiving they had lost many men and
as yet advanced but little towards the gaining either this
or the other castles remaining, thought to make use of
fireballs, which they threw with their hands, designing,
if possible, to burn the doors of the castle. But going
about to put this into execution, the Spaniards, from the
wall let fall great quantities of stones and earthen pots
full of powder and other combustible matter, which forced
them to desist from that attempt. Captain Morgan seeing this generous defence made by the Spaniards, began
to despair of the whole success of the enterprize. Hereupon many faint and calm meditations came into his
mind ; neither could he determine which way to turn
himself in that straitness of affairs. Being involved in
these thoughts, he was suddenly animated to continue the
assault, by seeing the English colours put forth at one of
the lesser castles, then entered by his men, of whom he
presently after spied a troop that came to meet him, pro-
claiming victory with loud shouts of joy. This instantly
put him upon new resolutions of making new efforts to
take the rest of the castles that stood out against him ;
especially seeing the chief citizens were fled to them, and
had conveyed thither great part of their riches, with all
the plate belonging to the churches, and other things
dedicated to divine service.

To this effect, therefore, he ordered ten or twelve
ladders to be made, in all possible haste, so broad that
three or four men at once might ascend by them. These
being finished, he commanded all the religious men and
women whom he had taken prisoners to fix them against

the walls of the castle. Thus much he had beforehand threatened the Governor to perform, in case he delivered not the castle. But his answer was : *He would never sur- render himself alive.* Captain Morgan was much persuaded that the Governor would not employ his utmost forces, seeing religious women and ecclesiastical persons, ex- posed in the front of the soldiers to the greatest dangers. Thus the ladders, as I have said, were put into the hands of religious persons of both sexes ; and these were forced, at the head of the companies, to raise and apply them to the walls. But Captain Morgan was fully de- ceived in his judgment of this design. For the Governor, who acted like a brave and courageous soldier, refused not, in performance of his duty, to use his utmost en- deavours to destroy whoever came near the walls. The religious men and women ceased not to cry to him and beg of him by all the Saints of Heaven he would deliver the castle, and hereby spare both his and their own lives. But nothing could prevail with the obstinacy and fierce- ness that had possessed the Governor's mind. Thus many of the religious men and nuns were killed before they could fix the ladders. Which at last being done, though with great loss of the said religious people, the Pirates mounted them in great numbers, and with no less valour ; having fireballs in their hands, and earthen pots full of powder. All which things, being now at the top of the walls, they kindled and cast in among the Spaniards.

This effort of the Pirates was very great: insomuch as the Spaniards could no longer resist nor defend the castle, which was now entered. Hereupon they all threw down their arms, and craved quarter for their lives. Only the Governor of the city would admit or crave no mercy ; but rather killed many of the Pirates with his own hands, and not a few of his own soldiers, because they did not stand to their arms. And although the Pirates asked him if he would have quarter, yet he constantly answered:

By no means : I had rather die as a valiant soldier than be hanged as a coward. They endeavoured, as much as they could, to take him prisoner. But he defended himself so obstinately that they were forced to kill him ; notwithstanding all the cries and tears of his own wife and daughter, who begged of him upon their knees he would demand quarter and save his life. When the Pirates had possessed themselves of the castle, which was about night, they enclosed therein all the prisoners they had taken, placing the women and men by themselves, with some guards upon them. All the wounded were put into a certain apartment by itself, to the intent their own complaints might be the cure of their own diseases ; for no other was afforded them.

This being done, they fell to eating and drinking after their usual manner ; that is to say, committing in both these things all manner of debauchery and excess. After such manner they delivered themselves up to all sort of debauchery, that if there had been found only fifty courageous men, they might easily have retaken the city, and killed all the Pirates. The next day, having plundered all they could find, they began to examine some of the prisoners (who had been persuaded by their companions to say they were the richest of the town), charging them severely to discover where they had hidden their riches and goods. But not being able to extort anything out of them, as they were not the right persons who possessed any wealth, they at last resolved to torture them. This they performed with such cruelty that many of them died upon the rack, or presently after. Soon after, the President of Panama had news brought him of the pillage and ruin of Porto Bello. This intelligence caused him to employ all his care and industry to raise forces, with design to pursue and cast out the Pirates thence. But these cared little for what extraordinary means the President used, as having their ships near at hand, and being determined to set fire

to the city, and retreat. They had now been at Porto
Bello fifteen days, in which space of time they had lost
many of their men, both by unhealthiness of the country
and the extravagant debaucheries they had committed.

Hereupon they prepared for a departure, carrying on
board their ships all the pillage they had got. But,
before all, they provided the fleet with sufficient victuals
for the voyage. While these things were getting ready,
Captain Morgan sent an injunction to the prisoners, that
they should pay him a ransom for the city, or else he
would by fire consume it to ashes, and blow up all the
castles into the air. Withal, he commanded them to send
speedily two persons to seek and procure the sum he demanded, which amounted to one hundred thousand pieces
of eight. To this effect, two men were sent to the
President of Panama, who gave him an account of all
these tragedies. The President having now a body of
men in a readiness, set forth immediately towards Porto
Bello, to encounter the Pirates before their retreat. But
these people, hearing of his coming, instead of flying
away, went out to meet him at a narrow passage through
which of necessity he ought to pass. Here they placed
an hundred men very well armed ; who, at the first encounter, put to flight a good party of those of Panama.
This accident obliged the President to retire for that
time, as not being yet in a posture of strength to proceed
any farther. Presently after this encounter, he sent a
message to Captain Morgan, to tell him : *That in case he
departed not suddenly with all his forces from Porto
Bello, he ought to expect no quarter for himself nor his
companions, when he should take them, as he hoped soon to
do.* Captain Morgan, who feared not his threats, knowing he had a secure retreat in his ships which were
near at hand, made him answer : *He would not deliver
the castles, before he had received the contribution-money
he had demanded. Which in case it were not paid down,
he would certainly burn the whole city, and then leave*

it ; demolishing beforehand the castles, and killing the prisoners.

The Governor of Panama perceived by this answer that no means would serve to mollify the hearts of the Pirates, nor reduce them to reason.   Hereupon he determined to leave them ; as also those of the city, whom he came to relieve, involved in the difficulties of making the best agreement they could with their enemies.   Thus, in few days more, the miserable citizens gathered the contribution wherein they were fined, and brought the entire sum of one hundred thousand pieces of eight to the Pirates, for a ransom of the cruel captivity they were fallen into.   But the President of Panama, by these transactions, was brought into an extreme admiration, considering that four hundred men had been able to take such a great city, with so many strong castles : especially seeing they had no pieces of cannon, nor other great guns, wherewith to raise batteries against them.   And what was more, knowing that the citizens of Porto Bello had always great repute of being good soldiers themselves, and who had never wanted courage in their own defence.   This astonishment was so great, that it occasioned him, for to be satisfied herein, to send a messenger to Captain Morgan, desiring him to send him some small pattern of those arms wherewith he had taken with such violence so great a city.   Captain Morgan received this messenger very kindly, and treated him with great civility.   Which being done, he gave him a pistol and a few small bullets of lead, to carry back to the President, his Master, telling him withal : *He desired him to accept that slender pattern of the arms wherewith he had taken Porto Bello, and keep them for a twelvemonth ; after which time he promised to come to Panama and fetch them away.*   The Governor of Panama returned the present very soon to Captain Morgan, giving him thanks for the favour of lending him such weapons as he needed not, and withal sent him a ring of gold, with this message : *That he desired him not to give himself the labour of coming to Panama, as he had done to Porto Bello; for he did certify to him, he should not speed so well here as he had done there.*

After these transactions, Captain Morgan (having provided his fleet with all necessaries, and taken with him the best guns of the castles, nailing the rest which he could not carry away) set sail from Porto Bello with all his ships. With these he arrived in few days at the Island of Cuba, where he sought out a place wherein with all quiet and repose he might make the dividend of the spoil they had got. They found in ready money two hundred and fifty thousand pieces of eight, besides all other merchandizes, as cloth linen, silks, and other goods. With this rich booty they sailed again thence to their common place of rendezvous, Jamaica. Being arrived, they passed here some time in all sorts of vices and debauchery, according to their common manner of doing, spending with huge prodigality what others had gained with no small labour and toil.

CHAPTER VII.

Captain Morgan takes the city of Maracaibo, on the coast of New Venezuela. Piracies committed in those Seas. Ruin of three Spanish ships, that were set forth to hinder the robberies of the Pirates.

NOT long after the arrival of the Pirates at Jamaica, being precisely that short time they needed to lavish away all the riches above-mentioned, they concluded upon another enterprize whereby to seek new fortunes. To this effect Captain Morgan gave orders to all the commanders of his ships to meet together at the island called De la Vaca, or Cow Isle, seated on the south side of the Isle of Hispaniola, as has been mentioned above. As soon as they came to this place, there flocked to them great numbers of other Pirates, both French and English, by reason the name of Captain Morgan was now rendered famous in all the neighbouring countries, for the great enterprizes he had performed. There was at that present at Jamaica an English ship newly come from New England, well mounted with thirty-six guns. This vessel likewise, by order of the Governor of Jamaica, came to join with Captain Morgan to strengthen his fleet, and give him greater courage to attempt things of huge consequence. With this supply Captain Morgan judged himself sufficiently strong, as having a ship of such port, being the greatest of his fleet, in his company. Notwithstanding, there being in the same place another great vessel that carried twenty-four iron guns, and twelve of brass, belonging to the French, Captain Morgan endeavoured as much as he could to join this ship in like manner to his own. But the French, not daring to repose any trust in the English, of whose actions they were not a little jealous, denied absolutely to consent to any such thing.

The French Pirates belonging to this great ship had accidentally met at sea an English vessel; and being then under an extreme necessity of victuals, they had taken some provisions out of the English ship without paying for them, having peradventure no ready money on board. Only they had given them bills of exchange, for Jamaica and Tortuga, to receive money there for what they had taken. Captain Morgan having notice of this accident, and perceiving he could not prevail with the French Captain to follow him in that expedition, resolved to lay hold on this occasion as a pretext to ruin the French, and seek his own revenge. Hereupon he invited, with dissimulation, the French commander and several of his men to dine with him on board the great ship that was come from Jamaica, as was said before. Being come thither, he made them all prisoners, pretending the injury aforementioned done to the English vessel in taking away some few provisions without pay.

This unjust action of Captain Morgan was soon followed by divine punishment, as we may very rationally conceive. The manner I shall instantly relate. Captain Morgan, presently after he had taken the French prisoners abovesaid, called a council to deliberate what place they should first pitch upon, in the course of this new expedition. At this council it was determined to go to the Isle of Savona, there to wait for the *flota* which was then expected from Spain, and take any of the Spanish vessels that might chance to straggle from the rest. This resolution being taken, they began on board the great ship to feast one another for joy of their new voyage and happy council, as they hoped it would prove. In testimony hereof, they drank many healths, and discharged many guns, as the common sign of mirth among

seamen used to be.   Most of the men being drunk, by
what accident is not known the ship suddenly was blown
up into the air, with three hundred and fifty Englishmen,
besides the French prisoners above-mentioned that were
in the hold.   Of all which number, there escaped only
thirty men, who were in the great cabin at some distance
from the main force of the powder.   Many more 'tis
thought might have escaped, had they not been so much
overtaken with wine.

The loss of such a great ship brought much consternation and conflict of mind upon the English.   They
knew not whom to blame ; but at last the accusation was
laid upon the French prisoners, whom they suspected to
have fired the powder of the ship wherein they were, out
of design to revenge themselves, though with the loss of
their own lives.   Hereupon they sought to be revenged
on the French anew, and accumulate new accusations
against the former, whereby to seize the ship and all
that was in it.   With this design they forged another
pretext against the said ship, by saying the French
designed to commit piracy upon the English.   The
grounds of this accusation were given them by a commission from the Governor of Barracoa, found on board
the French vessel, wherein were these words : *That the
said Governor did permit the French to trade in all
Spanish ports, etc. . . . As also to cruize upon the English
Pirates in what place soever they could find them, because
of the multitude of hostilities which they had committed
against the subjects of his Catholic Majesty, in time of
peace betwixt the two Crowns.*   This Commission for
trade was interpreted by the English as an express order
to exercise piracy and war against them, notwithstanding
it was only a bare licence for coming into the Spanish
ports ; the cloak of which permission were those words
inserted : *That they should cruize upon the English.*
And although the French did sufficiently expound the
true sense of the said Commission, yet they could not

clear themselves to Captain Morgan, nor his council. But, in lieu hereof, the ship and men were seized and sent to Jamaica. Here they also endeavoured to obtain justice and the restitution of their ship, by all the means possible. But all was in vain : for instead of justice, they were long time detained in prison, and threatened with hanging.

Eight days after the loss of the said ship, Captain Morgan commanded the bodies of the miserable wretches who were blown up to be searched for, as they floated upon the waters of the sea. This he did, not out of any design of affording them Christian burial, but only to obtain the spoil of their clothes and other attire. And if any had golden rings on their fingers, these were cut off for purchase, leaving them in that condition exposed to the voracity of the monsters of the sea. At last they set sail for the Isle of Savona, being the place of their assignation. They were in all fifteen vessels, Captain Morgan commanding the biggest, which carried only fourteen small guns. The number of men belonging to this fleet were nine hundred and threescore. In few days after, they arrived at the Cape called Cabo de Lobos, on the south side of the Isle of Hispaniola, between Cape Tiburon and Cape Punta d' Espada. Hence they could not pass, by reason of contrary winds that continued the space of three weeks, notwithstanding all the endeavours Captain Morgan used to get forth, leaving no means unattempted thereunto. At the end of this time they doubled the cape, and presently after spied an English vessel at a distance. Having spoken with her, they found she came from England, and bought of her, for ready money, some provisions they stood in need of.

Captain Morgan proceeded in the course of his voyage, till he came to the port of Ocoa. Here he landed some of his men, sending them into the woods to seek water and what provisions they could find, the better to spare

such as he had already on board his fleet. They killed
many beasts, and among other animals some horses. But
the Spaniards, being not well satisfied at their hunting,
attempted to lay a stratagem for the Pirates. To this
purpose they ordered three or four hundred men to come
from the city of San Domingo, not far distant from this
port, and desired them to hunt in all the parts thereabouts adjoining the sea, to the intent that if any Pirates
should return, they might find no subsistence. Within
a few days the same Pirates returned, with design to
hunt. But finding nothing to kill, a party of them, being
about fifty in number, straggled farther on into the
woods. The Spaniards, who watched all their motions,
gathered a great herd of cows, and set two or three
men to keep them. The Pirates having spied this herd,
killed a sufficient number thereof ; and although the
Spaniards could see them at a distance, yet they would
not hinder their work for the present. But as soon as
they attempted to carry them away, they set upon them
with all fury imaginable, crying : *Mata, mata !* that is,
Kill, kill. Thus the Pirates were soon compelled to
quit the prey, and retreat towards their ships as well as
they could. This they performed, notwithstanding, in
good order, retiring from time to time by degrees ;
and when they had any good opportunity, discharging
full volleys of shot upon the Spaniards. By this means
the Pirates killed many of the enemies, though with
some loss on their own side.

The rest of the Spaniards, seeing what damage they
had sustained, endeavoured to save themselves by flight,
and carry off the dead bodies and wounded of their companions. The Pirates perceiving them to flee, could not
content themselves with what hurt they had already
done, but pursued them speedily into the woods, and
killed the greatest part of those that were remaining.
The next day Captain Morgan, being extremely offended
at what had passed, went himself with two hundred men

The Towne of Puerto del Principe taken & sackt

into the woods, to seek for the rest of the Spaniards. But finding nobody there, he revenged his wrath upon the houses of the poor and miserable rustics that inhabit scatteringly those fields and woods ; of which he burnt a great number. With this he returned to his ships, something more satisfied in his mind, for having done some considerable damage to the enemy ; which was always his most ardent desire.

The huge impatience wherewith Captain Morgan had waited now this long while for some of the ships, which were not yet arrived, made him resolve to set sail without them, and steer his course for the Isle of Savona, the place he had always designed. Being arrived there, and not finding any of his ships yet come, he was more impatient and concerned than before, fearing their loss, or that he must proceed without them. Notwithstanding, he waited for their arrival some few days longer. In the meanwhile, having no great plenty of provisions, he sent a crew of one hundred and fifty men to the Isle of Hispaniola, to pillage some towns that were near the city of San Domingo. But the Spaniards, having had intelligence of their coming, were now so vigilant and in such good posture of defence, that the Pirates thought it not convenient to assault them, choosing rather to return empty-handed to Captain Morgan's presence than to perish in that desperate enterprize.

At last Captain Morgan, seeing the other ships did not come, made a review of his people, and found only five hundred men, more or less. The ships that were wanting were seven, he having only eight in his company, of which the greatest part were very small. Thus having hitherto resolved to cruize upon the coasts of Caracas, and plunder all the towns and villages he could meet, finding himself at present with such small forces, he changed his resolution, by the advice of a French Captain that belonged to his fleet. This Frenchman had served L'Ollonais in like enterprizes, and was at the taking

of Maracaibo ; whereby he knew all the entries, passages, forces and means how to put in execution the same
again in the company of Captain Morgan, to whom,
having made a full relation of all, he concluded to sack
it again the second time, as being himself persuaded,
with all his men, of the facility the Frenchman propounded. Hereupon they weighed anchor, and steered
their course towards Curaçoa. Being come within sight
of that island, they landed at another, which is near it,
and is called Ruba, seated about twelve leagues from
Curaçoa, towards the west. This island is defended but
by a slender garrison, and is inhabited by Indians, who
are subject to the Crown of Spain, and speak Spanish,
by reason of the Roman Catholic religion, which is
here cultivated by some few priests that are sent from
time to time from the neighbouring continent.

The inhabitants of this isle exercise a certain commerce or trade with the Pirates that go and come this
way. These buy of the islanders sheep, lambs and kids,
which they exchange unto them for linen, thread and
other things of this kind. The country is very dry and
barren, the whole substance thereof consisting in those
three things above-mentioned, and in a small quantity of
wheat, which is of no bad quality. This isle produces a
great number of venomous insects, as vipers, spiders
and others. These last are so pernicious here, that if
any man is bitten by them, he dies mad. And the
manner of recovering such persons, is to tie them very
fast both hands and feet, and in this condition to leave
them for the space of four and twenty hours without eating or drinking the least thing imaginable. Captain
Morgan, as was said, having cast anchor before this
island, bought of the inhabitants many sheep, lambs and
also wood, which he needed for all his fleet. Having
been there two days he set sail again, in the time of the
night, to the intent they might not see what course he
steered.

The next day they arrived at the sea of Maracaibo, having always great care of not being seen from Vigilias, for which reason they anchored out of the sight of the watch-tower. Night being come, they set sail again towards the land, and the next morning by break of day found themselves directly over against the bar of the lake above-mentioned. The Spaniards had built another fort since the action of L'Ollonais, whence they did now fire continually against the Pirates, while they were putting their men into boats to land. The dispute continued very hot on both sides, being managed with huge courage and valour from morning till dark night. This being come, Captain Morgan, in the obscurity thereof, drew nigh the fort; which having examined, he found nobody in it, the Spaniards having deserted it not long before. They left behind them a match kindled near a train of powder, wherewith they designed to blow up the Pirates and the whole fortress, as soon as they were in it. This design had taken effect, had the Pirates failed to discover it the space of one quarter of an hour. But Captain Morgan prevented the mischief by snatching away the match with all speed, whereby he saved both his own and his companions' lives. They found here great quantity of powder, whereof he provided his fleet; and afterwards demolished part of the walls, nailing sixteen pieces of ordnance, which carried from twelve to four and twenty pound of bullet. Here they found also great number of muskets and other military provisions.

The next day they commanded the ships to enter the bar; among which, they divided the powder, muskets and other things they found in the fort, These things being done, they embarked again, to continue their course towards Maracaibo. But the waters were very low, whereby they could not pass a certain bank that lies at the entry of the lake. Hereupon they were compelled to put themselves into canoes and small boats with which they arrived the next day before Maracaibo, having no other defence than some small pieces which they could carry in the said boats. Being landed, they ran immediately to the fort called De la Barra, which they found in like manner as the preceding, without any person in it: for all were fled before them into the woods, leaving also the town without any people, except a few miserable poor folk who had nothing to lose.

As soon as they had entered the town the Pirates searched every corner thereof, to see if they could find any people that were hidden who might offend them unawares. Not finding anybody, every party, according as they came out of their several ships, chose what houses they pleased to themselves, the best they could find. The church was deputed for the common *corps de garde*, where they lived after their military manner, committing many insolent actions. The next day after their arrival, they sent a troop of one hundred men to seek for the inhabitants and their goods. These returned the next day following, bringing with them to the number of thirty persons, between men, women and children, and fifty mules laden with several good merchandize. All these miserable prisoners were put to the rack, to make them confess where the rest of the inhabitants were and their goods. Amongst other tortures then used, one was to stretch their limbs with cords, and at the same time beat them with sticks and other instruments. Others had burning matches placed betwixt their fingers, which were thus burnt alive. Others had slender cords or matches twisted about their heads, till their eyes burst out of the skull. Thus all sort of inhuman cruelties were executed upon those innocent people. Those who would not confess, or who had nothing to declare, died under the hands of those tyrannical men. These tortures and racks continued for the space of three whole weeks; in which time they ceased not to send out, daily, parties of men to seek for more people to torment and rob ; they never returning home without booty and new riches.

Captain Morgan, having now got by degrees into his hands about one hundred of the chief families, with all their goods, at last resolved to go to Gibraltar, even as L'Ollonais had done before. With this design he equipped his fleet, providing it very sufficiently with all necessary things. He put likewise on board all the prisoners ; and, thus weighing anchor, set sail for the said place, with resolution to hazard the battle. They had sent before them some prisoners to Gibraltar, to denounce to the inhabitants they should surrender : otherwise Captain Morgan would certainly put them all to the sword, without giving quarter to any person he should find alive. Not long after, he arrived with his fleet before Gibraltar, whose inhabitants received him with continual shooting of great cannon-bullets. But the Pirates, instead of fainting hereat, ceased not to encourage one another, saying : *We must make one meal upon bitter things, before we come to taste the sweetness of the sugar this place affords.*

The next day, very early in the morning, they landed all their men. And being guided by the Frenchman above-mentioned, they marched towards the town, not by the common way but crossing through the woods ; which way the Spaniards scarce thought they would have come. For, at the beginning of their march, they made appearance as if they intended to come the next and open way that led to the town, hereby the better to deceive the Spaniards. But these remembering as yet full well what hostilities L'Ollonais had committed upon them but two years before, thought it not safe to expect the second brunt, and hereupon were all fled out of the town as fast as they could, carrying with them all their goods and riches, as also all the powder, and having nailed all the great guns : insomuch as the Pirates found not one person in the whole city, excepting only one poor and innocent

man who was born a fool. This man they asked whither
the inhabitants were fled, and where they had absconded
their goods.   To all which questions and the like he
constantly made answer: *I know nothing, I know nothing.*
But they presently put him to the rack, and tortured
him with cords; which torments forced him to cry out :
*Do not torture me any more, but come with me and I will
show you my goods and my riches.* They were persuaded,
as it should seem, he was some rich person who had
disguised himself under those clothes so poor as also that
innocent tongue.   Hereupon they went along with him ;
and he conducted them to a poor and miserable cottage,
wherein he had a few earthen dishes, and other things of
little or no value ; and amongst these, three pieces of
eight, which he had concealed with some other trumpery
underground.   After this, they asked him his name ; and
he readily made answer : *My name is Don Sebastian
Sanchez, and I am brother to the Governor of Maracaibo.*
This foolish answer, it must be conceived, these men,
though never so inhuman, took for a certain truth.   For
no sooner had they heard it, but they put him again upon
the rack, lifting him up on high with cords, and tying huge
weights to his feet and neck ; besides which cruel and
stretching torment, they burnt him alive, applying palm-
leaves burning to his face, under which miseries he died
in half-an-hour.   After his death they cut the cords
wherewith they had stretched him, and dragged him
forth into the adjoining woods, where they left him without burial.

The same day they sent out a party of Pirates to seek
for the inhabitants, upon whom they might employ their
inhuman cruelties.   These brought back with them an
honest peasant with two daughters of his, whom they had
taken prisoners, and whom they intended to torture as
they used to do with others, in case they showed not the
places where the inhabitants had absconded themselves.
The peasant knew some of the said places, and hereupon

seeing himself threatened with the rack, went with the Pirates to show them. But the Spaniards perceiving their enemies to range everywhere up and down the woods, were already fled thence much farther off into the thickest parts of the said woods, where they built themselves huts, to preserve from the violence of the weather those few goods they had carried with them. The Pirates judged themselves to be deceived by the said peasant; and hereupon, to revenge their wrath upon him, notwithstanding all the excuses he could make, and his humble supplications for his life, they hanged him upon a tree.

After this, they divided into several parties, and went to search the plantations. For they knew the Spaniards that were absconded could not live upon what they found in the woods, without coming now and then to seek provisions at their own country houses. Here they found a certain slave, to whom they promised mountains of gold, and that they would give him his liberty by transporting him to Jamaica, in case he would show them the places where the inhabitants of Gibraltar lay hidden. This fellow conducted them to a party of Spaniards, whom they instantly made all prisoners, commanding the said slave to kill some of them before the eyes of the rest ; to the intent that by this perpetrated crime he might never be able to leave their wicked company. The negro, according to their orders, committed many murders and insolent actions upon the Spaniards, and followed the unfortunate traces of the Pirates, who after the space of eight days, returned to Gibraltar with many prisoners and some mules laden with riches. They examined every prisoner by himself (who were in all about two hundred and fifty persons) where they had absconded the rest of their goods, and if they knew of their fellow-townsmen. Such as would not confess were tormented after a most cruel and inhuman manner. Among the rest, there happened to be a certain Portuguese, who by the information of a negro was reported, though falsely, to be very rich. This man was commanded to produce his riches. But his answer was, he had no more than one hundred pieces of eight in the whole world, and that these had been stolen from him two days before, by a servant of his. Which words, although he sealed with many oaths and protestations, yet they would not believe him. But dragging him to the rack, without any regard to his age, as being threescore years old, they stretched him with cords, breaking both his arms behind his shoulders.

This cruelty went not alone. For he not being able or willing to make any other declaration than the above-said, they put him to another sort of torment that was worse and more barbarous than the preceding. They tied him with small cords by his two thumbs and great-toes to four stakes that were fixed in the ground at a convenient distance, the whole weight of his body being pendent in the air upon those cords. Then they thrashed upon the cords with great sticks and all their strength, so that the body of this miserable man was ready to perish at every stroke, under the severity of those horrible pains. Not satisfied as yet with this cruel torture, they took a stone which weighed above two hundred pound, and laid it on his belly, as if they intended to press him to death. At which time they also kindled palm-leaves, and applied the flame to the face of this unfortunate Portuguese, burning with them the whole skin, beard and hair. At last these cruel tyrants, seeing that neither with these tortures nor others they could get anything out of him, they untied the cords, and carried him, being almost half dead, to the church, where was their *corps du garde*. Here they tied him anew to one of the pillars thereof, leaving him in that condition, without giving him either to eat or drink, except very sparingly, and so little as would scarce sustain life, for some days. Four or five being past, he desired that one of the prisoners might have the liberty to come to him, by whose means he promised he would endeavour to raise some money to satisfy their demands. The prisoner whom he required was brought to him; and he ordered him to promise the Pirates five hundred pieces of eight for his ransom. But they were both deaf and obstinate at such a small sum, and, instead of accepting it, did beat him cruelly with cudgels, saying unto him: *Old fellow, instead of five hundred you must say five hundred thousand pieces of eight; otherwise you shall here end your life.* Finally, after a thousand protestations that he was but a miserable man, and kept a poor tavern for his living, he agreed with them for the sum of one thousand pieces of eight. These he raised in few days, and having paid them to the Pirates, got his liberty; although so horribly maimed in his body, that 'tis scarce to be believed he could survive many weeks after.

Several other tortures besides these were exercised upon others, which this Portuguese endured not. If with this they were minded to show themselves merciful to those wretches, thus lacerated in the most tender parts of their bodies, their mercy was to run them through and through with their swords; and by this means rid them soon of their pains and life. Otherwise, if this were not done, they used to lie four or five days under the agonies of death, before dying. Others were crucified by these tyrants, and with kindled matches were burnt between the joints of their fingers and toes. Others had their feet put into the fire, and thus were left to be roasted alive. At last, having used both these and other cruelties with the white men, they began to practice the same over again with the negroes, their slaves; who were treated with no less inhumanity than their masters.

Among these slaves was found one who promised Captain Morgan to conduct him to a certain river belonging to the lake, where he should find a ship and four boats richly laden with goods that belonged to the inhabi-

tants of Maracaibo. The same slave discovered likewise
the place where the Governor of Gibraltar lay hidden, together with the greatest part of the women of the town.
But all this he revealed, through great menaces wherewith they threatened to hang him, in case he told not
what he knew. Captain Morgan sent away presently
two hundred men in two *saëties*, or great boats, towards
the river above-mentioned, to seek for what the slave had
discovered. But he himself, with two hundred and fifty
more, undertook to go and take the Governor. This
gentleman was retired to a small island seated in the
middle of the river, where he had built a little fort, after
the best manner he could, for his defence. But hearing
that Captain Morgan came in person with great forces
to seek him, he retired farther off to the top of a mountain not much distant from that place ; unto which
there was no ascent, but by a very narrow passage.
Yea, this was so straight, that whosoever did pretend to
gain the ascent, must of necessity cause his men to pass
one by one. Captain Morgan spent two days before he
could arrive at the little island above-mentioned. Thence
he designed to proceed to the mountain where the
Governor was posted, had he not been told of the im-
possibility he should find in the ascent, not only of the
narrowness of the path that led to the top, but also because the Governor was very well provided with all sorts
of ammunition above. Besides that, there was fallen a
huge rain, whereby all the baggage belonging to the
Pirates, and their powder, was wet. By this rain also
they had lost many of their men at the passage over a
river that was overflown. Here perished likewise some
women and children, and many mules laden with plate
and other goods ; all which they had taken in the fields
from the fugitive inhabitants. So that all things were in
a very bad condition with Captain Morgan, and the
bodies of his men as much harassed, as ought to be inferred from this relation. Whereby, if the Spaniards in

that juncture of time had had but a troop of fifty men well armed with pikes or spears, they might have entirely destroyed the Pirates, without any possible resistance on their sides. But the fears which the Spaniards had conceived from the beginning were so great, that only hearing the leaves on the trees to stir, they often fancied them to be Pirates. Finally, Captain Morgan and his people, having upon this march sometimes waded up to their middles in water for the space of half or whole miles together, they at last escaped for the greatest part. But of the woman and children they brought home prisoners, the major part died.

Thus twelve days after they set forth to seek the Governor, they returned to Gibraltar with a great number of prisoners. Two days after arrived also the two *saëties* that went to the river, bringing with them four boats and some prisoners. But as to the greatest part of the merchandize that were in the said boats, they found them not, the Spaniards having unladed and secured them, as having intelligence beforehand of the coming of the Pirates. Whereupon they designed also, when the merchandize were all taken out, to burn the boats. Yet the Spaniards made not so much haste as was requisite to unlade the said vessels, but that they left both in the ship and boats great parcels of goods, which, they being fled from thence, the Pirates seized, and brought thereof a considerable booty to Gibraltar. Thus, after they had been in possession of the place five entire weeks, and committed there infinite number of murders, robberies, and suchlike insolences, they concluded upon their departure. But before this could be performed, for the last proof of their tyranny, they gave orders to some prisoners to go forth into the woods and fields, and collect a ransom for the town ; otherwise they would certainly burn every house down to the ground. Those poor afflicted men went forth as they were sent. And after they had searched every corner of the adjoining fields and

woods, they returned to Captain Morgan, telling him they
had scarce been able to find anybody. But that to such
as they had found, they had proposed his demands ; to
which had they made answer that the Governor had
prohibited them to give any ransom for not burning the
town. But notwithstanding any prohibition to the contrary, they beseeched him to have a little patience, and
among themselves they would collect to the sum of
five thousand pieces of eight. And for the rest, they
would give him some of their own townsmen as hostages,
whom he might carry with him to Maracaibo, till such
time as he had received full satisfaction.

Captain Morgan having now been long time absent
from Maracaibo, and knowing the Spaniards had had
sufficient time wherein to fortify themselves, and hinder
his departure out of the lake, granted them their proposition above-mentioned ; and, withal, made as much haste
as he could to set things in order for his departure. He
gave liberty to all the prisoners, having beforehand put
them every one to the ransom ; yet he detained all the
slaves with him. They delivered to him four persons
that were agreed upon for hostages of what sums of
money more he was to receive from them ; and they
desired to have the slave of whom we made mention
above, intending to punish him according to his deserts.
But Captain Morgan would not deliver him, being persuaded they would burn him alive. At last they weighed
anchor, and set sail with all the haste they could, directing
their course towards Maracaibo. Here they arrived in
four days, and found all things in the same posture they
had left them when they departed. Yet here they received news, from the information of a poor distressed
old man, who was sick and whom alone they found in
the town, that three Spanish men of war were arrived at
the entry of the lake, and there waited for the return
of the Pirates out of those parts. Moreover, that the
castle at the entry thereof was again put into a good pos-

ture of defence, being well provided with great guns and
men and all sorts of ammunition.

This relation of the old man could not choose but
cause some disturbance in the mind of Captain Morgan,
who now was careful how to get away through those narrow passages of the entry of the lake. Hereupon he sent
one of his boats, the swiftest he had, to view the entry,
and see if things were as they had been related. The
next day the boat came back, confirming what was said,
and assuring they had viewed the ships so near that they
had been in great danger of the shot they had made at
them. Hereunto they added that the biggest ship was
mounted with forty guns, the second with thirty, and the
smallest with four and twenty. These forces were much
beyond those of Captain Morgan ; and hence they caused
a general consternation in all the Pirates, whose biggest
vessel had not above fourteen small guns. Every one
judged Captain Morgan to despond in his mind and be
destitute of all manner of hopes, considering the difficulty
either of passing safely with his little fleet amidst those
great ships and the fort, or that he must perish. How
to escape any other way by sea or by land, they saw no
opportunity nor convenience. Only they could have
wished that those three ships had rather come over the
lake to seek them at Maracaibo, than to remain at the
mouth of the strait where they were. For at that
passage they must of necessity fear the ruin of their fleet,
which consisted only for the greatest part of boats.

Hereupon, being necessitated to act as well as he could,
Captain Morgan resumed new courage, and resolved to
show himself as yet undaunted with these terrors. To
this intent he boldly sent a Spaniard to the Admiral of
those three ships, demanding of him a considerable
tribute or ransom for not putting the city of Maracaibo
to the flame. This man (who doubtless was received by
the Spaniards with great admiration of the confidence
and boldness of those Pirates) returned two days after,

bringing to Captain Morgan a letter from the said
Admiral, whose contents were as follows.

Letter of Don Alonso del Campo y Espinosa, Admiral of the Spanish Fleet, unto Captain Morgan, commander of the pirates.

*Having understood by all our friends and neighbours the
unexpected news, that you have dared to attempt and commit hostilities in the countries, cities, towns and villages
belonging to the dominions of his Catholic Majesty,
my Sovereign Lord and Master; I let you understand
by these lines, that I am come to this place, according
to my obligation, nigh unto that castle which you took
out of the hands of a parcel of cowards; where I have put
things into a very good posture of defence, and mounted
again the artillery which you had nailed and dismounted.
My intent is to dispute with you your passage out of the
lake, and follow and pursue you everywhere, to the end
you may see the performance of my duty. Notwithstanding, if you be contented to surrender with humility all that
you have taken, together with the slaves and all other
prisoners, I will let you freely pass, without trouble or
molestation; upon condition that you retire home presently
to your own country. But in case that you make any
resistance or opposition unto these things that I proffer unto
you, I do assure you I will command boats to come from
Caracas, wherein I will put my troops, and coming to
Maracaibo, will cause you utterly to perish, by putting
you every man to the sword. This is my last and absolute
resolution. Be prudent, therefore, and do not abuse my
bounty with ingratitude. I have with me very good soldiers,
who desire nothing more ardently than to revenge on you
and your people all the cruelties and base infamous actions
you have committed upon the Spanish nation in America.
Dated on board the Royal Ship named the* Magdalen, *lying*

at anchor at the entry of the Lake of Maracaibo, this 24th day of April, 1669.

Don Alonso del Campo y Espinosa.

As soon as Captain Morgan had received this letter, he called all his men together in the market-place of Maracaibo ; and, after reading the contents thereof, both in French and English, he asked their advice and resolutions upon the whole matter, and whether they had rather surrender all they had purchased, to obtain their liberty, than fight for it ?

They answered all unanimously : They had rather fight, and spill the very last drop of blood they had in their veins, than surrender so easily the booty they had got with so much danger of their lives. Among the rest, one was found who said to Captain Morgan : *Take you care for the rest, and I will undertake to destroy the biggest of those ships with only twelve men. The manner shall be, by making a brulot, or fire-ship, of that vessel we took in the river of Gibraltar. Which, to the intent she may not be known for a fire-ship, we will fill her decks with logs of wood, standing with hats and Montera-caps, to deceive their fight with the representation of men. The same we will do at the port-holes that serve for the guns, which shall be filled with counterfeit cannon. At the stern we will hang out the English colours, and persuade the enemy she is one of our best men-of-war that goes to fight them.* This proposition, being heard by the *Junta* (*i.e.*, council), was admitted and approved of by every one ; howbeit their fears were not quite dispersed.

For notwithstanding what had been concluded there, they endeavoured the next day to see if they could come to an accommodation with Don Alonso. To this effect Captain Morgan sent him two persons, with these following propositions. First : *That he would quit Maracaibo, without doing any damage to the town, nor exacting any ransom for the firing thereof.* Secondly : *That he would*

*set at liberty one half of the slaves, and likewise all other
prisoners, without ransom.* Thirdly: *That he would
send home freely the four chief inhabitants of Gibraltar,
which he had in his custody as hostages for the contribu-
tions those people had promised to pay.* These propositions from the Pirates, being understood by Don Alonso,
were instantly rejected every one, as being dishonourable
for him to grant. Neither would he hear any word more
of any other accommodation; but sent back this message:
*That in case they surrendered not themselves voluntarily
into his hands within the space of two days, under the
conditions which he had offered them by his letter, he
would immediately come and force them to do it.*

No sooner had Captain Morgan received this message
from Don Alonso, than he put all things in order to fight,
resolving to get out of the lake by main force, and without surrendering anything. In the first place, he commanded all the slaves and prisoners to be tied and
guarded very well. After this, they gathered all the
pitch, tar and brimstone they could find in the whole
town, therewith to prepare the fire-ship above-mentioned.
Likewise they made several inventions of powder and
brimstone, with great quantities of palm-leaves, very well
anointed with tar. They covered very well their counterfeit cannon, laying under every piece thereof many
pounds of powder. Besides which, they cut down many
outworks belonging to the ship, to the end the powder
might exert its strength the better. Thus they broke
open also ·new port-holes; where, instead of guns they
placed little drums, of which the negroes make use.
Finally, the decks were handsomely beset with many
pieces of wood dressed up in the shape of men with hats,
or monteras, and likewise armed with swords, muskets
and bandoliers.

The brulot or fire-ship, being thus fitted to their
purpose, they prepared themselves to go to the entry of
the port. All the prisoners were put into one great boat,

The Spanish Armada destroyed by Captaine Morgan

and in another of the biggest they placed all the women, plate, jewels and other rich things which they had. Into others they put all the bales of goods and merchandize, and other things of greatest bulk. Each of these boats had twelve men on board, very well armed. The brulot had orders to go before the rest of the vessels, and presently to fall foul with the great ship. All things being in readiness, Captain Morgan exacted an oath of all his comrades, whereby they protested to defend themselves against the Spaniards, even to the last drop of blood, without demanding quarter at any rate : promising them withal, that whosoever thus behaved himself should be very well rewarded.

With this disposition of mind and courageous resolution, they set sail to seek the Spaniards, on the 30th day of April, 1669. They found the Spanish fleet riding at anchor in the middle of the entry of the lake. Captain Morgan, it being now late and almost dark, commanded all his vessels to come to an anchor ; with design to fight thence even all night, if they should provoke him thereunto. He gave orders that a careful and vigilant watch should be kept on board every vessel till the morning, they being almost within shot, as well as within fight, of the enemy. The dawning of the day being come, they weighed anchors, and set sail again, steering their course directly towards the Spaniards; who observing them to move, did instantly the same. The fire-ship, sailing before the rest, fell presently upon the great ship, and grappled to her sides in a short while. Which by the Spaniards being perceived to be a fire-ship, they attempted to escape the danger by putting her off ; but in vain, and too late. For the flame suddenly seized her timber and tackling, and in a short space consumed all the stern, the forepart sinking into the sea, whereby she perished. The second Spanish ship, perceiving the Admiral to burn, not by accident but by industry of the enemy, escaped towards the castle, where the Spaniards

themselves caused her to sink; choosing this way of
losing their ship, rather than to fall into the hands of
those Pirates, which they held for inevitable.   The third,
as having no opportunity nor time to escape, was taken
by the Pirates.   The seamen that sank the second ship
near the castle, perceiving the Pirates to come towards
them to take what remains they could find of their shipwreck (for some part of the bulk was extant above water),
set fire in like manner to this vessel, to the end the Pirates
might enjoy nothing of that spoil.   The first ship being
set on fire, some of the persons that were in her swam
towards the shore.   These the Pirates would have taken
up in their boats; but they would neither ask nor admit
of any quarter, choosing rather to lose their lives than
receive them from the hands of their persecutors, for such
reasons as I shall relate hereafter.

The Pirates were extremely gladdened at this signal
victory, obtained in so short a time and with so great
inequality of forces; whereby they conceived greater
pride in their minds than they had before.   Hereupon
they all presently ran ashore, intending to take the castle.
This they found very well provided both with men, great
cannon and ammunition; they having no other arms than
muskets and a few fire-balls in their hands.   Their own
artillery they thought incapable, for its smallness, of
making any considerable breach in the walls.   Thus they
spent the rest of that day, firing at the garrison with their
muskets till the dusk of the evening, at which time they
attempted to advance nearer to the walls, with intent
to throw in the fire balls.   But the Spaniards, resolving
to sell their lives as dear as they could, continued firing
so furiously at them, that they thought it not convenient
to approach any nearer nor persist any longer in that
dispute.   Thus having experienced the obstinacy of the
enemy, and seeing thirty of their own men already
dead, and as many more wounded, they retired to their
ships.

The Spaniards believing the Pirates would return the next day to renew the attack, as also make use of their own cannon against the castle, laboured very hard all night to put all things in order for their coming. But more particularly they employed themselves that night in digging down and making plain some little hills and eminent places, whence possibly the castle might be offended.

But Captain Morgan intended not to come ashore again, busying himself the next day in taking prisoners some of the men who still swam alive upon the waters, and hoping to get part of the riches that were lost in the two ships that perished. Among the rest, he took a certain pilot, who was a stranger and who belonged to the lesser ship of the two, with whom he held much discourse, enquiring of him several things. Such questions were: What number of people those three ships had had in them? Whether they expected any more ships to come? From what port they set forth the last time, when they came to seek them out? His answer to all these questions was as follows, which he delivered in the Spanish tongue: *Noble sir, be pleased to pardon and spare me, that no evil be done to me, as being a stranger to this nation I have served, and I shall sincerely inform you of all that passed till our arrival at this lake. We were sent by orders from the Supreme Council of State in Spain, being six men-of-war well-equipped into these seas, with instructions to cruise upon the English pirates, and root them out from these parts by destroying as many of them as we could. These orders were given, by reason of the news brought to the Court of Spain of the loss and ruin of Porto Bello, and other places. Of all which damages and hostilities committed here by the English very dismal lamentations have oftentimes penetrated the ears both of the Catholic King and Council, to whom belongs the care and preservation of this New World. And although the Spanish Court has many times by their Ambassadors sent complaints hereof to the King of England, yet it has been the constant answer of his Majesty of Great Britain, That he never gave any Letters-patent nor Commissions for the acting any hostility whatsoever against the subjects of the King of Spain.   Hereupon the Catholic King, being resolved to avenge his subjects and punish these proceedings, commanded six men-of-war to be equipped, which he sent into these parts under the command of Don Augustin de Bustos, who was constituted Admiral of the said fleet. He commanded the biggest ship thereof, named* Nuestra Señora de la Soledad, *mounted with eight and forty great guns and eight small ones.   The Vice-Admiral was Don Alonso del Campo y Espinosa, who commanded the second ship, called* La Concepcion, *which carried forty-four great guns and eight small ones.   Besides which vessels, there were also four more ; whereof the first was named the* Magdalen, *and was mounted with thirty-six great guns and twelve small ones, having on board two hundred and fifty men.   The second was called* St. Lewis, *with twenty-six great guns, twelve small ones and two hundred men. The third was called* La Marquesa, *which carried sixteen great guns, eight small ones and one hundred and fifty men.   The fourth and last,* Nuestra Señora del Carmen, *with eighteen great guns, eight small ones and likewise two hundred and fifty men.*

We were now arrived at Cartagena, when the two greatest ships received orders to return into Spain, as being judged too big for cruizing upon these coasts.   With the four ships remaining, Don Alonso del Campo y Espinosa departed thence towards Campeche, to seek out the English. We arrived at the port of the said city, where being surprised by a huge storm that blew from the north, we lost one of our four ships ; being that which I named in the last place among the rest.   Hence we set sail for the Isle of Hispaniola ; in sight of which we came within few days, and directed our course to the port of San Domingo.   Here we received intelligence there had passed that way a fleet from Jamaica, and that some men thereof having landed at a place called *Alta Gracia*, the inhabitants had taken one of them prisoner, who confessed their whole design was to go and pillage the city of Caracas. With these news Don Alonso instantly weighed anchor, and set sail thence, crossing over to the continent, till we came in sight of Caracas. Here we found not the English; but happened to meet with a boat which certified us they were in the Lake of Maracaibo, and that the fleet consisted of seven small ships and one boat.

Upon this intelligence we arrived here; and coming nigh unto the entry of the lake, we shot off a gun to demand a pilot from the shore. Those on land perceiving that we were Spaniards, came willingly to us with a pilot, and told us that the English had taken the city of Maracaibo and that they were at present at the pillage of Gibraltar. Don Alonso, having understood this news, made a handsome speech to all his soldiers and mariners, encouraging them to perform their duty, and withal promising to divide among them all they should take from the English. After this, he gave order that the guns which we had taken out of the ship that was lost should be put into the castle, and there mounted for its defence, with two pieces more out of his own ship, of eighteen pounds port each. The pilots conducted us into the port, and Don Alonso commanded the people that were on shore to come to his presence, to whom he gave orders to repossess the castle, and re-inforce it with one hundred men more than it had before its being taken by the English. Not long after, we received news that you were returned from Gibraltar to Maracaibo; to which place Don Alonso wrote you a Letter, giving you account of his arrival and design, and withal exhorting you to restore all that you had taken. This you refused to do; whereupon he renewed his promises and intentions to his soldiers and seamen. And having given a very good supper to all his people, he persuaded them neither to take nor give any quarter to the English that

*should fall into their hands. This was the occasion of
so many being drowned, who dared not to crave any
quarter for their lives, as knowing their own intentions
of giving none. Two days before you came against us, a
certain negro came on board Don Alonso's ship, telling
him: Sir, be pleased to have great care of yourself; for
the English have prepared a fire-ship with design to burn
your fleet. But Don Alonso would not believe this intelligence, his answer being: How can that be? Have
they, peradventure, wit enough to build a fire-ship? or
what instruments have they to do it withal?*

The pilot above-mentioned having related so distinctly
all the aforesaid things to Captain Morgan, was very well
used by him, and, after some kind proffers made to
him, remained in his service.   He discovered moreover
to Captain Morgan, that in the ship which was sunk,
there was a great quantity of plate, even to the value of
forty thousand pieces of eight.   And that this was certainly the occasion they had oftentimes seen the Spaniards
in boats about the said ship.   Hereupon Captain Morgan ordered that one of his ships should remain there
to watch all occasions of getting out of the said vessel
what plate they could.   In the meanwhile he himself,
with all his fleet, returned to Maracaibo, where he refitted the great ship he had taken of the three afore-mentioned.   And now being well accommodated, he chose it
for himself, giving his own bottom to one of his captains.

After this he sent again a messenger to the Admiral,
who was escaped on shore and got into the castle, demanding of him a tribute or ransom of fire for the town
of Maracaibo; which being denied, he threatened he
would entirely consume and destroy it.   The Spaniards,
considering how unfortunate they had been all along
with those Pirates, and not knowing after what manner
to get rid of them, concluded among themselves to pay
the said ransom, although Don Alonso would not consent
to it.

Hereupon they sent to Captain Morgan to ask what sum he demanded. He answered them he would have thirty thousand pieces of eight, and five hundred beeves, to the intent his fleet might be well victualled with flesh. This ransom being paid, he promised in such case he would give no farther trouble to the prisoners, nor cause any ruin or damage to the town. Finally, they agreed with him upon the sum of twenty thousand pieces of eight, besides the five hundred beeves. The cattle the Spaniards brought in the next day, together with one part of the money. And while the pirates were busied in salting the flesh, they returned with the rest of the whole sum of twenty thousand pieces of eight, for which they had agreed.

But Captain Morgan would not deliver for that present the prisoners, as he had promised to do, by reason he feared the shot of the artillery of the castle at his going forth of the lake. Hereupon he told them he intended not to deliver them till such time as he was out of that danger, hoping by this means to obtain a free passage. Thus he set sail with all his fleet in quest of that ship which he had left behind, to seek for the plate of the vessel that was burnt. He found her upon the place, with the sum of fifteen thousand pieces of eight, which they had secured out of the wreck, besides many other pieces of plate, as hilts of swords and other things of this kind ; also great quantity of pieces of eight that were melted and run together by the force of the fire of the said ship.

Captain Morgan scarce thought himself secure, neither could he contrive how to evade the damages the said castle might cause to his fleet. Hereupon he told the prisoners it was necessary they should agree with the Governor to open the passage with security for his fleet ; to which point, if he should not consent, he would certainly hang them all up in his ships. After this warning the prisoners met together to confer upon the persons

they should depute to the said Governor Don Alonso ;
and they assigned some few among them for that embassy.   These went to him, beseeching and supplicating
the Admiral he would have compassion and pity on those
afflicted prisoners who were as yet, together with their
wives and children, in the hands of Captain Morgan ;
and that to this effect he would be pleased to give his
word to let the whole fleet of Pirates freely pass, without
any molestation, forasmuch as this would be the only
remedy of saving both the lives of them that came with
this petition, as also of those who remained behind in
captivity ; all being equally menaced with the sword and
gallows, in case he granted not this humble request.
But Don Alonso gave them for answer a sharp repre-
hension of their cowardice, telling them : *If you had been
as loyal to your King in hindering the entry of these
Pirates as I shall do their going out, you had never caused
these troubles, neither to yourselves, nor to our whole
nation ; which have suffered so much through your pusill-
animity.   In a word, I shall never grant your request ;
but shall endeavour to maintain that respect which is due
to my King, according to my duty.*

Thus the Spaniards returned to their fellow-prisoners
with much consternation of mind, and no hopes of obtaining their request ; telling Captain Morgan what answer
they had received.   His reply was : *If Don Alonso
will not let me pass, I will find means how to do it without
him.*   Hereupon he began presently to make a dividend
of all the booty they had taken in that voyage, fearing lest
he might not have an opportunity of doing it in another
place, if any tempest should arise and separate the ships,
as also being jealous that any of the commanders might
run away with the best part of the spoil which then lay
much more in one vessel than another.   Thus they all
brought in, according to their laws, and declared what
they had ; having beforehand made an oath not to conceal the least thing from the public.   The accounts

being cast up, they found to the value of two hundred and fifty thousand pieces of eight in money and jewels, besides the huge quantity of merchandize and slaves : all which booty was divided into every ship or boat, according to its share.

The dividend being made, the question still remained on foot, how they should pass the castle and get out of the Lake. To this effect they made use of a stratagem, of no ill invention, which was as follows. On the day that pre-ceeded the night wherein they determined to get forth, they embarked many of their men in canoes, and rowed towards the shore, as if they designed to land them. Here they concealed themselves under the branches of trees that hung over the coast for a while till they had laid themselves down along in the boats. Then the canoes returned to the ships, with the appearance only of two or three men rowing them back, all the rest being concealed at the bottom of the canoes. Thus much only could be perceived from the castle ; and this action of false-landing of men, for so we may call it, was repeated that day several times. Hereby the Spaniards were brought into persuasion the Pirates intended to force the castle by scaling it, as soon as night should come. This fear caused them to place most of their great guns on that side which looks towards the land, together with the main force of their arms, leaving the contrary side be-longing to the sea almost destitute of strength and defence.

Night being come, they weighed anchor, and by the light of the moon, without setting sail, committed them-selves to the ebbing tide, which gently brought them down the river, till they were nigh the castle. Being now almost over against it, they spread their sails with all the haste they could possibly make. The Spaniards, perceiving them to escape, transported with all speed their guns from the other side of the castle, and began to fire very furiously at the Pirates. But these having a

favourable wind were almost past the danger before those
of the castle could put things into convenient order of
offence.   So that the Pirates lost not many of their men,
nor received any considerable damage in their ships.
Being now out of the reach of the guns, Captain Morgan
sent a canoe to the castle with some of the prisoners ;
and the Governor thereof gave them a boat that every
one might return to his own home.   Nctwithstanding, he
detained the hostages he had from Gibraltar, by reason
those of that town were not as yet come to pay the rest
of the ransom for not firing the place.   Just as he departed Captain Morgan ordered seven great guns with
bullets to be fired against the castle, as it were to take his
leave of them.   But they answered not so much as with
a musket-shot.

The next day after their departure, they were surprised
with a great tempest, which forced them to cast anchor
in the depth of five or six fathom water.   But the storm
increased so much that they were compelled to weigh
again and put out to sea, where they were in great danger
of being lost.   For if on either side they should have been
cast on shore, either to fall into the hands of the Spaniards,
or of the Indians, they would certainly have obtained no
mercy.   At last the tempest being spent, the wind
ceased ; which caused much content and joy in the whole
fleet.

While Captain Morgan made his fortune by pillaging the towns above-mentioned, the rest of his companions, who separated from his fleet at the Cape de
Lobos to take the ship of which was spoken before,
endured much misery, and were very unfortunate in all
their attempts.   For being arrived at the Isle of Savona,
they did not find Captain Morgan there, nor any one of
their companions.   Neither had they the good fortune
to find a letter which Captain Morgan at his departure
left behind him in a certain place, where in all probability
they would meet with it.   Thus, not knowing what course

to steer, they at last concluded to pillage some town or other, whereby to seek their fortune. They were in all four hundred men, more or less, who were divided into four ships and one boat. Being ready to set forth they constituted an Admiral among themselves, by whom they might be directed in the whole affair. To this effect they chose a certain person who had behaved himself very courageously at the taking of Porto Bello, and whose name was Captain Hansel. This commander resolved to attempt the taking of the town of Comana, seated upon the continent of Caracas, nearly threescore leagues from the west side of the Isle of Trinidad. Being arrived there, they landed their men, and killed some few Indians that were near the coast. But approaching the town, the Spaniards, having in their company many Indians, disputed them the entry so briskly, that with great loss and in great confusion they were forced to retire towards their ships. At last they arrived at Jamaica, where the rest of their companions who came with Captain Morgan, ceased not to mock and jeer them for their ill success at Comana, often telling them : *Let us see what money you brought from Comana, and if it be as good silver as that which we bring from Maracaibo.*

The End of the Second Part.

PART III.

CHAPTER I.

Captain Morgan goes to the Isle of Hispaniola to equip a new fleet, with intent to pillage again upon the coasts of the West Indies.

CAPTAIN MORGAN perceived now that fortune favoured his arms, by giving good success to all his enterprizes, which occasioned him, as it is usual in human affairs, to aspire to greater things, trusting she would always be constant to him. Such was the burning of Panama; wherein fortune failed not to assist him, in like manner as she had done before, crowning the event of his actions with victory, howbeit she had led him thereto through thousands of difficulties. The history hereof I shall now begin to relate, as being so very remarkable in all its circumstances that peradventure nothing more deserving memory may occur to be read by future ages.

Not long after Captain Morgan arrived at Jamaica, he found many of his chief officers and soldiers reduced to their former state of indigence through their immoderate vices and debauchery. Hence they ceased not to importune him for new invasions and exploits, thereby to get something to expend anew in wine, as they had already wasted what was secured so little before. Captain Morgan being willing to follow fortune while she called him, hereupon stopped the mouths of many of the inhabitants of Jamaica, who were creditors to

his men for large sums of money, with the hopes and
promises he gave them, of greater achievements than
ever, by a new expedition he was going about. This
being done, he needed not give himself much trouble to
levy men for this or any other enterprize, his name being
now so famous through all those islands, that that alone
would readily bring him in more men than he could well
employ. He undertook therefore to equip a new fleet of
ships; for which purpose he assigned the south side of
the Isle of Tortuga, as a place of rendezvous. With this
resolution, he wrote divers letters to all the ancient and
expert Pirates there inhabiting, as also to the Governor
of the said isle, and to the planters and hunters of Hispaniola, giving them to understand his intentions, and
desiring their appearance at the said place, in case they
intended to go with him. All these people had no
sooner understood his designs than they flocked to the
place assigned in huge numbers, with ships, canoes and
boats, being desirous to obey his commands. Many,
who had not the convenience of coming to him by sea,
traversed the woods of Hispaniola, and with no small
difficulties arrived there by land. Thus all were present
at the place assigned, and in readiness, against the 24th
day of October, 1670.

Captain Morgan was not wanting to be there according to his punctual custom, who came in his ship to the
same side of the island, to a port called by the French
Port Couillon, over against the island De la Vaca, this
being a place which he had assigned to others. Having
now gathered the greatest part of his fleet, he called a
council, to deliberate about the means of finding provisions sufficient for so many people. Here they concluded
to send four ships and one boat, manned with four hundred
men, over to the continent, to the intent they should rifle
some country towns and villages, and in these get all the
corn or maize they could gather. They set sail for the
continent, towards the river De la Hacha, with design

to assault a small village, called La Rancheria, where is usually to be found the greatest quantity of maize of all those parts thereabouts. In the meanwhile Captain Morgan sent another party of his men to hunt in the woods, who killed there a huge number of beasts, and salted them. The rest of his companions remained in the ships, to clean, fit and rig them out to sea, so that at the return of those who were sent abroad, all things might be in readiness to weigh anchor, and follow the course of their designs.

CHAPTER II.

What happened in the river De la Hacha.

THE four ships abovementioned, after they had set sail from Hispaniola, steered their course till they came within sight of the river De la Hacha, where they were suddenly overtaken with a tedious calm. Being thus within sight of land becalmed for some days, the Spaniards inhabiting along the coast, who had perceived them to be enemies, had sufficient time to prepare themselves for the assault, at least to hide the best part of their goods, to the end that, without any care of preserving them, they might be in readiness to retire, when they found themselves unable to resist the force of the Pirates, by whose frequent attempts upon those coasts they had already learnt what they had to do in such cases. There was in the river at that present a good ship, which was come from Cartagena to lade maize, and was now when the Pirates came almost ready to depart. The men belonging to this ship endeavoured to escape, but not being able to do it, both they and the vessel fell into their hands. This was a fit booty for their mind, as being good part of what they came to seek for with so much care and toil. The next morning about break of day they came with their ships towards the shore, and landed their men, although the Spaniards made huge resistance from a battery which they had raised on that side, where of necessity they had to land : but notwithstanding what defence they could make, they were forced to retire towards a village, to which the Pirates followed them. Here the Spaniards, rallying again, fell upon them with

186

great fury, and maintained a strong combat, which lasted till night was come ; but then, perceiving they had lost great number of men, which was no smaller on the Pirates' side, they retired to places more occult in the woods.

The next day when the Pirates saw they were all fled, and the town left totally empty of people, they pursued them as far as they could possibly. In this pursuit they overtook a party of Spaniards, whom they made all prisoners and exercised the most cruel torments, to discover where they had hidden their goods : some were found who by the force of intolerable tortures confessed ; but others who would not do the same were used more barbarously than the former. Thus, in the space of fifteen days that they remained there, they took many prisoners, much plate and moveable goods, with all other things they could rob, with which booty they resolved to return to Hispaniola. Yet not contented with what they had already got, they dispatched some prisoners into the woods to seek for the rest of the inhabitants, and to demand of them a ransom for not burning the town. To this they answered, they had no money nor plate, but in case they would be satisfied with a certain quantity of maize, they would give as much as they could afford. The Pirates accepted this proffer, as being more useful to them at that occasion than ready money, and agreed they should pay four thousand hanegs, or bushels, of maize. These were brought in three days after, the Spaniards being desirous to rid themselves as soon as possible of that inhuman sort of people. Having laded them on board their ships, together with all the rest of their booty, they returned to the Island of Hispaniola, to give account to their leader Captain Morgan of all they had performed.

They had now been absent five entire weeks, about the commission aforementioned, which long delay occasioned Captain Morgan almost to despair of their

return, fearing lest they were fallen into the hands
of the Spaniards, especially considering that the place
whereto they went could easily be relieved from Cartagena and Santa Maria, if the inhabitants were at all
careful to alarm the country : on the other side he feared
lest they should have made some great fortune in that
voyage, and with it escaped to some other place.   But at
last seeing his ships return, and in greater number than
they had departed, he resumed new courage, this sight
causing both in him and his companions infinite joy.
This was much increased when, being arrived, they found
them full laden with maize, whereof they stood in great
need for the maintenance of so many people, by whose
help they expected great matters through the conduct of
their commander.

After Captain Morgan had divided the said maize, as
also the flesh which the hunters brought in, among all
the ships, according to the number of men that were in
every vessel, he concluded upon the departure, having
viewed beforehand every ship, and observed their being
well equipped and clean.   Thus he set sail, and directed
his course towards Cape Tiburon, where he determined
to take his measures and resolution, of what enterprize
he should take in hand.   No sooner were they arrived
there than they met with some other ships that came
newly to join them from Jamaica.   So that now the
whole fleet consisted of thirty-seven ships, wherein were
two thousand fighting men, besides mariners and boys ;
the Admiral hereof was mounted with twenty-two great
guns, and six small ones, of brass ; the rest carried some
twenty, some sixteen, some eighteen, and the smallest
vessel at least four, besides which they had great quantity
of ammunition and fire-balls, with other inventions of
powder.

Captain Morgan finding himself with such a great
number of ships, divided the whole fleet into two
squadrons, constituting a Vice-Admiral, and other

officers and commanders of the second squadron, distinct from the former. To every one of these he gave letters patent, or commissions, to act all manner of hostility against the Spanish nation, and take of them what ships they could, either abroad at sea or in the harbours, in like manner as if they were open and declared enemies (as he termed it) of the King of England, his pretended master. This being done, he called all his captains and other officers together, and caused them to sign some articles of common agreement between them, and in the name of all. Herein it was stipulated that he should have the hundredth part of all that was gotten to himself alone : That every captain should draw the shares of eight men, for the expenses of his ship, besides his own : That the surgeon, besides his ordinary pay, should have two hundred pieces of eight, for his chest of medicaments : And every carpenter, above his common salary, should draw one hundred pieces of eight. As to recompences and rewards, they were regulated in this voyage much higher than was expressed in the first part of this book. Thus, for the loss of both legs, they assigned one thousand five hundred pieces of eight or fifteen slaves, the choice being left to the election of the party ; for the loss of both hands, one thousand eight hundred pieces of eight or eighteen slaves ; for one leg, whether the right or the left, six hundred pieces of eight or six slaves ; for a hand, as much as for a leg ; and for the loss of an eye, one hundred pieces of eight or one slave. Lastly, unto him that in any battle should signalize himself, either by entering the first any castle, or taking down the Spanish colours and setting up the English, they constituted fifty pieces of eight for a reward. In the head of these articles it was stipulated that all these extraordinary salaries, recompences and rewards should be paid out of the first spoil or purchase they should take, according as every one should then occur to be either rewarded or paid.

This contract being signed, Captain Morgan commanded his Vice-admirals and Captains to put all things in order, every one in his ship, to go and attempt one of three places, either Cartagena, Panama or Vera Cruz; but the lot fell upon Panama as being believed to be the richest of all three : notwithstanding this city being situated at such distance from the Northern sea, as they knew not well the avenues and entries necessary to approach it, they judged it necessary to go beforehand to the isle of St. Catharine, there to find and provide themselves with some persons who might serve them for guides in this enterprize ; for in the garrison of that island are commonly employed many banditti and outlaws belonging to Panama and the neighbouring places, who are very expert in the knowledge of all that country. But before they proceeded any farther, they caused an act to be published through the whole fleet, containing that in case they met with any Spanish vessel, the first captain who with his men should enter and take the said ship, should have for his reward the tenth part of whatsoever should be found within her.

CHAPTER III.

Captain Morgan leaves the Island of Hispaniola, and goes to that of St. Catharine, which he takes.

CAPTAIN MORGAN and his companions weighed anchor from the Cape of Tiburon, the 16th day of December in the year 1670. Four days after they arrived within sight of the Isle of St. Catharine, which was now in possession of the Spaniards again, as was said in the Second Part of this history, and to which they commonly banish all the malefactors of the Spanish dominions in the West Indies. In this island are found huge quantities of pigeons at certain seasons of the year; it is watered continually by four rivulets or brooks, whereof two are always dry in the summer season. Here is no manner of trade nor commerce exercised by the inhabitants, neither do they give themselves the trouble to plant more fruits than what are necessary for the sustentation of human life; howbeit the country would be sufficient to make very good plantations of tobacco, which might render considerable profit, were it cultivated for that use.

As soon as Captain Morgan came near the island with his fleet, he sent before one of his best sailing vessels to view the entry of the river and see if any other ships were there who might hinder him from landing; as also fearing lest they should give intelligence of his arrival to the inhabitants of the island, and they by this means prevent his designs.

The next day before sunrise, all the fleet came to anchor near the island, in a certain bay called Aguada

Grande : upon this bay the Spaniards had lately built a
battery, mounted with four pieces of cannon.   Captain
Morgan landed with a thousand men, more or less, and
disposed them into squadrons, beginning his march
through the woods, although they had no other guides
than some few of his own men who had been there
before when Mansvelt took and ransacked the island.
The same day they came to a certain place where the
Governor at other times kept his ordinary residence :
here they found a battery called *The Platform,* but
nobody in it, the Spaniards having retired to the lesser
island, which, as was said before, is so near the great
one that a short bridge only may conjoin them.

This lesser island aforesaid was so well fortified with
forts and batteries round it as might seem impregnable.
Hereupon, as soon as the Spaniards perceived the pirates
to approach, they began to fire upon them so furiously
that they could advance nothing that day, but were contented to retreat a little, and take up their rest upon the
grass in the open fields, which afforded no strange beds
to these people, as being sufficiently used to such kind of
repose : what most afflicted them was hunger, having not
eaten the least thing that whole day.   About midnight
it began to rain so hard that those miserable people had
much ado to resist so much hardship, the greatest part of
them having no other clothes than a pair of seaman's
trousers or breeches, and a shirt, without either shoes or
stockings.   Thus finding themselves in great extremity,
they began to pull down a few thatched houses to make
fires withal : in a word, they were in such condition that
one hundred men, indifferently well armed, might easily
that night have torn them all in pieces.   The next morning about break of day the rain ceased, at which time
they began to dry their arms, which were entirely wet,
and proceed on their march.   But not long after, the
rain commenced anew, rather harder than before, as if
the skies were melted into waters, which caused them

to cease from advancing towards the forts, whence the Spaniards continually fired at the Pirates, seeing them to approach.

The Pirates were now reduced to great affliction and danger of their lives through the hardness of the weather, their own nakedness, and the great hunger they sustained. For a small relief hereof, they happened to find in the fields an old horse, which was both lean and full of scabs and blotches, with galled back and sides. This horrid animal they instantly killed and flayed, and divided into small pieces among themselves as far as it would reach, for many could not obtain one morsel, which they roasted and devoured without either salt or bread, more like ravenous wolves than men. The rain as yet ceased not to fall, and Captain Morgan perceived their minds to relent, hearing many of them say they would return on board the ships. Amongst these fatigues both of mind and body, he thought it convenient to use some sudden and almost unexpected remedy : to this effect he commanded a canoe to be rigged in all haste, and the colours of truce to be hanged out of it. This canoe he sent to the Spanish governor of the island with this message : *That if within a few hours he delivered not himself and all his men into his hands, he did by that messenger swear to him, and all those that were in his company, he would most certainly put them all to the sword, without granting quarter to any.*

After noon the canoe returned with this answer : *That the Governor desired two hours' time to deliberate with his officers in a full council about that affair ; which being past, he would give his positive answer to the message.* The time now being elapsed, the said Governor sent two canoes with white colours, and two persons, to treat with Captain Morgan ; but before they landed, they demanded of the Pirates two persons as hostages of their security. These were readily granted by Captain Morgan, who delivered to them two of his captains, for a mutual pledge

of the security required. With this the Spaniards propounded to Captain Morgan, that their Governor in a
full assembly had resolved to deliver up the island,
not being provided with sufficient forces to defend it
against such an armada or fleet. But withal he desired
that Captain Morgan would be pleased to use a certain
stratagem of war, for the better saving of his own credit,
and the reputation of his officers both abroad and at
home, which should be as follows: That Captain Morgan would come with his troops by night, near the bridge
that joined the lesser island to the great one, and there
attack the fort of St. Jerome: that at the same time all
the ships of his fleet would draw near the castle of Santa
Teresa, and attack it by sea, landing in the meanwhile
some more troops, near the battery called St. Matthew:
that these troops which were newly landed should by
this means intercept the Governor by the way, as he endeavoured to pass to St. Jerome's fort, and then take
him prisoner, using the formality, as if they forced him
to deliver the said castle; and that he would lead the
English into it, under the fraud of being his own troops;
that on one side and the other there should be continual
firing at one another, but without bullets, or at least into
the air, so that no side might receive any harm by this
device; that thus having obtained two such considerable forts, the chief of the isle, he needed not take care
for the rest, which of necessity must fall by course into
his hands.

These propositions, every one, were granted by
Captain Morgan, upon condition they should see them
faithfully observed, for otherwise they should be used
with all rigour imaginable: this they promised to do, and
hereupon took their leaves, and returned to give account
of their negotiation to the Governor. Presently after
Captain Morgan commanded the whole fleet to enter the
port, and his men to be in readiness to assault that
night the castle of St. Jerome. Thus the false alarm or

battle began, with incessant firing of great guns from both the castles against the ships, but without bullets, as was said before. Then the Pirates landed, and assaulted by night the lesser island, which they took, as also possession of both the fortresses, forcing all the Spaniards, in appearance, to fly to the church. Before this assault, Captain Morgan had sent word to the Governor he should keep all his men together in a body, otherwise if the Pirates met any straggling Spaniards in the streets, they should certainly shoot them.

The island being taken by this unusual stratagem, and all things put in due order, the Pirates began to make a new war against the poultry, cattle and all sort of victuals they could find. This was their whole employ for some days, scarce thinking of anything else than to kill those animals, roast and eat, and make good cheer, as much as they could possibly attain unto. If wood was wanting, they presently fell upon the houses, and, pulling them down, made fires with the timber, as had been done before in the field. The next day they numbered all the prisoners they had taken upon the whole island, which were found to be in all four hundred and fifty persons, between men, women and children, viz., one hundred and ninety soldiers, belonging to the garrison; forty inhabitants, who were married; forty-three children; thirty-four slaves, belonging to the King, with eight children; eight banditti; thirty-nine negroes, belonging to private persons, with twenty-seven female blacks and thirty-four children. The Pirates disarmed all the Spaniards, and sent them out immediately to the plantations, to seek for provisions, leaving the women in the church, there to exercise their devotions.

Soon after they took a review of the whole island, and all the fortresses belonging thereunto, which they found to be nine in all, as follows : the fort of St. Jerome, nearest to the bridge, had eight great guns, of 12, 6 and 8 pound carriage, together with six pipes of muskets, every pipe containing ten muskets. Here they found still sixty muskets, with sufficient quantity of powder and all other sorts of ammunition. The second fortress, called St. Matthew, had three guns, of 8 pound carriage each. The third and chief among all the rest, named Santa Teresa, had twenty great guns, of 18, 12, 8 and 6 pound carriage, with ten pipes of muskets, like those we said before, and ninety muskets remaining, besides all other warlike ammunition. This castle was built with stone and mortar, with very thick walls on all sides, and a large ditch round about it of twenty foot depth, which although it was dry was very hard to get over. Here was no entry but through one door, which corresponded to the middle of the castle. Within it was a mount or hill, almost inaccessible, with four pieces of cannon at the top, whence they could shoot directly into the port. On the sea side this castle was impregnable, by reason of the rocks which surrounded it and the sea beating furiously upon them. In like manner, on the side of the land, it was so commodiously seated on a mountain that there was no access to it, but by a path of three or four foot broad. The fourth fortress was named St. Augustine, having three guns, of 8 and 6 pound carriage. The fifth, named La Plattaforma de la Concepcion, had only two guns, of eight pound carriage. The sixth, by name San Salvador, had likewise no more than two guns. The seventh, being called Plattaforma de los Artilleros, had also two guns. The eighth, called Santa Cruz, had three guns. The ninth, which was called St. Joseph's Fort, had six guns, of 12 and 8 pound carriage, besides two pipes of muskets and sufficient ammunition.

In the store-house were found above thirty thousand pounds of powder, with all other sorts of ammunition, which were transported by the Pirates on board the ships. All the guns were stopped and nailed, and the fortresses demolished, excepting that of St. Jerome, where the Pirates kept their guard and residence. Captain Morgan enquired if any banditti were there from Panama or Porto Bello; and hereupon three were brought before him, who pretended to be very expert in all the avenues of those parts. He asked them if they would be his guides, and show him the securest ways and passages to Panama; which, if they performed, he promised them equal shares in all they should pillage and rob in that expedition, and that afterwards he would set them at liberty, by transporting them to Jamaica. These propositions pleased the banditti very well, and they readily accepted his proffers, promising to serve him very faithfully in all he should desire; especially one of these three, who was the greatest rogue, thief and assassin among them, and who had deserved for his crimes rather to be broken alive upon the wheel than punished with serving in a garrison. This wicked fellow had a great ascendancy over the other two banditti, and could domineer and command over them as he pleased, they not daring to refuse obedience to his orders.

Hereupon Captain Morgan commanded four ships and one boat to be equipped and provided with all things necessary, to go and take the castle of Chagre, seated upon the river of that name. Neither would he go himself with his whole fleet, fearing lest the Spaniards should be jealous of his farther designs upon Panama. In these vessels he caused to embark four hundred men, who went to put in execution the orders of their chief commander Captain Morgan, while he himself remained behind in the Island of St. Catharine, with the rest of the fleet. expecting to hear the success of their arms.

CHAPTER IV.

Captain Morgan takes the castle of Chagre, with four hundred men sent for this purpose from the Isle of St. Catharine.

CAPTAIN MORGAN sending these four ships and a boat to the river of Chagre, chose for Vice-Admiral thereof a certain person named Captain Brodely. This man had been a long time in those quarters, and committed many robberies upon the Spaniards when Mansvelt took the Isle of St. Catharine, as was related in the Second Part of this history. He, being therefore well acquainted with those coasts, was thought a fit person for this exploit, his actions likewise having rendered him famous among the Pirates, and their enemies the Spaniards. Captain Brodely being chosen chief commander of these forces, in three days after he departed from the presence of Captain Morgan arrived within sight of the said castle of Chagre, which by the Spaniards is called St. Lawrence. This castle is built upon a high mountain, at the entry of the river, and surrounded on all sides with strong palisades or wooden walls, being very well terre-pleined, and filled with earth, which renders them as secure as the best walls made of stone or brick. The top of this mountain is in a manner divided into two parts, between which lies a ditch, of the depth of thirty foot. The castle itself has but one entry, and that by a drawbridge which passes over the ditch aforementioned. On the land side it has four bastions, that of the sea containing only two more. That part thereof which looks towards the South is totally inaccessible and impossible to be climbed, through the infinite asperity of the mountain.

The North side is surrounded by the river, which here-abouts runs very broad. At the foot of the said castle, or rather mountain, is seated a strong fort, with eight great guns, which commands and impedes the entry of the river. Not much lower are to be seen two other batteries, whereof each hath six pieces of cannon, to defend likewise the mouth of the said river. At one side of the castle are built two great store-houses, in which are deposited all sorts of warlike ammunition and merchandize, which are brought thither from the inner parts of the country. Near these houses is a high pair of stairs, hewed out of the rock, which serves to mount to the top of the castle. On the West side of the said fortress lies a small port, which is not above seven or eight fathom deep, being very fit for small vessels and of very good anchorage. Besides this, there lies before the castle, at the entry of the river, a great rock, scarce to be perceived above water, unless at low tide.

No sooner had the Spaniards perceived the Pirates to come than they began to fire incessantly at them with the biggest of their guns. They came to an anchor in a small port, at the distance of a league more or less from the castle. The next morning very early they went on shore, and marched through the woods, to attack the castle on that side. This march continued until two o'clock in the afternoon, before they could reach the castle, by reason of the difficulties of the way, and its mire and dirt. And although their guides served them exactly, notwithstanding they came so near the castle at first that they lost many of their men with the shot from the guns, they being in an open place where nothing could cover nor defend them. This much perplexed the Pirates in their minds, they not knowing what to do, nor what course to take, for on that side of necessity they must make the assault, and being uncovered from head to foot, they could not advance one step without great danger. Besides that, the castle, both for its situation

and strength, caused them much to fear the success
of that enterprize. But to give it over they dared not,
lest they should be reproached and scorned by their
companions.

At last, after many doubts and disputes among themselves, they resolved to hazard the assault and their lives
after a most desperate manner. Thus they advanced
towards the castle, with their swords in one hand and
fire-balls in the other. The Spaniards defended themselves very briskly, ceasing not to fire at them with their
great guns and muskets continually, crying withal
*Come on, ye English dogs, enemies to God and our King;
let your other companions that are behind come on too; ye
shall not go to Panama this bout.* After the Pirates had
made some trial to climb up the walls, they were forced
to retreat, which they accordingly did, resting themselves until night. This being come, they returned to
the assault, to try if by the help of their fire-balls they
could overcome and pull down the pales before the wall.
This they attempted to do, and while they were about it
there happened a very remarkable accident, which gave
them the opportunity of the victory. One of the Pirates
was wounded with an arrow in his back, which pierced
his body to the other side. This instantly he pulled out
with great valour at the side of his breast; then taking
a little cotton that he had about him, he wound it about
the said arrow, and putting it into his musket, he shot it
back into the castle. But the cotton being kindled by
the powder, occasioned two or three houses that were
within the castle, being thatched with palm-leaves, to
take fire, which the Spaniards perceived not so soon
as was necessary. For this fire meeting with a parcel
of powder, blew it up, and thereby caused great ruin,
and no less consternation to the Spaniards, who were not
able to account for this accident, not having seen the
beginning thereof.

Thus the Pirates, perceiving the good effect of the

arrow and the beginning of the misfortune of the
Spaniards, were infinitely gladdened thereat. And while
they were busied in extinguishing the fire, which caused
great confusion in the whole castle, having not sufficient
water wherewithal to do it, the Pirates made use of this
opportunity, setting fire likewise to the palisades. Thus
the fire was seen at the same time in several parts about
the castle, which gave them huge advantage against the
Spaniards. For many breaches were made at once by
the fire among the pales, great heaps of earth falling
down into the ditch. Upon these the Pirates climbed up,
and got over into the castle, notwithstanding that some
Spaniards, who were not busied about the fire, cast down
upon them many flaming pots, full of combustible matter
and odious smells, which occasioned the loss of many of
the English.

The Spaniards, notwithstanding the great resistance
they made, could not hinder the palisades from being
entirely burnt before midnight. Meanwhile the Pirates
ceased not to persist in their intention of taking the
castle. To which effect, although the fire was great, they
would creep upon the ground, as nigh unto it as they
could, and shoot amidst the flames, against the Spaniards
they could perceive on the other side, and thus cause
many to fall dead from the walls. When day was come,
they observed all the moveable earth that lay between
the pales to be fallen into the ditch in huge quantity.
So that now those within the castle did in a manner lie
equally exposed to them without, as had been on the
contrary before. Whereupon the Pirates continued
shooting very furiously against them, and killed great
numbers of Spaniards. For the Governor had given
them orders not to retire from those posts which corresponded to the heaps of earth fallen into the ditch, and
caused the artillery to be transported to the breaches.

Notwithstanding, the fire within the castle still continued, and now the Pirates from abroad used what

means they could to hinder its progress, by shooting
incessantly against it. One party of the Pirates was
employed only to this purpose, and another commanded
to watch all the motions of the Spaniards, and take all
opportunities against them. About noon the English
happened to gain a breach, which the Governor himself
defended with twenty-five soldiers. Here was performed a very courageous and warlike resistance by the
Spaniards, both with muskets, pikes, stones and swords.
Yet notwithstanding, through all these arms the Pirates
forced and fought their way, till at last they gained the
castle. The Spaniards who remained alive cast themselves down from the castle into the sea, choosing rather
to die precipitated by their own selves (few or none surviving the fall) than ask any quarter for their lives.
The Governor himself retreated to the *corps du garde*,
before which were placed two pieces of cannon. Here he
intended still to defend himself, neither would he demand
any quarter. But at last he was killed with a musket
shot, which pierced his skull into the brain.

The Governor being dead, and the *corps du garde*
surrendered, they found still remaining in it alive to the
number of thirty men, whereof scarce ten were not
wounded. These informed the Pirates that eight or nine
of their soldiers had deserted their colours, and were
gone to Panama to carry news of their arrival and invasion. These thirty men alone were remaining of three
hundred and fourteen, wherewith the castle was garrisoned, among which number not one officer was found
alive. These were all made prisoners, and compelled to
tell whatsoever they knew of their designs and enterprizes. Among other things they declared that the
Governor of Panama had notice sent him three weeks
ago from Cartagena, how that the English were equipping a fleet at Hispaniola, with design to come and take
the said city of Panama. Moreover, that this their
intention had been known by a person, who was run

away from the Pirates, at the river De la Hacha, where
they provided their fleet with corn. That, upon this
news, the said Governor had sent one hundred and sixty
four men to strengthen the garrison of that castle, together with much provision and warlike ammunition ;
the ordinary garrison whereof did only consist of one
hundred and fifty men. So that in all they made the
number aforementioned of three hundred and fourteen
men, being all very well armed. Besides this they had
declared that the Governor of Panama had placed several
ambuscades all along the river of Chagre ; and that he
waited for their coming, in the open fields of Panama,
with three thousand six hundred men.

The taking of this castle of Chagre cost the Pirates
excessively dear, in comparison to the small numbers
they used to lose at other times and places. Yea, their
toil and labour here far exceeded what they sustained at
the conquest of the Isle of St. Catharine and its adjacent.
For coming to number their men, they found they had
lost above one hundred, besides those that were wounded,
whose number exceeded seventy. They commanded the
Spaniards that were prisoners to cast all the dead bodies
of their own men down from the top of the mountain to
the seaside, and afterwards to bury them. Such as were
wounded were carried to the church belonging to the
castle, of which they made a hospital, and where also
they shut up the women.

Captain Morgan remained not long time behind at the
Isle of St. Catharine, after taking the castle of Chagre ;
of which he had notice presently sent him. Yet notwithstanding, before he departed thence, he caused to be
embarked all the provisions that could be found, together
with great quantities of maize or Indian wheat, and
cassava, whereof in like manner is made bread in those
parts. He commanded likewise great store of provisions
should be transported to the garrison of the aforesaid
castle of Chagre, from what parts soever they could be

got. At a certain place of the island they cast into the
sea all the guns belonging thereto, with a design to return and leave that island well garrisoned, for the perpetual possession of Pirates. Notwithstanding he ordered
all the houses and forts to be set on fire, excepting only
the castle of St. Teresa, which he judged to be the
strongest and securest wherein to fortify himself at his
return from Panama. He carried with him all the
prisoners of the island, and thus set sail for the river of
Chagre, where he arrived in the space of eight days.
Here the joy of the whole fleet was so great, when they
spied the English colours upon the castle that they
minded not their way into the river, which occasioned
them to lose four of their ships at the entry thereof, that
wherein Captain Morgan went being one of the four.
Yet their fortune was so good as to be able to save all
the men and goods that were in the said vessels. Yea,
the ships likewise had been preserved, if a strong
northerly wind had not risen on that occasion, which cast
the ships upon the rock abovementioned, that lies at the
entry of the said river.

Captain Morgan was brought into the castle with great
acclamations of triumph and joy of all the Pirates, both
of those who were within, and also them that were but
newly come. Having understood the whole transactions
of the conquest, he commanded all the prisoners to begin to work, and repair what was necessary. Especially
in setting up new palisades, or pales, round about the
forts depending on the castle. There were still in the
river some Spanish vessels, called by them *chatten*, which
serve for the transportation of merchandize up and down
the said river, as also for going to Porto Bello and
Nicaragua. These are commonly mounted with two
great guns of iron and four other small ones of brass.
All these vessels they seized on, together with four
little ships they found there, and all the canoes, In the
castle they left a garrison of five hundred men, and in

the ships within the river one hundred and fifty more. These things being done, Captain Morgan departed towards Panama, at the head of one thousand two hundred men. He carried very small provisions with him, being in good hopes he should provide himself sufficiently among the Spaniards, whom he knew to lie in ambuscade at several places by the way.

CHAPTER V.

Captain Morgan departs from the Castle of Chagre, at the head of one thousand two hundred men, with design to take the city of Panama.

CAPTAIN MORGAN set forth from the castle of Chagre, towards Panama, the 18th day of August[1] in the year 1670. He had under his conduct one thousand two hundred men, five boats with artillery and thirty-two canoes, all which were filled with the said people. Thus he steered his course up the river towards Panama. That day they sailed only six leagues, and came to a place called De los Bracos. Here a party of his men went on shore, only to sleep some few hours and stretch their limbs, they being almost crippled with lying too much crowded in the boats. After they had rested a while, they went abroad, to see if any victuals could be found in the neighbouring plantations. But they could find none, the Spaniards being fled and carrying with them all the provisions they had. This day, being the first of their journey, there was amongst them such scarcity of victuals that the greatest part were forced to pass with only a pipe of tobacco, without any other refreshment.

The next day, very early in the morning, they continued their journey, and came about evening to a place called Cruz de Juán Gallego. Here they were compelled to leave their boats and canoes, by reason the river was

---

[1] "August" is probably intended for "January," for we note (p. 3 of 3rd part) that the assembly at Tortuga was on the 24th of October, 1670, that (p. 11) they sailed from Teburon on 16th December, 1670, and that (p. 70) they left Panama on the 24th February, 1671.

very dry for want of rain, and the many obstacles of trees that were fallen into it.

The guides told them that about two leagues farther on the country would be very good to continue the journey by land. Hereupon they left some companies, being in all one hundred and sixty men, on board the boats to defend them, with intent they might serve for a place of refuge, in case of necessity.

The next morning, being the third day of their journey, they all went ashore, excepting those above mentioned who were to keep the boats. To these Captain Morgan gave very strict orders, under great penalties, that no man, upon any pretext whatsoever, should dare to leave the boats and go ashore. This he did, fearing lest they should be surprised and cut off by an ambuscade of Spaniards, that might chance to lie thereabouts in the neighbouring woods, which appeared so thick as to seem almost impenetrable. Having this morning begun their march they found the ways so dirty and irksome, that Captain Morgan thought it more convenient to transport some of the men in canoes (though it could not be done without great labour) to a place farther up the river, called Cedro Bueno. Thus they re-embarked, and the canoes returned for the rest that were left behind. So that about night they found themselves altogether at the said place. The Pirates were extremely desirous to meet any Spaniards, or Indians, hoping to fill their bellies with what provisions they should take from them. For now they were reduced almost to the very extremity of hunger.

On the fourth day, the greatest part of the Pirates marched by land, being led by one of the guides. The rest went by water, farther up with the canoes, being conducted by another guide, who always went before them with two of the said canoes, to discover on both sides the river the ambuscades of the Spaniards. These had also spies, who were very dextrous, and could at any

time give notice of all accidents or of the arrival of the
Pirates, six hours at least before they came to any place.
This day about noon they found themselves near a post,
called Torna Cavallos.   Here the guide of the canoes
began to cry aloud he perceived an ambuscade.   His
voice caused infinite joy to all the Pirates, as persuading
themselves they should find some provisions wherewith
to satiate their hunger, which was very great.   Being
come to the place, they found nobody in it, the Spaniards
who were there not long before being every one fled, and
leaving nothing behind unless it were a small number of
leather bags, all empty, and a few crumbs of bread
scattered upon the ground where they had eaten.   Being
angry at this misfortune, they pulled down a few little
huts which the Spaniards had made, and afterwards fell
to eating the leathern bags, as being desirous to afford
something to the ferment of their stomachs, which now
was grown so sharp that it did gnaw their very bowels,
having nothing else to prey upon.   Thus they made a
huge banquet upon those bags of leather, which doubtless
had been more grateful unto them, if divers quarrels had
not risen concerning who should have the greatest share.
By the circumference of the place, they conjectured five
hundred Spaniards, more or less, had been there.   And
these, finding no victuals, they were now infinitely
desirous to meet, intending to devour some of them
rather than perish.   Whom they would certainly in that
occasion have roasted or boiled, to satisfy their famine,
had they been able to take them.

After they had feasted themselves with those pieces of
leather, they quitted the place, and marched farther on,
till they came about night to another post called Torna
Munni.   Here they found another ambuscade, but as
barren and desert as the former.   They searched the
neighbouring woods, but could not find the least thing to
eat.   The Spaniards having been so provident as not to
leave behind them anywhere the least crumb of sus-

tenance, whereby the Pirates were now brought to the extremity aforementioned. Here again he was happy, that had reserved since noon any small piece of leather whereof to make his supper, drinking after it a good draught of water for his greatest comfort. Some persons, who never were out of their mothers' kitchen, may ask how these Pirates could eat, swallow and digest those pieces of leather, so hard and dry. To whom I only answer: That could they once experiment what hunger, or rather famine, is, they would certainly find the manner, by their own necessity, as the Pirates did. For these first took the leather, and sliced it in pieces. Then did they beat it between two stones, and rub it, often dipping it in the water of the river, to render it by these means supple and tender. Lastly, they scraped off the hair, and roasted or broiled it upon the fire. And being thus cooked they cut it into small morsels, and eat it, helping it down with frequent gulps of water, which by good fortune they had near at hand.

They continued their march the fifth day, and about noon came to a place called Barbacoa. Here likewise they found traces of another ambuscade, but the place totally as unprovided as the two preceeding were. At a small distance were to be seen several plantations, which they searched very narrowly, but could not find any person, animal or other thing that was capable of relieving their extreme and ravenous hunger. Finally, having ranged up and down and searched a long time, they found a certain grotto which seemed to be but lately hewn out of a rock, in which they found two sacks of meal, wheat and like things, with two great jars of wine, and certain fruits called Platanos. Captain Morgan knowing that some of his men were now, through hunger, reduced almost to the extremity of their lives, and fearing lest the major part should be brought into the same condition, caused all that was found to be distributed amongst them who were in greatest necessity. Having refreshed themselves with these victuals, they began to march anew with greater courage than ever. Such as could not well go for weakness were put into the canoes, and those commanded to land that were in them before. Thus they prosecuted their journey till late at night, at which time they came to a plantation where they took up their rest. But without eating anything at all ; for the Spaniards, as before, had swept away all manner of provisions, leaving not behind them the least signs of victuals.

On the sixth day they continued their march, part of them by land through the woods, and part by water in the canoes. Howbeit they were constrained to rest themselves very frequently by the way, both for the ruggedness thereof and the extreme weakness they were under. To this they endeavoured to occur, by eating some leaves of trees and green herbs, or grass, such as they could pick, for such was the miserable condition they were in. This day, at noon, they arrived at a plantation, where they found a barn full of maize. Immediately they beat down the doors, and fell to eating of it dry, as much as they could devour. Afterwards they distributed great quantity, giving to every man a good allowance thereof. Being thus provided, they prosecuted their journey, which having continued for the space of an hour or thereabouts, they met with an ambuscade of Indians. This they no sooner had discovered, but they threw away their maize, with the sudden hopes they conceived of finding all things in abundance. But after all this haste, they found themselves much deceived, they meeting neither Indians, nor victuals, nor anything else of what they had imagined. They saw notwithstanding on the other side of the river a troop of a hundred Indians, more or less, who all escaped away through the agility of their feet. Some few Pirates there were who leapt into the river, the sooner to reach the shore to see if they could take any of the said Indians prisoners. But all was in vain ; for being much more nimble on their feet than the Pirates, they easily baffled their endeavours. Neither did they only baffle them, but killed also two or three of the Pirates with their arrows, shouting at them at a distance, and crying : *Ha ! perros, á la savana, á la savana. Ha ! ye dogs, go to the plain, go to the plain.*

This day they could advance no farther, by reason they were necessitated to pass the river hereabouts to continue their march on the other side. Hereupon they took up their repose for that night. Howbeit their sleep was not heavy nor profound, for great murmurings were heard that night in the camp, many complaining of Captain Morgan and his conduct in that enterprize, and being desirous to return home. On the contrary, others would rather die there than go back one step from what they had undertaken. But others who had greater courage than any of these two parties did laugh and joke at all their discourses. In the meanwhile they had a guide who much comforted them, saying : *It would not be long before they met with people, from whom they should reap some considerable advantage.*

The seventh day in the morning they all made clean their arms, and every one discharged his pistol or musket, without bullet, to examine the security of their firelocks. This being done, they passed to the other side of the river in the canoes, leaving the post where they had rested the night before, called Santa Cruz. Thus they proceeded on their journey till noon, at which time they arrived at a village called Cruz. Being at a great distance as yet from the place, they perceived much smoke to arise out of the chimneys. The sight hereof afforded them great joy and hopes of finding people in the town, and afterwards what they most desired, which was plenty of good cheer. Thus they went on with as much haste as they could, making several arguments to one another upon those external signs, though all like castles built in the air. *For*, said they, *there is smoke coming out of every house, therefore they are making good fires, to roast and boil what we are to eat.* With other things to this purpose.

At length they arrived there in great haste, all sweating and panting, but found no person in the town, nor anything that was eatable wherewith to refresh themselves, unless it were good fires to warm themselves, which they wanted not. For the Spaniards before their departure, had every one set fire to his own house, excepting only the store-houses and stables belonging to the King.

They had not left behind them any beast whatsoever, either alive or dead. This occasioned much confusion in their minds, they not finding the least thing to lay hold on, unless it were some few cats and dogs, which they immediately killed and devoured with great appetite. At last in the King's stables they found by good fortune fifteen or sixteen jars of Peru wine, and a leather sack full of bread. But no sooner had they began to drink of the said wine when they fell sick, almost every man. This sudden disaster made them think that the wine was poisoned, which caused a new consternation in the whole camp, as judging themselves now to be irrecoverably lost. But the true reason was, their huge want of sustenance in that whole voyage, and the manifold sorts of trash which they had eaten upon that occasion. Their sickness was so great that day as caused them to remain there till the next morning, without being able to prosecute their journey as they used to do, in the afternoon. This village is seated in the latitude of 9 degrees and 2 minutes, North, being distant from the river of Chagre twenty-six Spanish leagues, and eight from Panama. Moreover, this is the last place to which boats or canoes can come; for which reason they built here store-houses, wherein to keep all sorts of merchandize, which hence to and from Panama are transported upon the backs of mules. ·

Here, therefore, Captain Morgan was constrained to

leave his canoes and land all his men, though never so weak in their bodies. But lest the canoes should be surprized, or take up too many men for their defence, he resolved to send them all back to the place where the boats were, excepting one, which he caused to be hidden, to the intent it might serve to carry intelligence according to the exigence of affairs. Many of the Spaniards and Indians belonging to this village were fled to the plantations thereabouts. Hereupon Captain Morgan gave express orders that none should dare to go out of the village, except in whole companies of a hundred together. The occasion hereof was his fear lest the enemies should take an advantage upon his men, by any sudden assault. Notwithstanding, one party of English soldiers, stickled not to contravene these commands, being tempted with the desire of finding victuals. But these were soon glad to fly into the town again, being assaulted with great fury by some Spaniards and Indians, who snatched up one of the Pirates, and carried him away prisoner. Thus the vigilance and care of Captain Morgan was not sufficient to prevent every accident that might happen.

On the eighth day, in the morning, Captain Morgan sent two hundred men before the body of his army, to discover the way to Panama, and see if they had laid any ambuscades therein. Especially considering that the places by which they were to pass were very fit for that purpose, the paths being so narrow that only ten or twelve persons could march in a file, and oftentimes not so many. Having marched about the space of ten hours, they came to a place called Quebrada Obscura. Here, all on a sudden, three or four thousand arrows were shot at them, without being able to perceive whence they came, or who shot them. The place whence it was presumed they were shot was a high rocky mountain, excavated from one side to the other, wherein was a grotto that went through it, only capable of admitting one horse, or other beast laded. This multitude of arrows caused a huge alarm among the Pirates, especially because they could not discover the place whence they were discharged. At last, seeing no more arrows to appear, they marched a little farther, and entered into a wood. Here they perceived some Indians to fly as fast as they could possible before them, to take the advantage of another post, and thence observe the march of the Pirates. There remained notwithstanding one troop of Indians upon the place, with full design to fight and defend themselves. This combat they performed with huge courage, till such time as their captain fell to the ground wounded, who although he was now in despair of life, yet his valour being greater than his strength, would demand no quarter, but, endeavouring to raise himself, with undaunted mind laid hold of his azagaya, or javelin, and struck at one of the Pirates. But before he could second the blow, he was shot to death with a pistol. This was also the fate of many of his companions, who like good and courageous soldiers lost their lives with their captain, for the defence of their country.

The Pirates endeavoured, as much as was possible, to lay hold on some of the Indians and take them prisoners. But they being infinitely swifter than the Pirates, every one escaped, leaving eight Pirates dead upon the place and ten wounded. Yea, had the Indians been more dextrous in military affairs, they might have defended that passage and not let one sole man to pass. Within a little while after they came to a large campaign field open, and full of variegated meadows. From here they could perceive at a distance before them a parcel of Indians, who stood on the top of a mountain, very near the way by which the Pirates were to pass. They sent a troop of fifty men, the nimblest they could pick out, to see if they could catch any of them, and afterwards force them to declare whereabouts their companions had their mansions. But all their industry was in vain, for they escaped through their nimbleness, and presently afterwards showed themselves in another place, hallooing to the English, and crying : *Á la savana, á la savana cornudos, perros Ingleses;* that is, *To the plain, to the plain, ye cuckolds, ye English dogs !* While these things passed, the ten Pirates that were wounded a little before were dressed and plastered up.

At this place there was a wood, and on each side thereof a mountain. The Indians had possessed themselves of the one, and the Pirates took possession of the other that was opposite to it. Captain Morgan was persuaded that in the wood the Spaniards had placed an ambuscade, as lying so conveniently for that purpose. Hereupon he sent before two hundred men to search it. The Spaniards and Indians perceiving the Pirates to descend the mountains, did so too, as if they designed to attack them. But being got into the wood, out of sight of the Pirates, they disappeared, and were seen no more, leaving the passage open to them.

About night there fell a great rain, which caused the Pirates to march the faster and seek everywhere for houses wherein to preserve their arms from being wet. But the Indians had set fire to every one thereabouts, and transported all their cattle to remote places, to the end that the pirates, finding neither houses nor victuals, might be constrained to return homewards. Notwithstanding, after diligent search, they found a few little huts belonging to shepherds, but in them nothing to eat. These not being capable of holding many men, they placed in them out of every company a small number, who kept the arms of all the rest of the army. Those who remained in the open field endured much hardship that night, the rain not ceasing to fall until the morning.

The next morning, about break of day, being the ninth of this tedious journey, Captain Morgan continued his march while the fresh air of the morning lasted. For the clouds then hanging as yet over their heads were much more favourable to them than the scorching rays of the sun, by reason the way was now more difficult and laborious than all the preceding. After two hours' march, they discovered a troop of about twenty Spaniards, who observed the motions of the Pirates. They endeavoured to catch some of them, but could lay hold on none, they suddenly disappearing, and absconding themselves in caves among the rocks, totally unknown to the Pirates. At last they came to a high mountain, which, when they ascended, they discovered from the top thereof the South Sea. This happy sight, as if it were the end of their labours, caused infinite joy among all the Pirates. Hence they could descry also one ship, and six boats, which were set forth from Panama, and sailed towards the islands of Tovago and Tovagilla. Having descended this mountain, they came to a vale, in which they found great quantity of cattle, whereof they killed good store. Here while some were employed in killing and flaying of cows, horses, bulls and chiefly asses, of which there was greatest number, others busied themselves in kindling of fires and getting wood wherewith to roast them. Thus cutting the flesh of these animals into convenient pieces, or gobbets, they threw them into the fire, and, half carbonadoed or roasted, they devoured them with incredible haste and appetite. For such was their hunger that they more resembled cannibals than Europeans at this banquet, the blood many times running down from their beards to the middle of their bodies.

Having satisfied their hunger with these delicious meats, Captain Morgan ordered them to continue the march. Here again he sent before the main body fifty men, with intent to take some prisoners, if possibly they could. For he seemed now to be much concerned that in nine days time he could not meet one person who might inform him of the condition and forces of the Spaniards. About evening they discovered a troop of two hundred Spaniards, more or less, who hallooed to the Pirates, but these could not understand what they said.

A little while after they came the first time within sight
of the highest steeple of Panama. This steeple they no
sooner had discovered than they began to show signs of
extreme joy, casting up their hats into the air, leaping for
mirth, and shouting, even just as if they had already obtained the victory and entire accomplishment of their
designs. All their trumpets were sounded and every
drum beaten, in token of this universal acclamation and
huge alacrity of their minds. Thus they pitched their
camp for that night with general content of the whole
army, waiting with impatience for the morning, at which
time they intended to attack the city. This evening
there appeared fifty horse, who came out of the city,
hearing the noise of the drums and trumpets of the
Pirates, to observe, as it was thought, their motions.
They came almost within musket-shot of the army, being
preceded by a trumpet that sounded marvellously well.
Those on horseback hallooed aloud to the Pirates, and
threatened them, saying, *Perros ! nos veremos*, that is,
Ye dogs ! we shall meet ye. Having made this menace,
they returned into the city, excepting only seven or eight
horsemen who remained hovering thereabouts, to watch
what motions the Pirates made. Immediately after, the
city began to fire and ceased not to play with their
biggest guns all night long against the camp, but with
little or no harm to the Pirates, whom they could not
conveniently reach. About this time also the two hundred Spaniards whom the pirates had seen in the afternoon appeared again within sight, making resemblance
as if they would block up the passages, to the intent no
Pirates might escape the hands of their forces. But the
Pirates, who were now in a manner besieged, instead of
conceiving any fear of their blockades, as soon as they
had placed sentries about their camp, began every one
to open their satchels, and without any preparation of
napkins or plates, fell to eating very heartily the remaining pieces of bulls and horses flesh which they had re-

served since noon. This being done, they laid themselves down to sleep upon the grass with great repose and huge satisfaction, expecting only with impatience the dawning of the next day.

On the tenth day, betimes in the morning, they put all their men in convenient order, and with drums and trumpets sounding, continued their march directly towards the city. But one of the guides desired Captain Morgan not to take the common highway that led thither, fearing lest they should find in it much resistance and many ambuscades. He presently took his advice, and chose another way that went through the wood, although very irksome and difficult. Thus the Spaniards, perceiving the Pirates had taken another way, which they scarce had thought on or believed, were compelled to leave their stops and batteries, and come out to meet them. The Governor of Panama put his forces in order, consisting of two squadrons, four regiments of foot, and a huge number of wild bulls, which were driven by a great number of Indians, with some negroes and others, to help them.

The Pirates, being now upon their march, came to the top of a little hill, whence they had a large prospect of the city and campaign country underneath. Here they discovered the forces of the people of Panama, extended in battle array, which, when they perceived to be so numerous, they were suddenly surprised with great fear, much doubting the fortune of the day. Yea, few or none there were but wished themselves at home, or at least free from the obligation of that engagement, wherein they perceived their lives must be so narrowly concerned. Having been some time at a stand, in a wavering condition of mind, they at last reflected upon the straits they had brought themselves into, and that now they ought of necessity either to fight resolutely or die, for no quarter could be expected from an enemy against whom they had committed so many cruelties on all occasions. Hereupon they encouraged one another, and resolved either to conquer, or spend the very last drop of blood in their bodies. Afterwards they divided themselves into three battalions, or troops, sending before them one of two hundred buccaneers, which sort of people are infinitely dextrous at shooting with guns. Thus the Pirates left the hill and descended, marching directly towards the Spaniards, who were posted in a spacious field, waiting for their coming. As soon as they drew near them, the Spaniards began to shout, and cry, *Viva el Rey! God save the King!* and immediately their horse began to move against the Pirates. But the field being full of quags and very soft under foot, they could not ply to and fro and wheel about, as they desired. The two hundred buccaneers who went before, every one putting one knee to the ground, gave them a full volley of shot, wherewith the battle was instantly kindled very hot. The Spaniards defended themselves very courageously, acting all they could possibly perform, to disorder the Pirates. Their foot, in like manner, endeavoured to second the horse, but were constrained by the Pirates to separate from them. Thus finding themselves frustrated of their designs, they attempted to drive the bulls against them at their backs, and by this means put them into disorder. But the greatest part of that wild cattle ran away, being frightened with the noise of the battle. And some few that broke through the English companies did no other harm than to tear the colours in pieces : whereas the buccaneers, shooting them dead, left not one to trouble them thereabouts.

The battle having now continued for the space of two hours, at the end thereof the greatest part of the Spanish horse was ruined and almost all killed. The rest fled away. Which being perceived by the foot, and that they could not possibly prevail, they discharged the shot they had in their muskets, and throwing them on the ground, betook themselves to flight, every one which way he could run. The Pirates could not possibly follow them, as being too much harassed and wearied with the long journey they had lately made. Many of them, not being able to fly whither they desired, hid themselves for that present among the shrubs of the sea-side. But very unfortunately ; for most of them being found out by the Pirates, were instantly killed, without giving quarter to any. Some religious men were brought prisoners before Captain Morgan ; but he being deaf to their cries and lamentations, commanded them all to be immediately pistoled, which was accordingly done. Soon after they brought a captain to his presence, whom he examined very strictly about several things ; particularly, wherein consisted the forces of those of Panama. To which he answered : Their whole strength did consist in four hundred horse, twenty-four companies of foot, each being of one hundred men complete, sixty Indians and some negroes, who were to drive two thousand wild bulls and cause them to run over the English camp, and thus by breaking their files put them into a total disorder and confusion. He discovered more, that in the city they had made trenches, and raised batteries in several places, in all which they had placed many guns, and that at the entry of the highway which led to the city they had built a fort, which was mounted with eight great guns of brass, and defended by fifty men.

Captain Morgan, having heard this information, gave orders instantly they should march another way. But before setting forth, he made a review of all his men, whereof he found both killed and wounded a considerable number, and much greater than had been believed. Of the Spaniards were found six hundred dead upon the place, besides the wounded and prisoners. The Pirates were nothing discouraged, seeing their number so much diminished, but rather filled with greater pride than before, perceiving what huge advantage they had obtained against their enemies. Thus having rested themselves some while, they prepared to march courageously towards

the city, plighting their oaths to one another in general
they would fight till never a man was left alive. With
this courage they recommenced their march, either to
conquer or be conquered, carrying with them all the
prisoners.

They found much difficulty in their approach to the
city. For within the town the Spaniards had placed
many great guns, at several quarters thereof, some of
which were charged with small pieces of iron, and others
with musket-bullets. With all these they saluted the
Pirates, at their drawing nigh to the place, and gave them
full and frequent broadsides, firing at them incessantly.
Whence it came to pass that unavoidably they lost, at
every step they advanced, great numbers of men. But
neither these manifest dangers of their lives, nor the
sight of so many of their own as dropped down continually at their sides, could deter them from advancing
farther, and gaining ground every moment upon the
enemy. Thus, although the Spaniards never ceased to
fire and act the best they could for their defence, yet
notwithstanding they were forced to deliver the city
after the space of three hours' combat. And the Pirates,
having now possessed themselves thereof, both killed and
destroyed as many as attempted to make the least opposition against them. The inhabitants had caused the
best of their goods to be transported to more remote and
occult places. Howbeit they found within the city as
yet several warehouses, very well stocked with all sorts
of merchandize, as well silks and cloths as linen, and
other things of considerable value. As soon as the first
fury of their entrance into the city was over, Captain
Morgan assembled all his men at a certain place which
he assigned, and there commanded them under very
great penalties that none of them should dare to drink or
taste any wine. The reason he gave for this injunction
was, because he had received private intelligence that it
had been all poisoned by the Spaniards. Howbeit it was

the opinion of many that he gave these prudent orders to prevent the debauchery of his people, which he foresaw would be very great at the beginning, after so much hunger sustained by the way—fearing withal lest the Spaniards, seeing them in wine, should rally their forces and fall upon the city, and use them as inhumanly as they had used the inhabitants before.

CHAPTER VI.

Captain Morgan sends several canoes and boats to the South Sea. He sets fire to the City of Panama. Robberies and cruelties committed there by the Pirates till their re urn to the Castle of Chagre.

CAPTAIN MORGAN, as soon as he had placed guards at several quarters where he thought necessary, both within and without the city of Panama, immediately commanded twenty-five men to seize a great boat, which had stuck in the mud of the port for want of water at a low tide, so that she could not put out to sea. The same day, about noon, he caused certain men privately to set fire to several great edifices of the city, nobody knowing whence the fire proceeded nor who were the authors thereof, much less what motives persuaded Captain Morgan thereto, which are as yet unknown to this day. The fire increased so fast that before night the greatest part of the city was in a flame. Captain Morgan endeavoured to make the public believe the Spaniards had been the cause thereof, which suspicions he surmised among his own people, perceiving they reflected upon him for that action. Many of the Spaniards, as also some of the Pirates, used all the means possible either to extinguish the flame, or by blowing up houses with gunpowder, and pulling down others, to stop its progress. But all was in vain; for in less than half an hour it consumed a whole street. All the houses of this city were built with cedar, being of very curious and magnificent structure. and richly adorned within, especially with hangings and paintings, whereof part was

already transported out of the Pirates way, and another
great part was consumed by the voracity of the fire.

There belonged to this city (which is also the head of
a bishopric) eight monasteries, whereof seven were for men
and one for women, two stately churches and one hospital.
The churches and monasteries were all richly adorned
with altar-pieces and paintings, huge quantity of gold and
silver, with other precious things ; all which the ecclesiastics had hidden and concealed. Besides which ornaments,
here were to be seen two thousand houses of magnificent
and prodigious building, being all or the greatest part
inhabited by merchants of that country, who are vastly
rich. For the rest of the inhabitants of lesser quality
and tradesmen, this city contained five thousand houses
more. Here were also great number of stables, which
served for the horses and mules, that carry all the plate,
belonging as well to the King of Spain as to private men,
towards the coast of the North Sea. The neighbouring
fields belonging to this city are all cultivated with fertile
plantations and pleasant gardens, which afford delicious
prospects to the inhabitants the whole year long.

The Genoese had in this city of Panama a stately
and magnificent house, belonging to their trade and
commerce of negroes. This building likewise was commanded by Captain Morgan to be set on fire ; whereby it
was burnt to the very ground. Besides which pile of building, there were consumed to the number of two hundred
warehouses, and great number of slaves, who had hid
themselves therein, together with an infinite multitude of
sacks of meal. The fire of all which houses and build-
ings was seen to continue four weeks after the day it began. The Pirates in the meanwhile, at least the greatest
parts of them, camped some time without the city, fearing
and expecting that the Spaniards would come and fight
them anew. For it was known that they had an incomparable number of men more than the Pirates were.
This occasioned them to keep the field, thereby to pre-

serve their forces united, which now were very much diminished by the losses of the preceding battles ; as also because they had a great many wounded, all which they had put into one of the churches which alone remained standing, the rest being consumed by the fire. Moreover, beside these decreases of their men, Captain Morgan had sent a convoy one hundred and fifty men to the Castle of Chagre, to carry the news of his victory obtained against Panama.

They saw many times whole troops of Spaniards cruize to and fro in the campaign fields, which gave them occasion to suspect their rallying anew. Yet they never had the courage to attempt anything against the Pirates. In the afternoon of this fatal day Captain Morgan re-entered again the city with his troops, to the intent that every one might take up his lodgings, which now they could hardly find, very few houses having escaped the desolation of the fire. Soon after they fell to seeking very carefully among the ruins and ashes for utensils of plate or gold, which peradventure were not quite wasted by the flames. And of such things they found no small number in several places, especially in wells and cisterns, where the Spaniards had hid them from the covetous search of the Pirates.

The next day Captain Morgan dispatched away two troops of Pirates, of one hundred and fifty men each, being all very stout soldiers and well armed, with orders to seek for the inhabitants of Panama who were escaped from the hands of their enemies. These men, having made several excursions up and down the campaign fields, woods and mountains, adjoining to Panama, returned after two days' time, bringing with them above two hundred prisoners, between men, women and slaves. The same day returned also the boat above mentioned, which Captain Morgan had sent into the South Sea, bringing with her three other boats, which they had taken in a little while. But all

these prizes they could willingly have given, yea, although
they had employed greater labour into the bargain, for
one certain galleon, which miraculously escaped their
industry, being very richly laden with all the King's plate
and great quantity of riches of gold, pearl, jewels and
other most precious goods, of all the best and richest
merchants of Panama. On board of this galleon were
also the religious women, belonging to the nunnery of
the said city, who had embarked with them all the ornaments of their church, consisting in great quantity of gold,
plate and other things of great value.

The strength of this galleon was nothing considerable,
as having only seven guns, and ten or twelve muskets
for its whole defence, being on the other side very ill
provided of victuals and other necessaries, with great
want of fresh water, and having no more sails than the
uppermost sails of the main mast. This description of
the said ship, the Pirates received from certain persons,
who had spoken with seven mariners belonging to the
galleon, at such time as they came ashore in the cock-boat,
to take in fresh water. Hence they concluded for certain
they might easily have taken the said vessel, had they
given her chase, and pursued her, as they ought to have
done, especially considering the said galleon could not
long subsist abroad at sea. But they were impeded from
following this vastly rich prize, by gluttony and drunkenness, having plentifully debauched themselves with
several sorts of rich wines they found there ready to their
hands. So that they chose rather to satiate their appetite
with the things abovementioned, than to lay hold on the
occasion of such a huge advantage, although this only
prize would certainly have been of far greater value and
consequence to them than all they secured at Panama,
and other places thereabouts. The next day, repenting
of their negligence, and being totally wearied of the vices
and debaucheries aforesaid, they sent forth to sea another
boat well armed, to pursue with all speed imaginable the

said galleon. But their present care and diligence was in vain, the Spaniards who were on board the said ship having received intelligence of the danger they were in one or two days before, while the Pirates were cruizing so near them, whereupon they fled to places more remote and unknown to their enemies.

Notwithstanding, the Pirates found in the ports of the islands of Tavoga and Tavogilla several boats that were laden with many sorts of very good merchandize : all which they took and brought to Panama ; where, being arrived, they made an exact relation of all that had passed while they were abroad to Captain Morgan. The prisoners confirmed what the Pirates had said, adding thereto, that they undoubtedly knew whereabouts the said galleon might be at that present, but that it was very probable they had been relieved before now from other places. These relations stirred up Captain Morgan anew to send forth all the boats that were in the port of Panama, with design to seek and pursue the said galleon till they could find her. The boats aforesaid, being in all four, set sail from Panama, and having spent eight days in cruizing to and fro, and searching several ports and creeks, they lost all their hopes of finding what they so earnestly sought for. Hereupon they resolved to return to the isles of Tavoga and Tavogilla. Here they found a reasonable good ship, that was newly come from Payta, being laden with cloth, soap, sugar and biscuit, with twenty thousand pieces of eight in ready money. This vessel they instantly seized, not finding the least resistance from any person within her. Near to the said ship was also a boat, whereof in like manner they possessed themselves. Upon the boat they laded great part of the merchandizes they had found in the ship, together with some slaves they had taken in the said islands. With this purchase they returned to Panama, something better satisfied of their voyage, yet withal much discontented they could not meet with the galleon.

The convoy which Captain Morgan had sent to the
castle of Chagre returned much about the same time,
bringing with them very good news. For while Captain
Morgan was upon his journey to Panama, those he had
left in the castle of Chagre had sent forth to sea two
boats to exercise piracy. These happened to meet with
a Spanish ship, which they began to chase within sight of
the castle. This being perceived by the Pirates that
were in the castle, they put forth Spanish colours, thereby
to allure and deceive the ship that fled before the boats.
Thus the poor Spaniards, thinking to refuge themselves
under the castle and the guns thereof, by flying into the
port, were caught in a snare and made prisoners, where
they thought to find defence. The cargo which was
found on board the said vessel, consisted in victuals and
provisions, that were all eatable things. Nothing could
be more opportune than this prize for the castle, where
they had begun already to experience great scarcity of
things of this kind.

This good fortune of the garrison of Chagre gave
occasion to Captain Morgan to remain longer time than
he had determined at Panama. And hereupon he ordered
several new excursions to be made into the whole country round about the city. So that while the Pirates at
Panama were employed in these expeditions, those at
Chagre were busied in exercising piracy upon the North
Sea. Captain Morgan used to send forth daily parties
of two hundred men, to make inroads into all the fields
and country thereabouts, and when one party came back,
another consisting of two hundred more was ready to go
forth. By this means they gathered in a short time a
huge quantity of riches, and no lesser number of prisoners. These, being brought into the city, were presently
put to the most exquisite tortures imaginable, to make
them confess both other people's goods and their own.
Here it happened, that one poor and miserable wretch
was found in the house of a gentleman of great quality,

who had put on, amidst that confusion of things, a pair of taffety breeches belonging to his master with a little silver key hanging at the strings thereof. This, being perceived by the Pirates they immediately asked him where was the cabinet of the said key? His answer was: he knew not what was become of it, but only that finding those breeches in his master's house, he had made bold to wear them. Not being able to extort any other confession out of him, they first put him upon the rack, wherewith they inhumanly disjointed his arms. After this, they twisted a cord about his forehead, which they wrung so hard, that his eyes appeared as big as eggs, and were ready to fall out of his skull. But neither with these torments could they obtain any positive answer to their demands. Whereupon they soon after hung him up, giving him infinite blows and stripes, while he was under that intolerable pain and posture of body. Afterwards they cut off his nose and ears, and singed his face with burning straw, till he could speak nor lament his misery no longer. Then losing all hopes of hearing any confession from his mouth, they commanded a negro to run him through with a lance, which put an end to his life and a period to their cruel and inhuman tortures. After this execrable manner did many others of those miserable prisoners finish their days, the common sport and recreation of these Pirates being these and other tragedies not inferior.

They spared, in these their cruelties, no sex nor condition whatsoever. For as to religious persons and priests, they granted them less quarter than to others, unless they could produce a considerable sum of money, capable of being a sufficient ransom. Women themselves were no better used, and Captain Morgan, their leader and commander, gave them no good example in this point. For as soon as any beautiful woman was brought as a prisoner to his presence, he used all the means he could, both of rigour and mildness, to bend her to his

pleasure : for a confirmation of which assertion, I shall
here give my reader a short history of a lady, whose
virtue and constancy ought to be transmitted to posterity,
as a memorable example of her sex.

Among the prisoners that were brought by the Pirates
from the islands of Tavoga and Tavogilla, there was
found a gentlewoman of good quality, as also no less
virtue and chastity, who was wife to one of the richest
merchants of all those countries. Her years were but
few, and her beauty so great as peradventure I may
doubt whether in all Europe any could be found to sur-
pass her perfections either of comeliness or honesty.
Her husband, at that present, was absent from home,
being gone as far as the kingdom of Peru, about great
concerns of commerce and trade, wherein his employments did lie. This virtuous lady, likewise, hearing that
Pirates were coming to assault the city of Panama, had
absented herself thence in the company of other friends
and relations, thereby to preserve her life, amidst the
dangers which the cruelties and tyrannies of those hard-
hearted enemies did seem to menace to every citizen.
But no sooner had she appeared in the presence of Captain Morgan than he commanded they should lodge her
in a certain apartment by herself, giving her a negress,
or black woman, to wait upon her, and that she should
be treated with all the respect and regale due to her
quality. The poor afflicted lady did beg, with multitude
of sobs and tears, she might be suffered to lodge among
the other prisoners, her relations, fearing lest that
unexpected kindness of the commander might prove to
be a design upon her chastity. But Captain Morgan
would by no means hearken to her petition, and all he
commanded, in answer thereto, was, she should be
treated with more particular care than before, and have
her victuals carried from his own table.

This lady had formerly heard very strange reports
concerning the Pirates, before their arrival at Panama,

intimating to her, as if they were not men, but, as they said, heretics, who did neither invoke the Blessed Trinity, nor believe in Jesus Christ. But now she began to have better thoughts of them than ever before, having experienced the manifold civilities of Captain Morgan, especially hearing him many times to swear by the name of God, and of Jesus Christ, in whom, she was persuaded, they did not believe. Neither did she now think them to be so bad, or to have the shapes of beasts, as from the relations of several people she had oftentimes heard. For as to the name of *robbers* or *thieves*, which was commonly given them by others, she wondered not much at it, seeing, as she said, that among all nations of the universe, there were to be found some wicked men, who naturally coveted to possess the goods of others. Conformable to the persuasion of this lady was the opinion of another woman, of weak understanding, at Panama, who used to say, before the Pirates came thither, she desired very much and had a great curiosity to see one of those men called Pirates ; for as much as her husband had often told her, that they were not men, like others, but rather irrational beasts. This silly woman, at last happened to see the first of them, cried out aloud, saying : *Jesus bless me ! these thieves are like us Spaniards.*

This false civility of Captain Morgan, wherewith he used this lady, was soon after changed into barbarous cruelty. For, three or four days being past, he came to see her, and the virtuous lady constantly repulsed him, with all the civility imaginable and many humble and modest expressions of her mind. But Captain Morgan still persisted in his disorderly request, presenting her withal with much pearl, gold and all that he had got that was precious and valuable in that voyage. But the lady being in no manner willing to consent thereto, nor accept his presents, and showing herself in all respects like Susannah for constancy, he presently changed note, and began to speak to her in another tone, threatening her with a thousand cruelties and hard usages at his hands. To all these things she gave this resolute and positive answer, than which no other could be extorted from her : *Sir, my life is in your hands; but as to my body, in relation to that which you would persuade me to, my soul shall sooner be separated from it, through the violence of your arms, then I shall condescend to your request.* No sooner had Captain Morgan understood this heroic resolution of her mind than he commanded her to be stripped of the best of her apparel, and imprisoned in a darksome and stinking cellar. Here she had allowed her an extremely small quantity of meat and drink, wherewith she had much ado to sustain her life for a few days.

Under this hardship the constant and virtuous lady ceased not to pray daily to God Almighty, for constancy and patience against the cruelties of Captain Morgan. But he being now throughly convinced of her chaste resolutions, as also desirous to conceal the cause of her confinement and hard usage, since many of the Pirates, his companions, did compassionate her condition, laid many false accusations to her charge, giving to understand she held intelligence with the Spaniards, and corresponded with them by letters, abusing thereby his former lenity and kindness. I myself was an eye witness to these things here related, and could never have judged such constancy of mind and virtuous chastity to be found in the world, if my own eyes and ears had not informed me thereof. But of this incomparable lady I shall say something more hereafter in its proper place ; whereupon I shall leave her at present, to continue my history.

Captain Morgan, having now been at Panama the full space of three weeks, commanded all things to be put in order for his departure. To this effect, he gave orders to every company of his men, to seek out for so many beasts of carriage as might suffice to convey the whole spoil of the city to the river where his canoes lay. About this time a great rumour was spread in the city, of a considerable number of Pirates who intended to leave Captain Morgan ; and that, by taking a ship which was in the port, they determined to go and rob upon the South Sea till they had got as much as they thought fit, and then return homewards by the way of the East Indies into Europe. For which purpose, they had already gathered great quantity of provisions, which they had hidden in private places, with sufficient store of powder, bullets and all other sorts of ammunition : likewise some great guns, belonging to the town, muskets and other things, wherewith they designed not only to equip the said vessel but also to fortify themselves and raise batteries in some island or other, which might serve them for a place of refuge.

This design had certainly taken effect as they intended, had not Captain Morgan had timely advice thereof given him by one of their comrades. Hereupon he instantly commanded the mainmast of the said ship should be cut down and burnt, together with all the other boats that were in the port. Hereby the intentions of all or most of his companions were totally frustrated. After this Captain Morgan sent forth many of the Spaniards into the adjoining fields and country, to seek for money wherewith to ransom not only themselves but also all the rest of the prisoners, as likewise the ecclesiastics, both secular and regular. Moreover he commanded all the artillery of the town to be spoiled, that is to say, nailed and stopped up. At the same time he sent out a strong company of men to seek for the Governor of Panama, of whom intelligence was brought that he had laid several ambuscades in the way, by which he ought to pass at his return. But those who were sent upon this design returned soon after, saying they had not found any sign or appearance of any such ambuscades ; for a confirmation whereof, they brought with them some prisoners they had taken, who declared that the said Governor had had

an intention of making some opposition by the way, but
that the men whom he had designed to effect it were
unwilling to undertake any such enterprize; so that for
want of means, he could not put his design in execution.

On the 24th of February of the year 1671 Captain
Morgan departed from the city of Panama, or rather
from the place where the said city of Panama did stand;
of the spoils whereof he carried with him one hundred
and seventy-five beasts of carriage, laden with silver,
gold and other precious things, besides six hundred
prisoners, more or less, between men, women, children and slaves. That day they came to a river that
passes through a delicious campaign field, at the distance of a league from Panama. Here Captain Morgan put all his forces into good order of martial array,
in such manner that the prisoners were in the middle of
the camp, surrounded on all sides with Pirates. At which
present conjuncture nothing else was to be heard but
lamentations, cries, shrieks and doleful sighs, of so many
women and children, who were persuaded Captain
Morgan designed to transport them all, and carry them
into his own country for slaves. Besides that, among all
those miserable prisoners, there was extreme hunger
and thirst endured at that time; which hardship and
misery Captain Morgan designedly caused them to sustain, with intent to excite them more earnestly to seek
for money wherewith to ransom themselves, according
to the tax he had set upon every one. Many of the
women begged of Captain Morgan upon their knees,
with infinite sighs and tears, he would permit them to
return to Panama, there to live in company of their dear
husbands and children, in little huts of straw which they
would erect, seeing they had no houses until the rebuild-
ing of the city. But his answer was: he came not thither
to hear lamentations and cries, but rather to seek
money. Therefore they ought to seek out for that in

the first place, wherever it were to be had, and bring it to him, otherwise he would assuredly transport them all to such places whither they cared not to go.

The next day, when the march began, those lamentable cries and shrieks were renewed, in so much as it would have caused compassion in the hardest heart to hear them. But Captain Morgan, a man little given to mercy, was not moved therewith in the least. They marched in the same order as was said before ; one party of the Pirates preceding in the van, the prisoners in the middle, and the rest of the Pirates in the rear-guard, by whom the miserable Spaniards were, at every step, punched and thrust in their backs and sides, with the blunt end of their arms, to make them march the faster. That beautiful and virtuous lady, of whom we made mention heretofore for her unparalleled constancy and chastity, was led prisoner by herself, between two Pirates who guarded her. Her lamentations now did pierce the skies, seeing herself carried away into foreign captivity, often crying to the Pirates, and telling them : *That she had given order to two religious persons, in whom she had relied, to go to a certain place, and fetch so much money as her ransom did amount to. That they had promised faithfully to do it, but having obtained the said money, instead of bringing it to her, they had employed it another way, to ransom some of their own and particular friends.* This ill action of theirs was discovered by a slave, who brought a letter to the said lady. Her complaints, and the cause thereof, being brought to the ears of Captain Morgan, he thought fit to enquire thereinto. Having found the thing to be true, especially hearing it confirmed by the confession of the said religious men, though under some frivolous excuses, of having diverted the money but for a day or two, within which time they expected more sums to repay it, he gave liberty to the said lady, whom otherwise he designed to transport to Jamaica. But in the meanwhile he detained the said religious men,

as prisoners in her place, using them according to the
deserts of their incompassionate intrigues.

As soon as Captain Morgan arrived, upon his march,
at the town called Cruz, situated on the banks of the
river Chagre, as was mentioned before, he commanded
an order to be published among the prisoners, that within the space of three days every one of them should
bring in his ransom, under the penalty aforementioned
of being transported to Jamaica. In the meanwhile he
gave orders, for so much rice and maize to be collected
thereabouts as was necessary for the victualling all his
ships. At this place some of the prisoners were ransomed,
but many others could not bring in their moneys in so
short time. Hereupon he continued his voyage, leaving the village on the 5th day of March next following,
and carrying with him all the spoil that ever he could
transport. From this village he likewise led away some
new prisoners, who were inhabitants of the said place.
So that these prisoners were added to those of Panama
who had not as yet paid their ransoms, and all transported. But the two religious men, who had diverted
the money belonging to the lady, were ransomed three
days after their imprisonment, by other persons who had
more compassion for their condition than they had
showed for hers. About the middle of the way to the
castle of Chagre, Captain Morgan commanded them to
be placed in due order, according to their custom, and
caused every one to be sworn, that they had reserved
nor concealed nothing privately to themselves, even not
so much as the value of sixpence. This being done,
Captain Morgan having had some experience that those
lewd fellows would not much stickle to swear falsely
in points of interest, he commanded every one to be
searched very strictly, both in their clothes and satchels
and everywhere it might be presumed they had reserved
anything. Yea, to the intent this order might not be ill
taken by his companions, he permitted himself to be

searched, even to the very soles of his shoes. To this effect, by common consent, there was assigned one out of every company, to be the searchers of all the rest. The French Pirates that went on this expedition with Captain Morgan, were not well satisfied with this new custom of searching. Yet their number being less than that of the English, they were forced to submit to it, as well as the others had done before them. The search being over, they re-embarked in their canoes and boats, which attended them on the river, and arrived at the castle of Chagre on the 9th day of the said month of March. Here they found all things in good order, excepting the wounded men, whom they had left there at the time of their departure. For of these the greatest number were dead, through the wounds they had received.

From Chagre, Captain Morgan sent presently after his arrival, a great boat to Porto Bello, wherein were all the prisoners he had taken at the Isle of St. Catharine, demanding by them a considerable ransom for the castle of Chagre, where he then was, threatening otherwise to ruin and demolish it even to the ground. To this message those of Porto Bello made answer: They would not give one farthing towards the ransom of the said castle, and that the English might do with it as they pleased. This answer being come, the dividend was made of all the spoil they had purchased in that voyage. Thus every company, and every particular person therein included, received their portion of what was got: or rather, what part thereof Captain Morgan was pleased to give them. For so it was, that the rest of his companions, even of his own nation, complained of his proceedings in this particular, and feared not to tell him openly to his face, that he had reserved the best jewels to himself. For they judged it impossible that no greater share should belong to them than two hundred pieces of eight *per capita*, of so many valuable booties and robberies

as they had obtained. Which small sum they thought
too little reward for so much labour and such huge and
manifest dangers as they had so often exposed their lives
to. But Captain Morgan was deaf to all these and many
other complaints of this kind, having designed in his
mind to cheat them of as much as he could.

At last Captain Morgan finding himself obnoxious to
many obloquies and detractions among his people, began
to fear the consequence thereof, and hereupon thinking it
unsafe to remain any longer time at Chagre, he commanded the ordnance of the said castle to be carried on board
his ship. Afterwards he caused the greatest part of the
walls to be demolished, and the edifices to be burnt, and
as many other things spoiled and ruined as could conveniently be done in a short while. These orders being
performed, he went secretly on board his own ship, without giving any notice of his departure to his companions,
nor calling any council, as he used to do. Thus he set
sail, and put out to sea, not bidding anybody adieu, being
only followed by three or four vessels of the whole fleet.
These were such (as the French Pirates believed) as
went shares with Captain Morgan, towards the best and
greatest part of the spoil which had been concealed from
them in the dividend. The Frenchmen could very
willingly have revenged this affront upon Captain Morgan
and those that followed him, had they found themselves
with sufficient means to encounter him at sea. But they
were destitute of most things necessary thereto. Yea,
they had much ado to find sufficient victuals and provisions for their voyage to Jamaica, he having left them
totally unprovided of all things.

CHAPTER VII.

Of a voyage made by the Author, along the coasts of Costa Rica, at his return towards Jamaica. What happened most remarkable in the said voyage. Some observations made by him at that time.

CAPTAIN MORGAN left us all in such a miserable condition, as might serve for a lively representation of what reward attends wickedness at the latter end of life. Whence we ought to have learned how to regulate and amend our actions for the future. However it was, our affairs being reduced to such a posture, every company that was left behind, whether English or French, were compelled to seek what means they could to help themselves. Thus most of them separated from each other, and several companies took several courses, at their return homewards. As for that party to which I belonged, we steered our voyage along the coast of Costa Rica, where we intended to purchase some provisions, and careen our vessel in some secure place or other. For the boat wherein we were, was now grown so foul as to be rendered totally unfit for sailing. In few days we arrived at a great port, called Boca del Toro, where are always to be found huge quantity of good and eatable tortoises. The circumference hereof is ten leagues, more or less, being surrounded with little islands, under which vessels may ride very secure from the violence of the winds.

The said islands are inhabited by Indians, who never could be subjugated by the Spaniards, and hence they give them the name of *Indios bravos,* or Wild Indians

They are divided, according to the variety of idioms of their language, into several customs and fashions of people, whence arise perpetual wars against one another. Towards the east side of this port are found some of them, who formerly did much trade with the Pirates, selling to them the flesh of divers animals which they hunt in their countries, as also all sorts of fruits that the land produces. The exchange of which commodities was iron instruments, that the Pirates brought with them, beads and other toys, whereof they made great account for wearing, more than of precious jewels, which they knew not nor esteemed in the least. This commerce afterwards failed, because the Pirates committed many barbarous inhumanities against them, killing many of their men on a certain occasion, and taking away their women. These abuses gave sufficient cause for a perpetual cessation of all friendship and commerce between them and the Pirates.

We went ashore, with design to seek provisions, our necessity being now almost extreme. But our fortune was so bad that we could find nothing else than a few eggs of crocodiles, wherewith we were forced to content ourselves for that present. Hereupon we left those quarters, and steered our course eastwards. Being upon this tack, we met with three boats more of our own companions, who had been left behind by Captain Morgan. These told us they had been able to find no relief for the extreme hunger they sustained ; moreover, that Captain Morgan himself and all his people were already reduced to such misery, that he could afford them no more allowance than once a day, and that very short too.

We therefore hearing from these boats that little or no good was like to be done by sailing farther eastward, changed our course, and steered towards the west. Here we found an excessive quantity of tortoises, more than we needed for the victualling our boats, should we be never so long without any other flesh or fish. Having provided ourselves with this sort of victuals, the next thing we wanted was fresh water. There was enough to be had in the neighbouring islands, but we scarce dared to land on them, by reason of the enmity above mentioned between us Pirates and those Indians. Notwithstanding, necessity having no law, we were forced to do as we could, rather than as we desired to do. And hereupon we resolved to go all of us together to one of the said islands. Being landed, one party of our men went to range in the woods, while another filled the barrels with water. Scarce one whole hour was past, after our people were got ashore, when suddenly the Indians came upon us, and we heard one of our men cry : *Arm! Arm!* We presently took up our arms, and began to fire at them as hot as we could. This caused them to advance no farther, and in a short while put them to flight, sheltering themselves in the woods. We pursued them some part of the way, but not far, by reason we then esteemed rather to get in our water than any other advantages upon the enemy. Coming back, we found two Indians dead upon the shore, whereof the habiliments of one gave us to understand he was a person of quality amongst them. For he had about his body a girdle, or sash, very richly woven ; and on his face he wore a beard of massive gold—I mean, a small planch of gold hung down at his lips by two strings (which penetrated two little holes, made there on purpose), that covered his beard, or served instead thereof. His arms were made of sticks of palmetto-trees, being very curiously wrought, at one end whereof was a kind of hook, which seemed to be hardened with fire. We could willingly have had opportunity to speak with some of these Indians, to see if we could reconcile their minds to us, and by this means renew the former trade with them, and obtain provisions. But this was a thing impossible, through the wildness of their persons and savageness of their minds. Notwithstanding, this encounter hindered us not from filling our barrels with water, and carrying them aboard.

The night following we heard from the shore huge cries and shrieks among the Indians. These lamentations caused us to believe, because they were heard so far, they had called in much more people to aid them against us; as also, that they lamented the death of those two men who were killed the day before. These Indians never come upon the waters of the sea, neither have they ever given themselves to build canoes or any other sort of vessels for navigation—not so much as fisher-boats, of which art of fishery they are totally ignorant. At last, having nothing else to hope for in these parts, we resolved to depart thence for Jamaica, whither we designed to go. Being set forth, we met with contrary winds, which caused us to make use of our oars, and row as far as the river of Chagre. When we came near it, we perceived a ship that made towards us, and began to give us chase. Our apprehensions were that it was a ship from Cartagena, which might be sent to rebuild and retake possession of the castle of Chagre, now all the Pirates were departed thence. Hereupon we set all our sail and ran before the wind, to see if we could escape or refuge ourselves in any place. But the vessel, being much swifter and cleaner than ours, easily got the wind of us, and stopped our course. Then approaching near us, we discovered what they were, and knew them to be our former comrades, in the same expedition of Panama, who were but lately set out from Chagre. Their design was to go to Nombre de Dios, and thence to Cartagena, to seek some purchase or other, in or about that frequented port. But the wind at that present being contrary to their intention, they concluded to go in our company towards the same place where we were before, called Boca del Toro.

This accident and encounter retarded our journey, in the space of two days, more than we could regain in a whole fortnight. This was the occasion that obliged us to return to our former station, where we remained for a few days. Thence we directed our course for a place called Boca del Dragon, there to make provisions of flesh, especially of a certain animal which the Spaniards call manati,[1] and the Dutch, *sea-cows*, because the head, nose and teeth of this beast are very like those of a cow. They are found commonly in such places, as under the depth of the waters are very full of grass, on which, it is thought, they pasture. These animals have no ears, and only in place of them are to be seen two little holes, scarce capable of receiving the little finger of a man. Near to the neck they have two wings, under which are seated two udders or breasts, much like the breasts of a woman. The skin is very close and united together, resembling the skin of a Barbary, or Guinea Dog. This skin upon the back is of the thickness of two fingers, which, being dried, is as hard as any whale-bone, and may serve to make walking-staffs with. The belly is in all things like that of a cow, as far as the kidneys, or reins. Their manner of engendering, likewise, is the same with the usual manner of a land cow, the male of this kind being in similitude almost one and the same thing with a bull. Yet, notwithstanding, they conceive and breed but once. But the space of time that they go with calf, I could not as yet learn. These fishes have the sense of hearing extremely acute, in so much that in taking them the fishermen ought not to make the least noise, nor row, unless it be very slightly. For this reason they make use of certain instruments for rowing, which the Indians call *pagayos*, and the Spaniards name *caneletas*, with which although they row, yet it is performed without any noise that can fright the fish. While they are busied in

[1] The name manati was first applied to this animal by the early Spanish colonists in regard to the hand-like use of its fore limbs ; a good description of it is to be found in Dampier's Letters. It is of the order Sirenia ; there are two varieties—one (M. Latirostris) inhabits the West Indies and Florida, the other (M. australis) the coast of Brazil.

this fishery, they do not speak to one another, but all is transacted by signs. He that darts them with the javelin, uses it after the same manner as when they kill tortoises. Howbeit, the point of the said javelin is somewhat different, having two hooks at the extremity, and these longer than that of the other fishery. Of these fishes, some are found to be of the length of twenty to twenty-four foot. Their flesh is very good to eat, being very like in colour that of a land cow, but in taste, that of pork. It contains much fat, or grease, which the Pirates melt and keep in earthen pots, to make use thereof instead of oil.

On a certain day, wherein we were not able to do any good at this sort of fishery, some of our men went into the woods to hunt, and others to catch other fish. Soon after we espied a canoe, wherein were two Indians. These no sooner had discovered our vessels than they rowed back with all the speed they could towards the land, being unwilling to trade or have anything to do with us Pirates. We followed them to the shore, but through their natural nimbleness, being much greater than ours, they retired into the woods before we could overtake them. Yea, what was more admirable, they drew on shore, and carried with them their canoe into the wood, as easily as if it were made of straw, although it weighed above two thousand pounds. This we knew by the canoe itself, which we found afterwards, and had much ado to get into the water again, although we were in all eleven persons to pull at it.

We had at that time in our company a certain pilot, who had been divers times in those quarters. This man, seeing this action of the Indians, told us that, some few years before, a squadron of Pirates happened to arrive at that place. Being there, they went in canoes, to catch a certain sort of little birds, which inhabits the sea-coast, under the shade of very beautiful trees, which here are to be seen. While they were busied at that work, certain

Indians who had climbed up into the trees to view their actions, seeing now the canoes underneath, leaped down into the sea, and with huge celerity seized some of the canoes and Pirates that kept them, both which they transported so nimbly into the remotest parts of the woods, that the prisoners could not be relieved by their companions. Hereupon the admiral of the said squadron landed presently after with five hundred men, to seek and rescue the men he had lost. But they saw such an excessive number of Indians flock together to oppose them, as obliged them to retreat with all possible diligence to their ships, concluding among themselves that if such forces as those could not perform anything towards the recovery of their companions, they ought to stay no longer time there. Having heard this history, we came away thence, fearing some mischief might befall us, and bringing with us the canoe aforementioned. In this we found nothing else but a fishing-net, though not very large, and four arrows, made of palm-tree, of the length of seven foot each and of the figure, or shape, as follows.

These arrows, we believed, to be their arms. The canoe we brought away was made of cedar, but very roughly hewn and polished, which caused us to think that those people have no instruments of iron.

We left that place, and arrived in twenty four hours at another called Rio de Zuera, where we found some few houses belonging to the city of Cartagena. These houses are inhabited by Spaniards, whom we resolved to visit, not being able to find any tortoises, nor yet any of their eggs. The inhabitants were all fled from the said houses, having left no victuals, nor provisions behind them, in so much that we were forced to content ourselves with a certain

fruit, which there is called platano. Of these platanos
we filled our boats, and continued our voyage, coasting
along the shore. Our design was to find out some creek
or bay, wherein to careen our vessel, which now was
very leaky on all sides. Yea, in such a dangerous condition, that both night and day we were constrained to
employ several men at the pump, to which purpose we
made use of all our slaves. This voyage lasted a whole
fortnight, all which time we lay under the continual
frights of perishing every moment. At last we arrived
at a certain port, called The Bay of Bleevelt, being so
named from a Pirate who used to resort thither, with the
same design that we did. Here one party of our men
went into the woods to hunt, while another undertook to
refit and careen our vessel.

Our companions who went abroad to hunt found hereabouts porcupines, of a huge and monstrous bigness.
But their chief exercise was killing of monkeys, and
certain birds called by the Spaniards *faisanes*, or phea-
sants. The toil and labour we had in this employment
of shooting, seemed at least to me, to be sufficiently com-
pensated with the pleasure of killing the said monkeys.
For at these we usually made fifteen to sixteen shots
before we could kill three or four of them, so nimbly
would they escape our hands and aim, even after being
desperately wounded. On the other side, it was delightful to see the female monkeys carry their little ones upon
their backs, even just as negresses do their children.
Likewise, if shooting at a parcel of them, any monkey
happens to be wounded, the rest of the company will
flock about him, and lay their hands upon the wound,
to hinder the blood from issuing forth. Others will
gather moss that grows upon the trees, and thrust it into
the wound, and hereby stop the blood. At other times
they will gather such or such herbs, and, chewing them
in their mouth, apply them after the manner of a poultice,
or cataplasm. All which things did cause in me great

admiration, seeing such strange actions in those irrational creatures, which testified the fidelity and love they had for one another.

On the 9th day after our arrival at that place, our women-slaves being busied in their ordinary employments of washing dishes, sewing, drawing water out of wells, which we had made on the shore, and the like things, we heard great cries of one of them, who said she had seen a troop of Indians appear towards the woods, whereby she began immediately to cry out: *Indians, Indians.* We, hearing this rumour, ran presently to our arms, and their relief. But, coming to the wood, we found no person there, excepting two of our women-slaves killed upon the place, with the shot of arrows. In their bodies we saw so many arrows sticking as might seem they had been fixed there with particular care and leisure ; for otherwise we knew that one of them alone was sufficient to bereave any human body of life. These arrows were all of a rare fashion and shape, their length being eight foot, and their thickness of a man's thumb. At one of the extremities hereof, was to be seen a hook made of wood, and tied to the body of the arrow with a string. At the other end was a certain case, or box, like the case of a pair of tweezers, in which we found certain little pebbles or stones. The colour thereof was red, and very shining, as if they had been locked up some considerable time. All which, we believed, were arms belonging to their captains and leaders.

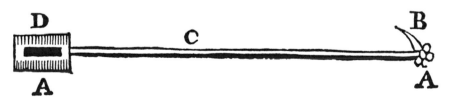

A. *A marcasite, which was tied to the extremity of the arrow.*
B. *A hook, tied to the same extremity.*
C. *The arrow.*
D. *The case, at the other end.*

These arrows were all made without instruments of iron. For whatsoever the Indians make, they harden it first very artificially with fire, and afterwards polish it with flints.

As to the nature of these Indians, they are extremely robust of constitution, strong and nimble at their feet. We sought them carefully up and down the woods, but could not find the least trace of them, neither any of their canoes, nor floats, whereof they make use to go out to fish. Hereupon we retired to our vessels, where, having embarked all our goods, we put off from the shore, fearing lest finding us there they should return in any considerable number, and overpowering our forces tear us all in pieces.

CHAPTER VIII.

The Author departs towards the Cape of Gracias à Dios. Of the Commerce which here the Pirates exercise with the Indians. His arrival at the Island De los Pinos; and finally, his return to Jamaica.

THE fear we had, more than usual, of those Indians above mentioned, by reason of the death of our two women-slaves, of which we told you in the former chapter, occasioned us to depart as fast as we could from that place. We directed our course thence, towards the Cape of Gracias à Dios, where we had fixed our last hopes of finding provisions. For thither do usually resort many Pirates, who entertain a friendly correspondence and trade with the Indians of those parts. Being arrived at the said cape, we hugely rejoiced, and gave thanks to God Almighty, for having delivered us out of so many dangers, and brought us to this place of refuge, where we found people who showed us most cordial friendship, and provided us with all necessaries whatsoever.

The custom of this island is such that, when any Pirates arrive there, every one has the liberty to buy for himself an Indian woman, at the price of a knife, or any old axe, wood-bill or hatchet. By this contract the woman is obliged to remain in the custody of the Pirate all the time he stayeth there. She serves him in the meanwhile, and brings him victuals of all sorts, that the country affords. The Pirate moreover has liberty to go when he pleases, either to hunt, or fish, or about any other divertisements of his pleasure; but withal is not to commit any hostility, or depredation upon the inhabitants, seeing the Indians bring him in all that he stands in need of, or that he desires.

Through the frequent converse and familiarity these Indians have with the Pirate they sometimes go to sea with them, and remain among them for whole years, without returning home. Whence it comes that many of them can speak English, and French, and some of the Pirates their Indian language. They are very dextrous at darting with the javelin, whereby they are very useful to the Pirates, towards the victualling their ships, by the fishery of tortoises, and *manitas*, a sort of fish so called by the Spaniards. For one of these Indians is alone sufficient to victual a vessel of an hundred persons. We had among our crew two Pirates who could speak very well the Indian language. By the help of these men, I was so curious as to enquire into their customs, lives and policy, whereof I shall give you here a brief account.

This island contains about thirty leagues in circumference, more or less. It is governed after the form of a little commonwealth, they having no king nor sovereign prince among them. Neither do they entertain any friendship or correspondence with other neighbouring islands, much less with the Spaniards. They are in all but a small nation, whose number does not exceed sixteen or seventeen hundred persons. They have among them some few negroes, who serve them in quality of slaves. These happened to arrive there, swimming, after shipwreck made upon that coast. For being bound for Terra Firma, in a ship that carried them to be sold in those parts, they killed the captain and mariners, with design to return to their country. But through their ignorance in marinery, they stranded their vessel hereabouts. Although, as I said before, they make but a small nation, yet they live divided, as it were, into two several provinces. Of these, the one sort employ themselves in cultivating the ground, and making several plantations. But the others are so lazy that they have not courage to build themselves huts, much less houses, to dwell in. They frequent chiefly the sea-coast, wandering disorderly up and down, without knowing, or caring so much as to cover their bodies from the rains, which are very frequent in those parts, unless it be with a few palm-leaves. These they put upon their heads, and keep their backs always turned to the wind that blows. They use no other clothes than an apron, tied to their middle ; such aprons are made of the rinds of trees, which they strongly beat upon stones till they are softened. Of these same they make use for bed-clothes, to cover themselves when they sleep. Some make to themselves bed-clothes of cotton, but these are but few in number. Their usual arms are nothing but azagayas, or spears, which they make fit for their use with points of iron or teeth of crocodiles.

They know, after some manner, that there is a God, yet they live without any religion or divine worship. Yea, as far as I can learn, they believe not in nor serve the devil, as many other nations of America do both believe, invoke and worship him. Hereby they are not so much tormented by him, as other nations are. Their ordinary food, for the greatest part, consists in several fruits ; such as are called bananas, racoven, ananas, potatos, cassava; as also crabs, and some few fish of other sorts, which they kill in the sea with darts. As to their drink, they are something expert in making certain pleasant and delicate liquors. The commonest among them is called *achioc*. This is made of a certain seed of palm-tree, which they bruise, and afterwards steep or infuse in hot water, till it be settled at the bottom. This liquor being strained off has a very pleasant taste, and is very nourishing. Many other sorts of liquors they prepare, which I shall omit for brevity. Only I shall say something, in short, of that which is made of *platanos*. These they knead betwixt their hands with hot water, and afterwards put into great calabashes, which they fill up with cold water, and leave in repose for the space of eight days, during which time it ferments as well as the best sort of wine. This liquor they drink for pleasure, and as a great regale, in so much that when these Indians invite their friends or relations they cannot treat them better than to give them some of this pleasant drink.

They are very unskilful in dressing of victuals; and hence it is that they very seldom treat one another with banquets. For this purpose, when they go or send to any house, to invite others, they desire them to come and drink of their liquors. Before the invited persons come to their house, those that expect them comb their hair very well, and anoint their faces with oil of palm, mingled with a certain black tincture which renders them very hideous. The women, in like manner, daub their faces with another sort of stuff, which cause them to look as red as crimson. And such are the greatest civilities they use in their ornaments and attire. Afterwards, he that invites the other takes his arms, which are three or four *azagayas*, and goes out of his cottage the space of three or four hundred steps, to wait for and receive the persons that are to come to visit him. As soon as they draw near him, he falls down upon the ground, lying flat on his face, in which posture he remains without any motion, as if he were dead. Being thus prostrate before them, the invited friends take him up and set him upon his feet, and thus they go altogether to the hut. Here the persons who are invited use the same ceremony, falling down on the ground, as the inviter did before. But he lifts them up one by one, and, giving them his hand, conducts them into his cottage, where he causes them to sit. The women on these occasions perform few or no ceremonies.

Being thus brought into the house, they are presented every one with a calabash full of the liquor abovementioned, made of *platanos*, which is very thick, almost like water-gruel, or children's pap, wherein is contained four quarts, more or less, of the said liquor. These they are to drink off as well as they can, and get down at any rate. The calabashes being emptied into their stomachs, the master of the house, with many ceremonies, goes about the room, and gathers his calabashes. And this drinking hitherto is reckoned but for one welcome, whereas every invitation ought to contain several welcomes. Afterwards, they begin to drink of the clear liquor abovementioned, for which they were called to this treat. Hereunto follow many songs and dances and a thousand caresses to the women that are present.

They do not marry any young maid without the consent of her parents. Hereupon, if any one desires to take a wife, he is first examined by the damsel's father concerning several points relating to good husbandry. These are most commonly : whether he can make *azagayas*, darts for fishing or spin a certain thread which they use about their arrows. Having answered to satisfaction, the examiner calls to his daughter, for a little calabash full of the liquor above mentioned. Of this he drinks first ; then gives the cup to the young man ; and he finally to the bride, who drinks it up ; and with this only ceremony the marriage is made. When any one drinks to the health of another, the second person ought to drink up the liquor which the other person has left in the calabash. But in case of marriage, as was said before, it is consumed alone among those three, the bride obtaining the greatest part to her share.

When the woman lies in, neither she nor her husband observe the time, as is customary among the Caribbees. But as soon as the woman is delivered, she goes instantly to the next river, brook or fountain, and washes the new-born creature, swaddling it up afterwards in certain rollers, or swaddling bands, which there are called *cabalas*. This being done, she goes about her ordinary labour, as before. At their entertainments it is usual, that when the man dies, his wife buries him with

all his *azagayas*, aprons and jewels that he used to wear
at his ears.　Her next obligation is, to come every day
to her husband's grave, bringing him meat and drink for
a whole year together.　Their years they reckon by the
moons, allowing fifteen to every year, which make their
entire circle, as our twelve months do ours.

Some historians, writing of the Caribbee Islands,
affirm that this ceremony of carrying victuals to the dead
is generally observed among them.　Moreover, that the
devil comes to the sepulchres, and carries away all the
meat and drink which is placed there.　But I myself am
not of this opinion, seeing I have oftentimes with my
own hands taken away these offerings, and eaten them
instead of other victuals.　To this I was moved, because
I knew that the fruits used on these occasions were the
choicest and ripest of all others, as also the liquors of the
best sort they made use of for their greatest regale and
pleasure.　When the widow has thus completed her year,
she opens the grave, and takes out all her husband's
bones.　These she scrapes and washes very well, and
afterwards dries against the beams of the sun.　When
they are sufficiently dried, she ties them all together, and
puts them into a *cabala*, being a certain pouch or satchel,
and is obliged for another year to carry them upon her
back in the daytime, and to sleep upon them in the night,
until the year be completely expired.　This ceremony
being finished, she hangs up the bag and bones against
the post of her own door, in case she be mistress of any
house.　But having no house of her own, she hangs
them at the door of her next neighbour, or relation.

The widows cannot marry a second time, according to
the laws or customs of this nation, until the space of the
two years above mentioned be completed.　The men are
bound to perform no such ceremonies towards their
wives. But if any Pirate marries an Indian Woman, she is
bound to do with him, in all things, as if he were an Indian
man born.　The negroes that are upon this Island, live

here in all respects according to the customs of their own country. All these things I have thought fit to take notice of in this place, though briefly, as judging them worthy the curiosity of some judicious and inquisitive persons. Now I shall continue the account of our voyage.

After we had refreshed and provided ourselves, as well as we could, at the island aforesaid, we departed thence, and steered our course towards the island De los Pinos. Here we arrived in fifteen days, and were constrained to refit again our vessel, which now the second time was very leaky and not fit for sailing any farther. Hereupon we divided ourselves, as before, and some went about that work of careening the ship, while others betook themselves to fishing. In this last we were so successful as to take in six or seven hours as much fish as would abundantly suffice to feed a thousand persons. We had in our company some Indians from the cape of Gracias à Dios, who were very dextrous both in hunting and fishing. With the help of these men we killed likewise, in a short while, and salted, a huge number of wild cows, sufficient both to satiate our hungry appetites and to victual our vessel for the sea. These cows were formerly brought into this island by the Spaniards, with design they should here multiply and stock the country with cattle of this kind. We salted, in like manner, a vast number of tortoises, whereof in this island huge quantities are to be found. With these things our former cares and troubles began to dissipate, and our minds to be so far recreated as to forget the miseries we had lately endured. Hereupon, we began to call one another again by the name of brothers, which was customary amongst us but had been disused in our miseries and scarce remembered without regret.

All the time we continued here, we feasted ourselves very plentifully, without the least fear of enemies. For as to the Spaniards that were upon the island, they were

here in mutual league and friendship with us. Thus
we were only constrained to keep watch and ward every
night, for fear of the crocodiles, which are here in great
plenty all over the island. For these, when they are
hungry, will assault any man whatsoever, and devour
him ; as it happened in this conjuncture to one of our
companions. This man being gone into the wood, in
company with a negro, they fell into a place where a
crocodile lay concealed. The furious animal, with incredible agility, assaulted the Pirate, and fastening upon
his leg, cast him upon the ground, the negro being fled,
who should assist him. Yet he, notwithstanding, being
a robust and courageous man, drew forth a knife he had
then about him, and with the same, after a dangerous
combat, overcame and killed the crocodile. Which
having done, he himself, both tired with the battle, and
weakened with the loss of blood, that ran from his
wounds, lay for dead upon the place, or at least beside
his senses. Being found in this posture some while after
by the negro, who returned to see what was become of
his master, he took him upon his back, and brought him
to the sea-side, distant thence the space of a whole league,
Here we received him into a canoe, and conveyed him
on board our ship.

After this misfortune, none of our men dared be so
bold as to enter the woods without good company. Yea,
we ourselves, desirous to revenge the disaster of our
companion, went in troops the next day to the woods,
with design to find out crocodiles to kill. These animals
would usually come every night to the sides of our ship,
and make resemblance of climbing up into the vessel.
One of these, on a certain night, we seized with an iron
hook, but he instead of flying to the bottom, began to
mount the ladder of the ship, till we killed him with other
instruments. Thus, after we had remained there some
considerable time, and refitted ourselves with all things
necessary, we set sail thence for Jamaica. Here we

arrived within few days, after a prosperous voyage, and found Captain Morgan, who was got home before us, but had seen as yet none of his companions whom he left behind, we being the first that arrived there after him.

The said Captain at that present was very busy, endeavouring to persuade and levy people to transport to the isle of St. Catharine, which he designed to fortify and hold as his own, thinking to make it a common refuge to all sorts of Pirates, or at least of his own nation, as was said before. But he was soon hindered in the prosecution of this design, by the arrival of a man-of-war from England. For this vessel brought orders from his Majesty of Great Britain, to recall the Governor of Jamaica from his charge over that island, to the court of England, there to give an account of his proceedings and behaviour in relation to the Pirates whom he had maintained in those parts, to the huge detriment of the subjects of the King of Spain. To this purpose, the said man-of-war brought over also a new Governor of Jamaica, to supply the place of the preceding. This gentleman, being possessed of the government of the island, presently after gave notice to all the ports thereof, by several boats which he sent forth to that intent, of the good and entire correspondence which his master the King of England designed henceforwards to maintain in those Western parts of the world towards his Catholic Majesty and all his subjects and dominions. And that to this effect, for the time to come, he had received from his Sacred Majesty and Privy Council strict and severe orders, not to permit any Pirate whatsoever to set forth from Jamaica, to commit any hostility or depredation upon the Spanish nation, or dominions, or any other people of those neighbouring islands.

No sooner these orders were sufficiently divulged than the Pirates, who as yet were abroad at sea, began to fear them, insomuch that they dared not return home to the said island. Hereupon they kept the seas as long

as they could, and continued to act as many hostilities as came in their way.   Not long after, the same
Pirates took and ransacked a considerable town, seated
in the Isle of Cuba, called La Villa de los Cayos, of which
we made mention in the description of the said island.
Here they committed again all sorts of hostility, and
inhuman and barbarous cruelties.   But the new Governor
of Jamaica behaved himself so constant to his duty, and
the orders he had brought from England, that he apprehended several of the chief actors herein, and condemned
them to be hanged, which was accordingly done.   From this
severity many others still remaining abroad took warning,
and retired to the isle of Tortuga, lest they should fall
into his hands.   Here they joined in society with the
French Pirates, inhabitants of the said island, in whose
company they continue to this day.

CHAPTER IX.

The Relation of the shipwreck, which Monsieur Bertram Ogeron, Governor of the Isle of Tortuga, suffered near the Isles of Guadanillas. How both he and his companions fell into the hands of the Spaniards. By what arts he escaped their hands, and preserved his life. The enterprize which he undertook against Porto Rico, to deliver his people. The unfortunate success of that design.

AFTER the expedition of Panama abovementioned, the inhabitants of the French islands in America, in the year 1673 (while the war was so fierce in Europe between France and Holland) gathered a considerable fleet, to go and possess themselves of the islands belonging to the States-General of the United Provinces in the West Indies. To this effect, their admiral called together and levied all the Pirates and volunteers that would, by any inductions whatsoever, sit down under his colours. With the same design the Governor of Tortuga caused to be built in that island a good strong man-of-war, to which vessel he gave the name of *Ogeron*. This ship he provided very well with all sorts of ammunition, and manned with five hundred buccaneers, all resolute and courageous men, as being the vessel he designed for his own safety. Their first intention was to go and take the Isle of Curaçoa, belonging to the said States of Holland. But this design met with very ill success, by reason of a shipwreck, which impeded the course of their voyage.

Monsieur Ogeron set sail from the port of Tortuga as soon as all things were in readiness, with intent to join the rest of the said fleet and pursue the enterprize aforementioned. Being arrived on the West side of the Island of St. John de Puerto Rico, he was suddenly surprized with a violent storm. This increased to such a degree, that it caused his new frigate to strike against the rocks that neighbour upon the islands, called Guadanillas, where the vessel broke into a thousand pieces. Yet being near the land of Porto Rico, all his men escaped, by saving their lives in boats, which they had at hand.

The next day, all being now got on shore, they were discovered by Spaniards who inhabit the island. These instantly took them to be French Pirates, whose intent was to take the said island anew, as they had done several times before. Hereupon they alarmed the whole country, and, gathering their forces together, marched out to their encounter. But they found them unprovided of all manner of arms, and consequently not able to make any defence, craving for mercy at their hands, and begging quarter for their lives, as the custom is. Yet notwithstanding, the Spaniards, remembering the horrible and cruel actions those Pirates had many times committed against them, would have no compassion on their condition. But answering them *Ha ! ye thievish dogs, here's no quarter for you;* they assaulted them with all the fury imaginable, and killed the greatest part of the company. At last perceiving they made no resistance, nor had any arms to defend themselves, they began to relent in their cruelty, and stay their blows, taking prisoners as many as remained alive. Yet still they would not be persuaded but that those unfortunate were come thither with design to take again and ruin the island.

Hereupon they bound them with cords, by two and two or three and three together, and drove them through the woods, into the campaign, or open fields. Being come thus far with them, they asked them : What was become of their captain and leader ? Unto these questions they constantly made answer : he was drowned in the shipwreck at sea ; although they knew full well it was false. For Monsieur Ogeron, being unknown to the Spaniards, behaved himself among them as if he were a fool and had no common use of reason. Notwithstanding, the Spaniards, scarce believing what the prisoners had answered, used all the means they could possibly to find him, but could not compass their desires. For Monsieur Ogeron kept himself very close, to all the features and mimical actions that might become any innocent fool. Upon this account, he was not tied as the rest of his companions, but let loose, to serve the divertisement and laughter of the common soldiers. These now and then would give him scraps of bread and other victuals, whereas the rest of the prisoners had never sufficient wherewith to satisfy their hungry stomachs. For as to the allowance they had from the Spaniards, their enemies, it was scarce enough to preserve them alive.

It happened there was found among the French Pirates a certain surgeon, who had done some remarkable service to the Spaniards. In consideration of these merits, he was unbound, and set at liberty, to go freely up and down, even as Monsieur Ogeron did. To this surgeon Monsieur Ogeron, having a fit opportunity thereto, declared his resolution of hazarding his life, to attempt an escape from the cruelty and hard usage of those enemies. After mature deliberation, they both performed it, by flying to the woods, with design there to make something or other that might be navigable, whereby to transport themselves elsewhere, although to this effect they neither had nor could obtain any other thing in the world that could be serviceable in building of vessels than one hatchet. Thus they joined company, and began their march towards the woods that lay nearest the sea-coast. Having travelled all day long, they came about evening to the sea-side almost unexpectedly. Here they found themselves without anything to eat, nor any secure place wherein to rest their wearied limbs.

At last they perceived nigh the shore a huge quantity .
of fishes, called by the Spaniards *corlabados.* These
frequently approach the sands of the shore, in pursuit of
other little fishes that serve them for their food. Of
these they took as many as they thought necessary, and,
by rubbing two sticks tediously together, they kindled
fire, wherewith they made coals to roast them. The
next day they began to cut down and prepare timber,
wherewith to make a kind of small boat, in which they
might pass over to the Isle of Santa Cruz, which belongs
to the French.

While they were busied about their work, they discovered, at a great distance, a certain canoe, which steered
directly towards the place where they were. This occasioned in their minds some fears lest they should be
found, and taken again by the Spaniards; and hereupon
they retired into the woods, till such time as they could
see thence and distinguish what people were in the
canoe. But at last, as their good fortune would have it,
they perceived them to be no more than two men, who
in their disposition and apparel seemed to be fishermen.
Having made this discovery, they concluded unanimously
betwixt themselves to hazard their lives, and overcome
them, and afterwards seize the canoe. Soon after they
perceived one of them, who was a mulatto, to go with
several calabashes hanging at his back towards a spring,
not far distant from the shore, to take in fresh water.
The other, who was a Spaniard, remained behind, waiting for his return. Seeing them divided, they assaulted
the mulatto first, and discharging a great blow on his head
with the hatchet, they soon bereaved him of life. The
Spaniard, hearing the noise, made instantly towards the
canoe, thinking to escape. But this he could not perform so soon, without being overtaken by the two, and
there massacred by their hands. Having now compassed
their design, they went to seek for the corpse of the
mulatto, which they carried on board the canoe. Their

intent was to convey them into the middle of the sea, and there cast them overboard, to be consumed by the fish, and by this means conceal this fact from being known to the Spaniards, either at a short or long distance of time.

These things being done, they took in presently as much fresh water as they could, and set sail to seek some place of refuge. That day they steered along the coast of Porto Rico, and came to the cape called by the Spaniards Cabo Roxo. Hence they traversed directly to the Isle of Hispaniola, where so many of their own comrades and companions were to be found. Both the currents of the waters and winds were very favourable to this voyage, in so much that in a few days they arrived at a place called Samana, belonging to the said island, where they found a party of their own people.

Monsieur Ogeron, being landed at Samana, gave orders to the surgeon to levy all the people he could possibly in those parts, while he departed to revisit his government of Tortuga. Being arrived at the said port, he used all his endeavours to gather what vessels and men he could to his assistance. So that within a few days he compassed a good number of both, very well equipped and disposed to follow and execute his designs. These were to go to the Island of St. John de Puerto Rico, and deliver his fellow prisoners, whom he had left in the miserable condition as was said before. After having embarked all the people which the surgeon had levied at Samana, he made them a speech, exhorting them to have good courage, and telling them : *You may all expect great spoil and riches from this enterprize, and therefore let all fear and cowardice be set on side. On the contrary, fill your hearts with courage and valour, for thus you will find yourselves soon satisfied, of what, at present, bare hopes do promise.* Every one relied much on these promises of Monsieur Ogeron, and, from his words, conceived no small joy in their minds. Thus they set sail from Tortuga, steering their course directly for the coasts of Porto Rico. Being come within sight of land, they made use only of their lower sails, to the intent they might not be discovered at so great a distance by the Spaniards, till they came somewhat near the place where they intended to land.

The Spaniards, notwithstanding this caution, had intelligence beforehand of their coming, and were prepared for a defence, having posted many troops of horse all along the coast, to watch the descent of the French Pirates. Monsieur Ogeron, perceiving their vigilance, gave order to the vessels to draw near the shore, and shoot off many great guns, whereby he forced the cavalry to retire to places more secure within the woods. Here lay concealed many companies of foot, who had prostrated themselves upon the ground. Meanwhile the Pirates made their descent at leisure, and began to enter among the trees, scarce suspecting any harm to be there, where the horsemen could do no service. But no sooner were they fallen into this ambuscade than the Spaniards arose with great fury, and assaulted the French so courageously that in a short while they destroyed great part of them. And thus leaving great numbers of dead on the place, the rest with difficulty escaped by retreating in all haste to their ships.

Monsieur Ogeron, although he escaped this danger, yet could willingly have perished in the fight, rather than suffer the shame and confusion the unfortunate success of this enterprize was like to bring upon his reputation, especially considering that those whom he had attempted to set at liberty were now cast into greater miseries through this misfortune. Hereupon they hastened to set sail, and go back to Tortuga the same way they came, with great confusion in their minds, much diminished in their number, and nothing laden with those spoils, the hopes whereof had possessed their hearts, and caused them readily to follow the promises of unfortunate Monsieur Ogeron. The Spaniards were very vigilant, and kept their posts near the sea-side, till such time as the fleet of Pirates was totally out of sight. In the meanwhile they made an end of killing such of their enemies as being desperately wounded could not escape by flight. In like manner, they cut off several limbs from the dead bodies, with design to show them to the former prisoners, for whose redemption these others had crossed the seas.

The fleet being departed, the Spaniards kindled bonfires all over the island, and made great demonstrations of joy for the victory they had obtained. But the French prisoners who were there before had more hardship showed them from that day than ever. Of their misery and misusage was a good eye witness, Jacob Binkes, Governor at that time in America for the States-General of the United Provinces. For he happened to arrive in that conjuncture at the Island of Porto Rico, with some men-of-war, to buy provisions and other necessaries for his fleet. His compassion on their misery was such as caused him to bring away by stealth five or six of the said prisoners, which served only to exasperate the minds of the Spaniards. For soon after they sent the rest of the prisoners to the chief city of the island, there to work and toil about the fortifications which then were making, forcing them to bring and carry stones and all sorts of materials belonging thereto. These being finished, the Governor transported them to Havana, where they employed them in like manner, in fortifying that city. Here they caused them to work in the day-time, and by night they shut them up as close prisoners, fearing lest they should enterprize upon the city. For of such attempts the Spaniards had had divers proofs on other occasions, which afforded them sufficient cause to use them after that manner.

Afterwards at several times, wherein ships arrived there from New Spain, they transported them by degrees into Europe, and landed them at the city of Cadiz. But notwithstanding this care of the Spaniards to disperse them, they soon after met almost all together in France, and resolved among themselves to return again to Tortuga with the first opportunity should proffer. To this effect, they assisted one another very lovingly with what necessaries they could spare, according to every one's condition: so that in a short while the greatest part of those Pirates had nested themselves again at Tortuga, their common place of rendezvous. Here, some time after, they equipped again a new fleet, to revenge their former misfortunes on the Spaniards, under the conduct of one Le Sieur Maintenon, a Frenchman by nation. With this fleet he arrived at the Island of Trinidad, situated between the Isle of Tobago and the neighbouring coasts of Paria. This island they sacked, and afterwards put to the ransom of ten thousand pieces of eight. Hence they departed, with design to take and pillage the city of Caracas, situated over against the Island of Curaçoa, belonging to the Hollanders.

CHAPTER X.

A relation of what encounters lately happened at the Islands of Cayana and Tobago, between the Count de Estres, Admiral of France, in America, and the Heer Jacob Binkes, Vice-Admiral of the United Provinces, in the same parts.

It is a thing already known to the greatest part of Europe that the Prince of Courland began to establish a colony in the Island of Tobago. As also, that somewhile after, his people, for want of timely recruits from their own country, abandoned the said island, leaving it to the first that should come and possess it. Thus it fell into the hands of the Heers Adrian and Cornelius Lampsius, natives of the city of Flushing, in the province of Zeeland. For being arrived at the said Island of Tobago, in the year 1654, they undertook to fortify it, by command of their sovereigns, the States-General. Hereupon they built a goodly castle, in a convenient situation, capable of hindering the assaults of any enemies that might enterprize upon the island.

The strength of this castle was afterwards sufficiently tried by Monsieur de Estres, as I shall presently relate, after I have first told you what happened before at Cayana, in the year 1676. This year the States-General of the United Provinces sent their Vice-Admiral, Jacob Binkes, to the Island of Cayana, then in possession of the French, to retake the said island, and hereby restore it to the dominions of the United Provinces aforementioned. With these orders he set forth from Holland, on the 16th day of March in the said year, his fleet consisting of seven men-of-war, one fireship and five other

small vessels of less account.   This fleet arrived at
Cayana the 4th day of the month of May next following.
Immediately after their arrival, the Heer Binkes landed
nine hundred men, who, approaching the castle, summoned
the Governor to surrender, at their discretion.   His
answer was : He thought of nothing less than surrendering, but that he and his people were resolved to defend
themselves, even to the utmost of their endeavours.
The Heer Binkes having received this answer, presently
commanded his troops to attack the castle on both sides
at once.   The assault was very furious.   But at length,
the French being few in number and overwhelmed with
the multitude of their enemies, surrendered both their
arms and the castle.   In it were found thirty-seven
pieces of cannon.   The Governor, who was named
Monsieur Lesi, together with two priests, were sent into
Holland.   The Heer Binkes lost in the combat fourteen
men only, and had twenty two wounded.

The King of France no sooner understood this success
than he sent in the month of October following the
Count de Estres, to retake the said island from the
Hollanders.   He arrived there in the month of December, with a squadron of men-of-war, all very well
equipped and provided.   Being come on his voyage as
far as the river called Aperovaco, he met there with a
small vessel of Nantes, which had set forth from the said
Island of Cayana but a fortnight before.   This ship gave
him intelligence of the present state and condition,
wherein he might be certain to find the Hollanders at
Cayana.   They told him there were three hundred men
in the castle ; that all about it they had fixed strong
palisades, or empalements ; and that within the castle
were mounted twenty-six pieces of cannon.

Monsieur de Estres, being enabled with this intelligence to take his own measures, proceeded on his voyage,
and arrived at a port of the said island, three leagues
distant from the castle.   Here he landed eight hundred

men, whom he divided into two several parties. The one he placed under the conduct of the Count de Blinac, and the other he gave to Monsieur de St. Faucher. On board the fleet he left Monsieur Gabaret, with divers other principal troops, which he thought not fit or necessary to be landed. As soon as the men were set on shore, the fleet weighed anchor, and sailed very slowly towards the castle, while the soldiers marched by land. These could not travel otherwise than by night, by reason of the excessive heat of the sun and intolerable exhalations of the earth, which here is very sulphurous, and consequently no better than a smoky and stinking oven.

On the 19th day of the said month the Count de Estres sent Monsieur de Lesi (who had been Governor of the island, as was said before), demanding of them, to deliver the castle to the obedience of the King, his master, and to him in his sovereign's name. But those who were within resolved not to deliver themselves up, but at the expense of their lives and blood, which answer they sent to Monsieur de Estres. Hereupon the French, the following night, assaulted and stormed the castle on seven several sides thereof all at once. The defendants, having performed their obligation very stoutly, and fought with as much valour as was possible, were as last forced to surrender. Within the castle were found thirty-eight persons dead, besides many others that were wounded. All the prisoners were transported into France, where they were used with great hardship.

Monsieur de Estres, having put all things in good order at the Isle of Cayana, departed thence for that of Martinique. Being arrived at the said island, he was told that the Heer Binkes was at that present at the Island of Tobago, and his fleet lay at anchor in the bay. Having received this intelligence, Monsieur de Estres made no long stay there, but set sail again, steering his course directly for Tobago. No sooner was he come

near the island than Vice-Admiral Binkes sent his land-
forces, together with a good number of mariners, on
shore, to manage and defend the artillery that was there.
These forces were commanded by the Captains Van der
Graef, Van Dongen and Ciavone, who laboured very
hard all that night in raising certain batteries and filling
up the palisades, or empalements, of the fortress called
Sterreschans.

Two days after, the French fleet came to an anchor in
the Bay of Palmit, and immediately, with the help of
eighteen boats, they landed all their men. The Heer
Binkes, perceiving the French to appear upon the hills,
gave orders to burn all the houses that were near the
castle, to the intent the French might have no place to
shelter themselves thereabouts. On the 23rd day of
February, Monsieur de Estres sent a drum over to the
Hollanders, to demand the surrender of the fort, which
was absolutely denied. In this posture of affairs things
continued until the 3rd of March. On this day the
French fleet came with full sail, and engaged the Dutch
fleet. The Heer Binkes presently encountered them,
and the dispute was very hot on both sides. In the
meanwhile the land-forces belonging to the French being
sheltered by the thickness of the woods, advanced towards the castle, and began to storm it very briskly,
with more than ordinary force, but were repulsed by the
Dutch with such vigor as caused them after three distinct
attacks to retire, with the loss of above one hundred and
fifty men, and two hundred wounded. These they carried
off, or rather dragged away, with no small difficulty, by
reason of their disorderly retreat.

All this while the two fleets continued the combat, and
fought very desperately, until on both sides some ships
were consumed between Vulcan and Neptune. Of this
number was Monsieur de Estres' own ship, mounted
with twenty-seven guns of prodigious bigness, besides
other pieces of lesser port. The battle continued from

break of day until the evening. A little before which time, Monsieur de Estres quitted the bay with the rest of his ships, unto the Hollanders, excepting only two, which were stranded under sail, as having gone too high within the port. Finally, the victory remained on the side of the Hollanders, howbeit with the loss of several of their ships that were burnt.

Monsieur de Estres finding himself under the shame of the loss of this victory, and that he could expect no advantage for that present, over the Island of Tobago, set sail from those quarters the 18th day of March, and arrived the 21st day of June next following at the port of Brest in France. Having given an account of these transactions to his most Christian Majesty, he was pleased to command him to undertake again the enterprize of Tobago. To this effect, he gave orders for eight great men-of-war to be equipped with all speed, together with eight others of smaller account: with all which vessels he sent again Monsieur de Estres into America the same year. He set sail from the said port of Brest on the 3rd day of October following, and arrived the 1st of December at the Island of Barbados. Afterwards, having received some recruits from the Isle of Martinique, he sent beforehand to review the Island of Tobago, and consider the condition thereof. This being done, he weighed anchor and set sail directly for the said island, where he arrived the 7th day of the said month of December with all his fleet.

Immediately after his arrival he landed five hundred men, under the conduct of Monsieur de Blinac, Governor of the French islands in America. These were followed soon after by one thousand more. The 9th day of the said month they approached within six hundred paces of a certain post called Le Cort, where they landed all the artillery designed for this enterprize. On the 10th day Monsieur de Estres went in person to take a view of the castle, and demanded of the Heer Binkes, by a messenger, the surrender thereof, which was generously denied. The next day the French began to advance towards the castle, and on the 12th of the said month, the Dutch from within began to fire at them with great perseverance. The French made a beginning to their attack by casting fire-balls into the castle with main violence. The very third ball that was cast in happened to fall in the path-way that led to the store-house, where the powder and ammunition was kept, belonging to the castle. In this path was much powder scattered up and down, through the negligence of those that carried it to and fro for the necessary supplies of the defendants. By this means the powder took fire in the path, and thence ran in a moment as far as the store-house above mentioned, so that suddenly both the store-house was blown up, and with it Vice-Admiral Binkes himself, then Governor of the island, and all his officers. Only Captain Van Dongen remained alive. This mischance being perceived by the French, they instantly ran with five hundred men, and possessed themselves of the castle. Here they found three hundred men alive, whom they took prisoners, and transported into France. Monsieur de Estres after this commanded the castle to be demolished, together with other posts that might serve for any defence, as also all the houses standing upon the island. This being done, he departed thence the 27th day of the said month of December, and arrived again in France, after a prosperous voyage.

COSIMO

COSIMO is a specialty publisher of books and publications that inspire, inform and engage readers. Our mission is to offer unique books to niche audiences around the world.

COSIMO CLASSICS offers a collection of distinctive titles by the great authors and thinkers throughout the ages. At **COSIMO CLASSICS** timeless classics find a new life as affordable books, covering a variety of subjects including: *Biographies, Business, History, Mythology, Personal Development, Philosophy, Religion and Spirituality,* and much more!

COSIMO-on-DEMAND publishes books and publications for innovative authors, non-profit organizations and businesses. **COSIMO-on-DEMAND** specializes in bringing books back into print, publishing new books quickly and effectively, and making these publications available to readers around the world.

COSIMO REPORTS publishes public reports that affect your world: from global trends to the economy, and from health to geo-politics.

FOR MORE INFORMATION CONTACT US AT
INFO@COSIMOBOOKS.COM

＊ If you are a book-lover interested in our current catalog of books.

＊ If you are an author who wants to get published

＊ If you represent an organization or business seeking to reach your members, donors or customers with your own books and publications

**COSIMO BOOKS ARE ALWAYS
AVAILABLE AT ONLINE BOOKSTORES**

———— **VISIT COSIMOBOOKS.COM** ————
BE INSPIRED, BE INFORMED